All That Crumbles
A Cascadian Earthquake Novel

Bridget Shannon Good

Misadventures Publishing
216 S 2nd Street
PO BOX 443
Independence, OR 97351

First paperback edition September 2021
Library of Congress Control Number: 2021916567

Jacket photograph copyright © 2021 by Jennifer Astorga/jjeanportraits
Book design by Rick Yurk/BAM Agency, Inc.
Pitch Consultation: David Henry Sterry/The Book Doctors

ISBN 978-1-7370241-1-8 (paperback)
ISBN 978-1-7370241-0-1 (ebook)

For more information about
Cascadia Subduction Zone earthquakes, visit my website
SurvivingCascadia.com

Dedication

Several years ago, I had the privilege of working for the University of Oregon under a remarkable woman named Annie Elling. One day, she encouraged me to attend an American Red Cross earthquake preparedness training on campus. That single hour lit a passion in me I never saw coming.

I've been a volunteer with Salem, Oregon's Community Emergency Response Team (CERT) since 2015. Mine is a small role in a large effort aimed at helping Pacific Northwest communities prepare for a Cascadia Subduction Zone earthquake. That effort would not exist if it weren't for the scientific community.

The scientists listed below have inspired me along my preparedness journey. Because of them and countless other dedicated scientists from around the globe, local building codes have evolved, seismic retrofitting has occurred, and infrastructure has improved. Their work boosts preparedness efforts through this battle against time. Though considerable work remains, one thing is certain: when that inevitable time comes, lives will be saved. These are my heroes.

Dr. Yumei Wang, Portland State University
Dr. Althea Turner Rizzo, Oregon Office of Emergency Management
Dr. Noel Bartlow, University of Kansas
Dr. Lucy Jones, Dr. Lucy Jones Center for Science and Society
Dr. Erin Wirth Moriarty, Dr. Brian Atwater, and Dr. Aaron Wech,
United States Geological Survey
Dr. Chris Goldfinger and Dr. Robert Yeats, Oregon State University
Dr. John Vidale, University of Southern California
Dr. Zhen Liu and Dr. Yingdi Luo, NASA's
Jet Propulsion Laboratory
Dr. Steve Malone and Dr. Harold Tobin, University of Washington
Dr. Seth Stein, Northwestern University
Dr. Tim Walsh, Washington State Department of Natural Resources
Dr. Jason Robert Patton, California Geological Survey

"Civilization exists by geological consent, subject to change without notice."
— William Durant, Historian and author of The Story of Civilization

Chapter One

Sunday, February 18th, 2029 3:00 am

The large room reeked of urine and soot. The stench, encased in the swirling hot air, slammed into her, coating her mouth and throat as it forced its way to unwilling lungs. She nearly gagged.

The temptation to turn, escape from the heat back into the freezing rain was undeniable. She could retreat to the thickening layer of ice that now blanketed every surface, climb in her Geo Prism, and drive home.

But she'd given her word.

She took another step inside. Warmer weather would undoubtedly have led to a door propped open, airing the room like a good spring cleaning, but with temperatures in the mid-twenties, an open door would defeat the night's purpose.

Brooke Halliwell shivered as she listened to the door of the warming center click shut at her back.

Large flat panel LEDs lit the space, a sharp contrast to the sunless sky she'd just abandoned. While her eyes adjusted to the change, she glanced to her right.

A white plastic chair sat behind a foldup card table. The chair, nicked with various scratches, supported an equally worn man.

He rose. "Can I help you?"

"Oh…"

"Have a few mattresses left," the man added, speaking a hair above a whisper. "Could find a place for ya to rest if you'd like some shuteye before morning."

Brooke's eyes widened, the question as shocking to her as the grotesque smell had been moments earlier.

She glanced down. Her body resembled more of a two-by-four than anything with curves, a fact that remained obvious through her lack of multi-layered clothing.

When she'd woken for the 3:00 am to 7:30 am shift, she'd dressed in what few winter clothes she owned. Brooke didn't own many. She had just moved up from the deserts of New Mexico, after all. And damn it, she thought, Albuquerque had been seventy-three degrees when she'd left – mere days earlier.

Days.

Her lips pursed. There was no denying her inadequate outfit gave her a very scrapped-together appearance, she decided.

But did she really look like one of them?

Brooke brought her gaze to the man watching her now with his quiet patience, a man who'd just mistaken her for being homeless.

Fear crawled over her skin, causing the goosebumps on her arms to deliver the sensation of dancing. She rubbed them with shaky hands. The thought of becoming homeless terrified her—a fear she'd acquired in her early teens.

I will never be one of them.

"No." She took a deep breath, focused on keeping the volume of her voice low. "I'm here to volunteer."

"Geez." The older man looked at his watch. "Time's flyin'. Didn't realize it was shift change already. Your name?"

"I'm Brooke, Elizabeth Noel's granddaughter."

The man came around the table. "Oh. Yeah. Yeah, of course." He grinned at her now as if they were old friends. "Your grandma talked about you. Made her proud, you did."

"Thanks."

"I, I didn't hear you were in town. Of course, you would be this week."

Color flooded his wrinkled cheeks. "Of course, you would be. Sorry. Tru- truly sorry for your loss."

Brooke nodded, unsure how to accept condolences from yet another stranger.

"It's mighty nice of you to have come."

He turned to pick up the sign-in sheet. "Tell you what, head up them there stairs." He gestured with a wave of his hand toward the back of the open room.

"My purse?"

"Tommy'll take your bag and lock it in the cabinets until end of shift. The..." he twitched his nose, paused, sneezed into his sleeve in an attempt to muffle the noise. "The other volunteers should be showin' soon. I'll be by, oh just a minute or two I'd be guessin'."

"Okay." She turned toward the stairs.

The building, a former car dealership, had once showcased top-of-the-line Hondas through floor-to-ceiling windowed walls. Now, those windows displayed forty of Salem, Oregon's poorest residents.

Brooke glanced outside, watched as a single car approached. Headlights illuminated the sleeping bodies as the car rounded the corner to make its way south down Commercial Street.

For the first time since she'd walked in, Brooke made herself look at those sleeping guests, showcased for the passing car like animals at a zoo.

At 2:45 am, most of them slept, but not on cots, as she'd expected to see. The man at the front had offered her a mattress.

He'd been generous with the term, she thought.

Red, plastic-covered sleeping pads no more than an inch thick lay atop concrete flooring, reminding Brooke more of cheap yoga mats than actual mattresses.

They sprawled out with no more than a foot or two of separation. Brooke scanned them as she eyed the sixty-foot-long path to the stairs that stretched out in front of her.

She took a step, making her way down an empty row between those who slept in the main display room and the couples who took up residence in offices lining the fourth and only non-windowed wall.

A man grunted. He rolled over in his sleep, his thin disposable emergency blanket slipping off to expose a naked rear end. Brooke's eyes widened. Before she could look away, she glimpsed his too-large pajama pants that had wiggled down to his thighs sometime in the night.

Was she supposed to wake him? Tell him? God, she hoped not.

Moving faster toward the stairs, she spotted another man lifting himself off his mat onto all fours. To Brooke's horror, vomit began to spew from his mouth. It hit the concrete and sprayed clothing that lay between mats.

"Oh, God," she mouthed. "What the hell am I doing here?"

Stepping back, she bumped into one of the office door jams. A dog growled, the deep tone telling her its owner wasn't a Chihuahua. She spun, terrified she was about to be attacked. Through the open office door, the Doberman bared his teeth. Brooke had no doubt she'd be in danger if it weren't for the kennel that held him.

Her hand lifted over her heart. She took several deep breaths to calm herself before noticing the clumps of missing fur on the dog's back and neck.

His teeth, sharp as they were, lacked the white sheen of the dogs in upper-middle-class neighborhoods. He looked, Brooke decided, in desperate need of a vet visit. Brooke's fear eased as her heart broke for the disheveled canine.

Sparks, her dog, lay cuddled in a warm bed three times thicker than the Warming Center's mats. He was up to date on vet visits, safe, fed, and not homeless.

She couldn't stand the thought of Sparks living on the streets.

This dog snarling at her had been able to come inside for the night while Salem endured one of its coldest winters in

4

recent memory. Would he be as lucky the next night, she wondered, continuing toward the stairs at the back.

The old building used an extensive heating system, one of many reasons the space worked so well as a Warming Center.

But heat rises.

As she climbed to the second story, the odors condensed, fused with the fresh spray of vomit. Its tangible film snaked along her nasal passage.

I made a promise.

"Sup."

Brooke lifted her gaze from the stairs to the face of a man in his early twenties.

In a skater's tee and jeans, he stood resting his arms on the counter behind him. He had a kind smile, so out of place in the situation. It threw her further off balance.

"Hey..."

"Old Joe," he said, pointing to the man who'd greeted Brooke at the front door. "He's in charge, but I can give ya a rundown. Name's Tommy."

She stuck out her hand. "Brooke."

"No offense," he said, holding up his latex-gloved hands as if she were about to shoot him, "but shakin' isn't something you wanna do tonight."

"I don't?"

"You saw the vomit, yeah?"

"Hard to miss."

He laughed at the expression on her face. "Germs. Man, they are rampant in here. Not that you don't have hot hands or anything."

He winked at her, a gesture more playful than serious.

She shook her head. "I'm sorry?"

Seeing her bewilderment, he waved it off, laughing. "Trust me. It's best not to touch anything or anyone without gloves."

She glanced at her outstretched hand, pulled it back.

From her vantage point on the landing of the stairs, she surveyed the scene below. The pitifully thin mats made her think of a war zone, one of those medic camps she'd seen in documentaries.

Tommy was right, she decided. A good majority of the residents looked ill. Coughing held a rhythm of its own above the sounds of snores, moans, and the steady flow of the heater.

She took in the grungy state of the clothing, the matted hair, and the soot-covered skin left from the fires they had huddled around to stay warm in the daylight hours. Try as she might, Brooke couldn't fathom how next-to-impossible life would be as a homeless person in the dead of winter with a nasty virus.

The Warming Center was only open at night, from 8:00 pm to 6:30 am. Volunteers stayed until 7:30 am to clean up, but the guests were forced back out into the cold at 6:30 am sharp, regardless of weather conditions, their mental state or health.

Pity swarmed her as she continued scanning the first floor.

Brooke let out a long slow sigh. The Volunteer Coordinator she'd spoken with the previous afternoon had been blunt. She'd explained that the warming center would not have been able to open for the night had Brooke not filled that seventh slot due to staff-to-guest ratio requirements.

In a town of nearly two-hundred-thousand people, they'd been struggling to find seven for the shift. Seven.

It was why she didn't depend on others, she admitted. Few were willing to help. Others weren't always able, even when they wanted to be.

Brooke thought of her mother, let the sadness flow through as it always did, then let the wave pass.

These forty people needed help, she thought. They depended on the center, on the volunteers. Her grandmother had volunteered for years with the organization, helping with the warming centers in the winters, cooling centers during summer heatwaves, and soup kitchens year-round.

Now Brooke, true to her promise, was trying to fill her late grandmother's shoes, for one night anyway.

Brooke supposed her fear of becoming homeless gave her an empathetic edge. She'd damn well use it. She'd make sure the warming center guests knew they had the support of seven of their community members. They weren't alone tonight.

She met Tommy's gaze. Goofy, young Tommy – one of seven who hadn't turned down the opportunity to help. One of the few who hadn't chosen a warm bed and free time.

One of the few she now respected.

Chapter Two

Brooke knocked on her best friend's door. Jennifer Monroy opened it with a welcoming smile while her newly three-year-old daughter, Maddie, jumped in front of her.

"Auntie Brooke! I stay up for ten extra minutes! Evewy night! I'm big now," the girl announced.

Jen and Brooke weren't sisters, but they'd been friends for the better part of two decades. The honorary title of Auntie made Brooke smile every time. She needed that smile today.

"What will you do with those ten minutes?"

Maddie spun to face her mom.

"Home! Mommy, watch *Home*? Pweeese?"

Jen hesitated for only a second before giving in. "For ten minutes. You can pick up where you left off. Then it's up to bed with you."

Maddie began dancing, her arms pumping up and down, her feet moving in a tip-toeing jig while she laughed.

Her excitement inspired Sparks, a sixty-pound basset hound, to let out a short, excited bark. Brooke bent slightly to scratch behind Sparks' ears, where his coarse fur gave way to a small patch of fluff. He'd been her best travel companion for nearly eleven years, going anywhere a dog was allowed to go, including Jen's house.

Maddie dropped to her knees to hug him. Sparks met her love with a slow, sloppy lick across her cheek. She giggled and took off running.

"Deprive her much?" Brooke wondered.

"No, she gets screen time more than she should," Jen admitted, moving toward the family room, tucked around the corner from the dining area and sliding glass patio door.

Jen paused just outside the room and smiled over her shoulder at her friend. "But, well, you'll see."

Intrigued, Brooke signaled for Sparks to follow. When they reached the family room, she stopped to gape.

Atop luscious light-blue carpet stood a vertical entertainment center made of solid oak and extending just over seven feet tall.

Brooke's jaw dropped—but not at the stand that had replaced their old, much smaller one. No, her eyes zeroed in on the sixty-inch flat-screen nestled into place.

"What! When did you get this?!"

Jen messed with the remote and waved a dismissive hand. "Oh no. I had nothing to do with this. Come on, me? Pick out electronics? I don't think so. Seth picked it up yesterday morning," she said, speaking of Maddie's dad, "and it is all Maddie wants to do right now, at least when we're inside."

"Pretty cold out," Brooke observed.

"Yes, it is. And yep, that definitely means we are indoors more this week than normal."

"The entertainment center's pretty unusual. I'm used to TVs just hanging on walls or on something." Brooke swept her arms out, palms facing the floor at thigh level.

"Yeah," Jen agreed. "Seth found this at the Restore. You know, the Habitat for Humanity secondhand store down Twelfth Street."

Brooke shrugged.

"I'll take you over there some time. Anyway, we think it's handmade. When Seth brought it home, the entire thing was broken into these cubbies." She indicated the squares around the TV that held plants and photos of her, Seth, and Maddie.

"So it's not even meant to hold the TV?"

"Nope. Seth sawed off the squares in the middle to make room for it. He loved the piece. I couldn't talk him out of it."

The movie started. They left Maddie in her blissful state and made their way back to the kitchen.

Brooke rummaged around and made a pot of coffee. They'd been friends too long to ask for a cup. It would have offended Jen more if she had. The rule between them was, and always had been, make yourself at home.

The aroma of Black Butte Gold Coffee, with its hints of dark chocolate and roasted almonds, wafted to her. "Sister's Oregon makes some excellent coffee." She moaned.

"Amen to that."

"So, where is Seth, buyer of all electronics, anyways?"

"Astoria." Jen told her, reaching down to pet Sparks, who was now plopping down on her feet. "His company just had some sort of major software breakthrough. He tried explaining it to me in his computer-geek lingo."

"Bet that was fun."

"Torture."

They both laughed.

"All I understood was that it should make for a nice profit this year."

"That's great. Isn't it?"

"Yeah, except the software is very different than what his clients have been using, so he's spending time this week training."

Brooke poured water into the coffee maker. "How long will he be there?"

"In Astoria? Last night and tonight, I think. Then he moves south until he hits Newport next Thursday."

"You going to meet him there?"

"Should I?"

"Don't they have some great aquarium in Newport? I bet Maddie loves it."

"She does," Jen admitted. "And yeah, she'd probably love to go. Me? I'd rather meet up with him in Seaside. I'm pretty sure he's headed there tomorrow, but it might have been today. He has so many stops. I should double-check that with him, but I'm pretty sure that's where he's going to be tomorrow."

Brooke remembered the town. She hadn't grown up in Oregon, but her grandmother lived there for all of Brooke's life. Brooke visited a couple of times as a young kid. Then her mom died in a car accident a week after her fourteenth birthday.

Brooke's dad, unable to afford summer camps, sent her to spend summers with her grandmother. It was a tradition that continued every summer until Brooke left for college.

With her grandmother's house just two down from Jen's, out in the country ten minutes from town, she and Jen had been so glad to have each other.

In high school, she and Jen had taken day trips to the various Oregon beaches, with Seaside ranking in the top five of their favorite destinations.

Now, twenty years later, Jen still lived in the very same house, having purchased it from her parents when they'd moved south. With Brooke's inheritance of her grandmother's house, she and Jen were truly neighbors—a silver lining to a gut-wrenching month . . . if she could nail tomorrow's interview and land the job. She had to land the job.

"Seaside is gorgeous," Brooke said. "The touristy family-owned shops. That amazing promenade."

"They have these cottages you can rent right on the beach. There's this one with cedar siding . . ."

"With a natural picket fence?" Brooke finished.

"How did you know that?"

Brooke swiveled in a barstool. "Sounds like the place you and Seth rented for your honeymoon. I think you used up half your phone's life photographing it."

Jen blushed. "Yeah. I guess I did."

She giggled, and a brand-new glint entered her eyes. "Great memories of the house that week. When Seth calls tonight, I'll ask where he's headed tomorrow. If he's going to be in Seaside, Maddie and I could go over and surprise him."

"Maddie would love it."

"Yep." Jen's smile turned a little wicked. "Then Seth and I could make all kinds of new memories after Maddie falls asleep at her new 7:10 bedtime."

"Eek! Do NOT need that image in my head," Brooke managed.

Jen laughed. "Maybe I will. Maybe I'll just pack up in the morning, drive Maddie and me over during her naptime around noon, and surprise him. Speaking of sex, Ian's back in town."

The freshly poured coffee sloshed out of Brooke's cup. It covered her wrist and the floor at her feet, making her grateful for the added milk that kept the temp from scalding her flesh.

Jen laughed harder this time and threw her friend the towel off the oven handle.

"Thanks." Brooke managed to say through clenched teeth as she wiped her arm. She could feel the heat rising in her cheeks, and she knew she was blushing. She hated blushing because it gave away emotions she'd rather hide.

She also hated the way her heart was now racing, just at the mention of his name.

"We never had sex," she said as she bent to wipe the drops of coffee off the floor.

"No." Jen waited for a beat before adding, "But you wanted to."

Chapter Three

Brooke threw the coffee-soaked towel at Jen with a speed that was just a hair above playful.

Jen caught it. "And besides, didn't he kiss you once?"

Brooke's blush intensified at the memory of that night, years back. She'd been twenty-five, he twenty-seven. She'd been on summer break from teaching fourth-graders at Aspen Elementary and had come to visit Jen and her grandmother.

"Yes," she said absentmindedly, remembering how much that kiss had meant.

Ian had been attending a family reunion at his grandparents' house on the same small road that split off Liberty Street south of town. Because their grandparents had been neighbors, Brooke had known Ian for years, yet he rarely visited for more than a week or two. It had made the intense feelings between them pointless to pursue.

Long-distance relationships had always given Brooke a sense of failure before they'd begun. She'd told him as much that not-so-long-ago summer. He'd kissed her anyway.

Jen smiled. "Do me a favor."

"Depends."

"When he does it again, have sex this time."

Brooke gaped at her friend. "Ian's married."

"Seriously?"

"What?" Brooke asked.

Jen burst out laughing.

"What? What did I miss?"

"Oh, hun. Ian's divorced." Her laugh bubbled out.

"Ouch." Brooke's eyebrows furrowed. "Why is that funny?"

"The divorce happened," Jen thought, biting her lip, "a good two years ago. You seriously didn't know?"

Brooke shook her head. How did she miss it? She'd been living in New Mexico, but she and Jen talked at least once a month. A part of her felt hurt that Jen didn't tell her right away. She'd had feelings for Ian for nearly as long as she'd known Jen.

Of course, she'd purposefully avoided talking about him a lot after his marriage five years earlier. Maybe, Brooke thought, Jen had just assumed she'd gotten over him. In all the years they'd known each other, Jen had never done anything to purposefully upset her, and because of that, Brooke was able to relax.

God, it had been a long week." She topped off her half-empty flowery mug. "You want?"

"No, I'm good. Hey, you okay?"

As Brooke was trying to find the right words, a song playing from the family room made her pause. The melody sent chills through her—not the kind of chills that come with fear, but the kind one feels when in awe of something or someone.

She loved any music that had that effect on her.

"What's that?"

Without waiting for a response, she took her coffee to the family room, where she watched a cartoon spaceship suck up strange aliens as a young girl searched for her mother. Brooke listened to the words as she let the music fill her.

The chills zinged straight toward Brooke's heart, which suddenly felt constricted.

"Wow."

Long month, Brooke thought, hating that a kid's movie had the back of her eyes burning and her throat aching.

"Rihanna."

Brooke looked over to see Jen standing at her side, concern evident on her face. "Maddie has the soundtrack. I must have heard this song a thousand times."

Brooke rubbed slightly at the goosebumps on her arms. "She likes it that much, huh?"

"Her fav. At the moment, anyway. You okay?" Jen repeated.

Brooke nodded. "Just nervous."

It wasn't a complete lie. There was so much at stake. At that moment, hearing the song, she didn't even know what she was feeling, only that the emotions rushed waves of energy across her skin, strong, intense. Nerves were part of it, she supposed.

"About tomorrow," Jen said.

She didn't have to ask. Jen didn't know the whole story about the move, but she knew Brooke. She understood that getting the job was a big deal.

Brooke closed her eyes. "Terrified might be more accurate," she admitted.

"Don't be. Candalaria would be stupid not to hire you."

"Goes without saying," Brooke joked, wishing she had half the confidence her voice portrayed.

"I've heard it's an awesome elementary school. You'll love it there." Jen waited for the song to end before moving to pause the movie.

"That's ten minutes, Maddie."

Maddie's face fell. "Pweese, Mommy, five more minutes."

"It's time, baby. See," she said, pointing to the darkness outside the bay window.

Brooke wasn't sure what that proved. It was winter in Oregon, the daylight short-lived, the sun setting before 6:00 p.m.

"What am I seeing?" From the brightly lit room, Brooke stared out at what looked like dozens of tiny lights.

Jen followed Brooke's gaze out toward the backyard and winced.

"Oh! Mommy, we haven't showed Auntie Brooke the fairies."

"Fairies?"

"We decided to give Maddie a fairy garden to play in out in the tree grove," Jen said, referring to the large pine trees wrapped in a near-perfect circle at the edge of Jen's property.

Brooke smiled at Maddie. "Every girl needs her own fairy garden."

"Pweese, we show her, Mommy?"

"It's so dark out. Am I actually going to be able to see much?"

Jen nodded at Brooke. "Yes."

Maddie spun in a circle. "I very love fairies."

"It's hard to tell from this distance just how much light there is in the center of those trees. Seth and his friends strung a ton of lights." Her voice filled with pride, Jen said, "I hung fairies in the lowest branches. It's fun during the day, but it's actually beautiful at night. Speaking of fairies . . ."

Jen left the room, returning moments later holding a six-inch-high fairy princess. "I found this one in the garden."

Maddie pouted and stared at her feet.

"Can I see?" Brooke asked.

Jen passed it to her.

"Tell me about her," Brooke said to Maddie.

"She is the specialist," Maddie said.

"Most special," Brooke corrected.

After trying out the new phrase, Maddie pointed to the wings on the back of the fairy princess. "See? I not have wings. I have crown. Not real like fairy. She is me when I growed up. I'm a fairy pwincess."

Brooke studied the doll more closely. "It does look like Maddie. A lot like her. How?"

"There is a 3D printing place in town. You go and have photos taken, and then they print 3D dolls of the person with any added features you want."

"That's very cool."

Jen nodded. "A mom was there turning her son into a centaur."

"The half-horse thing?"

"Uh-huh. It was a little creepy if you ask me, but it gave me an idea. I hired the business to take some photos of Maddie and create this doll."

"Yep, yep." Maddie reached for the doll. "Have it back?"

Brooke handed the doll over. "Well, she is beautiful."

"Yes, and it's also not supposed to leave your bedroom, Madelyn Lee Monroy."

Maddie twisted a toe on the ground and pouted. "Sorry, Mommy. I very love her. Want her to fly. Like other fairies."

"Can't she fly in your room?" Brooke asked.

"No, the tea is out there," Maddie said, pointing to the lights.

"I'm missing something," Brooke decided.

"The tea she keeps out there is special fairy tea," Jen explained, slipping on her winter boots and coat. "It's what makes the fairies fly."

Brooke's eyebrows knitted together. "Whatever happened to pixie dust?"

Jen waived that off, "New generation," then turned to put a jacket on her daughter. "I love that you want her to fly, baby, but I'd rather you take tea inside for her than bring her outside. I want to keep her safe."

Chapter Four

Monday, February 19, 2029, 7:00 am

Seth woke just before dawn. Although his little girl wasn't in the Seaside rental home, climbing into bed for cuddles with him and Jen the way Maddie usually did first thing in the morning, he was wide awake.

He sat and marveled for a second at the room's silence. Maddie's morning cuddles morphed quickly to never-ending energy. With her and Jen still in Salem, the stillness felt surreal.

Should be loving the quiet, he thought, shaking his head at himself, chuckling. He enjoyed a break now and then but damned if he didn't miss the hell out of Jen and Maddie when his work took him out of town for more than a night or two.

His feet hit the cold tiled floors as he headed to the kitchen. Opening cupboards, Seth frowned at the box of cereal.

Umph. He missed his family, but that didn't mean he had to eat like he was still home. He was traveling, damnit—only a few hours from home, but still—he wanted something more.

An image of the Neskowin Trading Company flashed in his mind. Just the thought of the terabyte-level of flavor in their breakfast burritos had Seth salivating. His stomach set off a solid growl as if in answer. No, boxed cereal wasn't what he was in the mood for.

Lucky for him, he had several hours free. His first stop in Astoria had been a headache. Seaside, though, had been a breeze. Thanks to the client's new young intern, a recent University of Oregon grad—Go Ducks—with a Master's in computer science, the previous evening's training had gone twice as fast as he'd planned for, erasing the need for a morning follow-up.

Seth grinned. He had until 3:00 pm to do... whatever. Reaching absentmindedly for a mug in the freshly painted cupboards, he hit brew on the machine and, hearing the victorious sound of water beginning to percolate, looked at the display on his phone.

7:15. Two-hour drive to Neskowin. The breakfast burritos were only available until 10:00. He could easily be there before 10:00... if he left soon.

"Oh, man. Hell yes."

Thinking not just of the burrito, massive with its eggs, potatoes, bell peppers, onions, cheese, and the extra bacon he planned to get, visions of a double-shot expresso had him clanking the mug on the counter.

He managed a shower in record time, barely waiting for the water to reach full temp before climbing in. Dressing, he packed his computer, laid it down in the front seat of his SUV. Then he gathered all the rest of his crap and just threw it in the back. He could deal with it later.

His phone buzzed in the back pocket of his jeans. Pulling it out, he read the text from Jen. Missing you. Check out the sun Maddie painted for you. Pretty good for a three-year-old, huh!

He made his way back into the kitchen, the smell of coffee now filling the room. Pouring a cup, Seth brought up the picture she'd texted. His eyebrows rose. Damned if the painting didn't look like a sun. It made him smile.

Missing my girls, he replied.

He hesitated, wondering if he should tell Jen he was leaving Seaside early. It occurred to him that maybe his last client meeting hadn't just gone fast because of the sharp intern. Seth knew his skills in training and sales had improved considerably over the past five years.

If he could manage another shorter-than-expected training this afternoon, he could drive home and surprise them.

Give our artist a hug for me, he wrote.

Seth went through the house one last time while drinking the coffee, wishing the rental had provided to-go cups so he could have a second cup on the drive. He straightened up the rooms. Following the checkout directions he'd found on the kitchen counter upon arrival, Seth turned the heat down, lowered the shades, locked up, and hit the road.

It was warmer on the coast than in the Valley; there wouldn't be any ice on the roads. Looking at the clouds, Seth decided they were mist-bringers, not rain-dumpers.

The drive would be a cinch.

He turned on his playlist, let Keith Urban and Pink's "One Too Many" sync to the car speakers. Driving down 1st Ave, he took the exit and headed south on Highway 101.

Seaside's flat landscape disappeared in Seth's rearview mirror. In front of him, the land began to rise and fall with cliffs overlooking the Pacific Ocean.

He cracked the window, listened to the unrelenting winter waves batter the North Jetty outside of Garibaldi. The smell of shellfish, their dull-white discarded remains piled twelve feet high, filled the car in Bay City. He didn't mind that scent, but as the highway pulled inland through Tillamook and the strong odor of cows replaced it, Seth rolled up his window.

Just past the Tillamook city limits, Seth glanced at the clock on his dashboard.

Cutting it close, he thought, running his hand through ruthlessly short blond hair that curled like Maddie's if he let grow long. He never did.

Hoping he didn't pass any state troopers, Seth gunned the engine. He wanted that damn burrito.

Farmlands sprawled on either side of him, their light green grasses a subtle contrast to the dark greens of the coastal mountain range to the east. He flew past them, slowing only through the small town of Hebo until the highway veered west to the edge of the ocean just outside Neskowin.

Like many small towns lining the Oregon coast, Neskowin held a deep tourist-free quiet during the winter months. Seth imagined that silence could be downright eerie to some under the darkening clouds.

He just loved the fact that he wouldn't have to wait in a long line for food.

A wooden fish totem hung at the town entrance. He parked by it in the small lot of the Neskowin Trading Company and glanced at the dashboard. 10:05.

"Crap!"

Seth all but dove out of the car, leaving his briefcase and jacket in the back, and jogged the short distance to the entry.

Inside the tiny grocery store, a young woman stood behind a counter where pastries lined windowed displays beneath her. She sported a baby on her hip. It made Seth smile.

Only in a small town, he thought.

As the baby squirmed, the woman repositioned the little boy, then forced a smile. "Good morning."

"Hey. Breakfast burrito. Please. Please tell me I didn't miss it. I know the Hawk Creek Café is open next store," he said, referring to one of the only other businesses in the small community, "but the burritos here are to die for."

"Agree. Hungry, hun?" Her smile softened.

"Starving."

She glanced over her shoulder at the cut-out in the wall dividing her from the kitchen. "Hey, you able to do one last burrito?"

"Yup," came a deep voice from the back.

"What kind?"

"Bacon. Lots of it," Seth told her. "And a double-shot expresso."

"Size?"

"Large."

She rang it up, swiped his debit card. "It'll be about ten minutes."

"Thanks. I can't remember. Is there a bathroom here?"

"In the main parking lot across the street."

"Right. Thanks."

Seth headed outside, stopped at his car for his coat. A steady rain had started to fall from the darkening clouds he'd noticed when he'd parked. With it, the wind cut right through his polo shirt.

Throwing on the green and gold Oregon Ducks coat, he headed toward the State Park-style bathrooms, crossing the street and making his way through the parking lot that hosted farmer's markets in the summer.

He was five parking spaces from the restrooms when the FAA's emergency siren blared out of his iPhone's speakers. He froze.

What the Hell?

Chapter Five

Monday, February 19, 2029, 10:00 am.

"So, how did it go?"

With her phone on speaker, Brooke half wished she hadn't answered the phone. Embarrassment floated hot and heavy somewhere in her, but molten panic oozed dominantly over it.

"I didn't get the job."

Brooke heard a high-pitched squeal. "Shhh," Jen said. "Sorry, Brooke. I talked with Seth last night and he was already in Seaside. I'm planning to surprise him there, so I'm trying to pack. It's been a little crazy trying to get Maddie ready."

"I bet."

"I couldn't hear you over her babbling. Tell me they hired you on the spot and you don't have to wait?"

"No. No, I didn't get the job."

Through the speakers, Jen's voice pitched an octave. "What do you mean you didn't get the job? They didn't hire you? Wait, did they tell you on the spot? Aren't they—"

"What am I going to do, Jen?"

Brooke bit back a sob. She'd had solid answers to Principal Neilson's questions during the interview. She'd felt the interview had been going well, had even felt an easy connection with the man. Then, he'd stood and reached out a hand to shake hers as he gently told her she wasn't a good fit.

At that moment, all her hopes of finally making a life in Salem, putting down roots where her grandmother and mother had grown up, her hopes of moving close to Jen and of finding stability, had crumbled.

So had her heart.

"Brooke, are you sure you didn't get the job, or is this just a hunch?" Jen asked.

"He thanked me for coming in," Brooke said. "Then he told me he just didn't think I was the right fit for his *team*."

"Are you serious?"

"Yes. He turned me down on the spot, just like that. I must have really screwed it up, but I don't have any idea how. I was ready."

Silence filled the car. Brooke felt her body shake slightly, but not from the chill. Her car's heater blew over her high-heel-covered feet, blasting her face.

"I'm scared. God, shit, I'm terrified," Brooke admitted. "I don't have a job, and there aren't any other openings for teachers in the area. Even if one comes up, it'll be for next year. I need a job, Jen. I don't want to lose my grandma's house. I don't want to leave. And more, I have no idea where I'd even go."

"I don't want you to leave either. And you're not going to."

Brooke opened her window a crack to let the cool air flow in soft against her face. "I don't see how."

"Brooke, you know I love you, right?"

"Yes."

"Then know I say this with that love. You really aren't all that good at asking for help or leaning on people."

"I know I can lean on you."

"Yep, you can. Hang on," Jen told Brooke. "Maddie, go turn on your movie, okay?"

Brooke heard Maddie squeal again.

"Sorry. God, she is just full of crazy amounts of energy today," Jen said. "My head just can't take anymore today. So I'm snippy with her. I hate that. It'll do us both some good if she watches TV while I finish packing. At any rate, Brooke, even with me, your strong independence rears its ugly head sometimes. Let me do this. You're staying. I think I've got an idea."

"What idea? Jen?" Brooke glanced at the screen on the phone. "She hung up on me."

Brooke scowled. From the time she'd hit high school, she'd had that fierce sense of independence Jen had mentioned. And yes, the thought of needing someone's help to get a job had her stomach sinking.

Then she rolled her eyes. It's Jen, Brooke reminded herself. Not some employment office. Please don't let me need an employment office.

Nervous, she decided to go over to Jen's when she got home, see what her best friend of twenty years had up her sleeve. Considering the woman's sizable network in town, Brooke felt a glimmer of hope.

They say it's all about who you know. I hope she can find something. Fast. How the hell did I blow that interview? I had planned answers for everything.

She looked at the grocery bag filled with all the fixings she needed to make herself a hot fudge sundae.

She hadn't intended on stopping at the store on her way home from the interview. But she hadn't gotten the job. If an eat-your-stress pity party helped her feel better, it was worth the calories despite spending the past five months working diligently to eat healthier.

Screw it.

Gaining weight had never been a problem for her, but with the diabetes epidemic raging across the US——something she witnessed too many times in her classrooms——she'd wanted her sugar cravings under control.

Today, she'd cave, Brooke thought, hating the fact that she had a reason to. She sent one smoldering glare toward the Tillamook Vanilla Bean ice cream peeking out of the bag.

The previous day's clouds over the valley had vanished sometime during the night, along with the minimal heat they'd managed to trap in.

Her tires skidded slightly on ice as she rounded the driveway to her house, a home that wouldn't be hers for much longer since she had no way to pay even the monthly state property taxes now.

Putting the car in park, she grabbed her phone, glanced at the time.

"God. 10:15, sorry, Sparks."

Two hours wasn't all that long for a dog to hold it if he had to pee, but in Sparks' old age, that was stretching it.

"I shouldn't have stopped for the groceries," she mumbled. "Shouldn't have gone out at all. It's not like it got me a job anyway."

She shoved open the car door, got out, and all but kicked it closed. Moving to the passenger side, she opened the door, grabbing the single grocery bag by its handle. Purse over her shoulder and keys in her free hand, she elbowed the car door closed, then took a step toward the house.

Her phone shrilled, its pitch and rhythm sending the hairs on her neck dancing.

Moving quickly, Brooke balanced the grocery bags and her purse in one hand then dug the phone out of her pocket.

Emergency Alerts. Earthquake Detected!
Drop, Cover, Hold On. Protect Yourself.
- USGS ShakeAlert.

She stood, dumbfounded, staring at the message displayed on her lock screen.

Earthquake? It had to be a test alert. Right? She blinked hard and reread it, hoping she'd missed words to that effect. Nothing. Her heartbeat quickened.

She glanced nervously at the ancient oak tree, its large branches dangling over her. Would they come crashing down?

Drop, cover, hold. Cover under what?

Her feet were frozen in place. She glanced behind her at the gravel road, knowing it would probably be safe. Then her quickening heart slammed into her throat.

"Oh my God, Sparks!"

Shoving the phone back into her purse, she took her first running steps toward her home.

The quiver coursed beneath her. She heard a low roar like an approaching stampede riding on the edge of rolling thunder.

Brooke stumbled, skidding in her heels on the icy ground. Even as her feet fought for purchase, the quiver beneath her strengthened, and her concrete driveway undulating like chilled Jell-O.

Hands flying out, she slapped one against the car for balance. The cold metal of the door stung her fingers on impact.

Before she could gain control, she slammed against the car as the compression in the ground at her feet fell victim to a vicious tortuosity.

Grocery bags tumbled to the ground. Brooke fell, her left hip taking the brunt of the impact. Her brain barely registered the pain. Her fear was too great.

The energy equivalent of five hundred million tons of TNT breaking earth was deafening.

Brooke tried to stand.

"Sparks," she screamed.

She couldn't gain her balance.

A brick from her home crashed. It missed her by a foot, and she jumped backward.

"Sparks!"

Crawling toward him now, she screamed as sharp rocks in the gravel dug into the soft flesh below her kneecaps. Her cry morphed from one of pain into one of terror as the rest of the bricks—a failed turn in the game of Jenga—came crashing down.

Chapter Six

The ground quieted. For a moment, Brooke couldn't be sure the shaking had actually stopped. Like a sailor coming ashore, she continued to feel the sensation of rolling earth.

Distant car alarms echoed in her ears, taking on a tunnel-like quality. Dust particles rained down around her like volcanic ash, making it hard to see, hard to breathe.

Coughing, she stood, adrenaline pushing her like a runner taking off their mark. Aimed toward the massive pile of bricks and broken pipes, she barreled toward what was left of her home.

She had only one thought, one goal: dig Sparks out of the wreckage. She had to save him.

Sanity as distant to her as the shaking now, she began yanking broken bricks from the wreckage that held so many wonderful childhood memories.

She didn't feel their sharp edges scraping across her palms or the jagged window shards that intermixed.

Desperate for the sound of his barking, his whimpering, some noise that would tell her he was alive, Brooke ran around the exterior of the pile.

"Sparks! Sparks!" she cried out. "Damn it!" She threw a broken piece of drywall. It hit the trunk of an oak tree.

"Sparks!"

She listened for a reply, then stilled. Had she heard him? She could have sworn he'd moaned. She'd heard it. Hadn't she?

Frantic, she began to climb the pile of debris towards the sound.

"Come on, baby. Where are you? Sparks?"

She stopped, listening again.

Anger filled her. Her ears were still ringing from the earthquake's auditory assault. It was like having a flashlight shown directly in her eyes and then being told to look at details on a small photo.

She strained, willing her ears to tune in, desperate for a sound that would tell her where to go. She heard another moan.

Moving toward it, she climbed higher. As she moved, she tossed shattered boards from the frame of a window and stumbled across precarious bricks to where the debris peaked.

Could there be a safe place beneath the peak, perhaps a gap between furniture? He could be trapped in some hole, terrified but alive?

She hoisted herself up another step. Her balance wavered as the debris moved beneath her weight.

Chapter Seven

Ian Russick moved down the gravel road in a dead run, cutting across the street, not even bothering to turn toward George and Carol Sims's place.

All his eyes could see was the destruction that had, just thirty minutes ago, been Brooke's home.

Thirty minutes earlier, he'd walked out to check his grandparent's mailbox for them. He hadn't seen her car.

When he'd learned that she'd moved to town, he'd wanted to go and say hello, had planned on it even, but had heard she was in a serious relationship back in New Mexico. That hadn't sat well with him.

Brooke mattered to Ian, boyfriend in the picture or not, so he'd spent the past few days figuring out how to stop by and say hi. Casually.

Casual wasn't what he felt for her. For ten years now, he'd never thought "casually" when he thought of Brooke Halliwell.

So he hadn't stopped by.

What if her serious relationship was moving up to Oregon with her, moving in with her? Thirty minutes earlier, that possibility had sickened him. He had decided then and there to find out more when Seth made it back from the coast.

It had been stupid to wait.

Filled with dread, with too many regrets, he ran.

That's when Ian saw her. Brooke's head peeked over the top of a pile of rubble opposite him.

For a second, it looked as though she were climbing out of the rubble. Ian's heart slammed into his chest. His mind raced, wondering how she could possibly still be alive.

In the next moment, he realized she wasn't climbing out but over. Wonder, dread, and regrets quickly turned to confusion. *What on Earth?*

With her outstretched arms, Brooke gripped bricks from the tallest point of the rubble. She was certain she was close to where she'd heard the moaning. Convinced it was Sparks, she guided herself up to the next foothold. She wanted to get to the top, to start moving bricks from the very peak. She was terrified that her weight might cause a collapse, but she had to believe she could save him—she had to try.

"Sparks! I'm coming. Hang on, honey. I'm coming."

The bricks turned and ground under her torn heels. She didn't notice, didn't think of anything but saving her one consistent companion who'd been by her side through everything over the past eleven years.

Using her knees now, she moved another foot toward the top of the raised mound.

Arms wrapped quickly around her waist. She felt herself being lifted up and backward. Away from the pile. Away from her dog.

She yelped in surprise, and the arms pulled again, inching her down the rubble.

"Stop!" she yelled, not bothering to turn around.

In her shocked state, she didn't consider who it was or why they were there. Sparks was family. Her family member was trapped. She was going to find a way to get him out, and no one was going to stop her.

"Stop! Damn it, let me go! I have to save him. Sparks is in there. I have to get him out."

Another yank backward had her losing ground again. Again, the pile unculated and then settled under the weight of their two bodies The arms around her gripped harder, ignoring her pleas, her thrashing body.

"Let me go!"

Her feet skidded and slipped. A brick scraped the side of her foot.

"Ahh!"

"Sorry, shit."

Brooke heard the undeniable frustration in the male voice.

"If you weren't squirmin' so damn much, I'd have us off here by now."

The familiar low drawl stunned her into complacency for a moment. She knew that frustrated voice.

"Ian." It wasn't a question.

They'd known each other for too long for the voice to go unrecognized. Besides, Ian had one of those deep voices, full of kindness and a hint of arrogance that was impossible to forget.

"Yeah,' he responded. "Now help me out here, will you? It'd be a whole lot easier to get down alive if you were helping."

"Sparks is in there. I can't just leave. You have to help me!" She was furious with him for dragging her backward. Now she'd have to work her way back up the pile again, wasting precious time.

"I can't"

Brooke lowered her upper body as much as she could manage in his hold, dug her feet into the rubble, and tried for another step just as Ian stepped back. The result had both crashing into the heap, not three feet from solid ground, three feet from safety. A brick struck her left hip where she'd fallen during the first nasty thrust of the earthquake.

Another cry of pain escaped her throat.

"Why are you doing this!?"

32

Ignoring Brooke, Ian grabbed her again, this time looping an arm under hers and around her waist. He lifted to his feet, bent for balance, and guided her down the last three feet, though "guide" was probably too nice a word.

Her struggles to go back up made every step more difficult, but with her body facing his direction now, he had the upper hand.

When their feet finally hit the grass lawn, she shoved his hand off her, rounded on him.

"Why?"

"You were going to kill yourself up there."

Ian wiped his bloody knuckles on his dust-covered jeans.

"No. I was going to save my dog. No thanks to you," Brooke spat the words out. "I have to make my way back up. This is something I have to do. You can either help, Ian, or get out of my way."

She swiped at a tear tracking down her cheek, furious.

Surprising her, he took her gently by the shoulders. "Fools rush into something like this, Brooke. What the blazes were you thinking?"

Scowling, she looked at him, really looked, for the first time and saw he was pleading with her.

His brown eyes, not multitone as so many tended to be but simply golden brown, were understanding.

"You don't think Sparks is alive?"

He said nothing in reply, just held Brooke's gaze.

Taking in a deep breath, she turned toward her ruined house. She looked at the pile again.

"But I heard a moan," she said, more to herself than to him.

As if in answer, the house settled, sounding eerily familiar.

Her eyes focused on the mound she had climbed. There was another mound off to the side she hadn't seen. She took a step back and scanned again. Her stomach dropped. Rather than looking like a single stratovolcano, the rubble looked more like a mountain range.

The peak she'd headed toward had been the tallest but not the only. Looking with fresh eyes, she no longer saw the peaks as possible shelters though. There was too much debris, too many small pieces.

She saw no possible sanctuaries for an old dog, a dog who should have been outside in the backyard waiting for her to return from her interview, except it was in the twenties outside so she'd left him in to stay warm.

But he should have been let out twenty minutes earlier, Brooke thought, bile rising in her throat. Sparks would have been outside if she'd come straight home from an interview rather than going to the grocery store for ice cream. He'd be alive.

Her heart broke. "No."

"I'm sorry."

His phrase reminded Brooke of Old Joe at the warming center when he'd given her his condolences for her grandmother's passing.

Brooke looked at the house that had belonged to them both. Seeing it in ruins felt like losing her grandmother all over again, and now she'd lost Sparks, too. Her heart constricted, suddenly wishing her dad lived in town. God, she missed him at the moment.

Ian stuck his hands in his pockets. "We have a pretty full house right now, but there's room for one more."

Brooke looked back toward him, unable to reply.

"You'll need a place to stay."

She nodded. She would need a place to stay, but she didn't want to stay with Ian. They had too much history, and she just couldn't deal with it at the moment. She needed a friend.

"Oh, my God! Jen! Maddie!"

Ian held up a hand to stop her from bolting. "I haven't been inside to see them, but her house looked fine when I went by."

Brooke shook her head, confused. "How is that possible?"

34

She'd just watched her house collapse like a house of cards. The other three homes were made from wood. Images flashed in her mind, first of a cartoon wolf blowing down the second pig's house made of wood, then of the third and carefully-made brick home standing strong. Wasn't brick stronger?

Yet as she let her vision take her past her house for the first time since the earthquake, she could see the other three homes down the gravel road: George and Carol Sims next door; across the street and down Ian's grandparents, Henry and Irene Russick; and past them at the end of the road, Jen's house.

With the distance between the homes, details were hard for Brooke to make out, but she could see that the homes were standing. To her, they looked much like they had before the earthquake.

Relief roared through her. "Good," she managed, though her throat seemed too tight. "Good. I'll go down to her place, stay with her. You said your house was full. Is everyone okay?"

Jen had mentioned he was back in town, but Brooke hadn't imagined he was staying at his grandparent's house. Didn't he have his own place?

"Banged up a bit, I think. Cuts and bruises like you."

She nodded.

"I took off kinda fast there. I should go check on everyone, but I'll stop by Jen's later, see if you guys need anything."

He squeezed her shoulder and headed off.

Chapter Eight

Didn't they call the place where an earthquake started an epicenter? Brooke wondered, feeling certain she'd been right in the heart of the damn thing.

Thoughts rammed into Brooke with only chaos to guide them as she watched Ian walk back toward his house where the structure had held.

Since when does Oregon have earthquakes? California gets the earthquakes, she fumed. The Midwest gets its tornados. The North East has its massive winter snow and ice storms. The Southwest gets fires and droughts, and the Southeast has hurricanes. Oregon had some localized flooding and summer fires.

She shook her head. In all her years spending summers there, she'd never heard of a fault that ran beneath Salem.

It'd have to be a big one, too, she considered. After all, didn't most earthquakes last seconds? Though time during the shaking had passed strangely, Brooke could have sworn it had lasted several minutes. What kind of earthquake did that?

The kind that had left her homeless. No, damn it!

Turning to face the devastation behind her, she stared. It was like seeing a car accident, wanting to look away, and not being able to.

That's my home. Salem is supposed to be my home. One I can keep.

A permanent town to call home had always seemed elusive in her life. She never felt connected to her location at the moment, except when she'd been in Salem. She'd always felt a connection to the city.

Her New Mexico life had been filled with colorful clays and cacti, with tumbleweeds, painful burrs of goatheads, and iron-filled arroyos that lay victim to flash floods during the summer's thunderstorms.

Salem couldn't have been more different, with its breathtaking ferns and colorful moss, its liken-covered trees, and explosions of flowers and fruit.

Now, the dream of putting down roots in that beauty felt unattainable. More, Brooke was all alone. Her eyes stung, fighting back the tears. Somewhere in that pile of rubble and ruined dreams lay Sparks.

"I should have come home." She choked the words out. "I should have never left the house this morning for that damn interview."

The school. Oh my God.

Was the school, at this very moment, in ruins like her house?

The very idea had her heartbreaking. *It's Monday morning. Kids were in school, parents at work.*

She prayed the school had been lucky, that it stood tall like Jen's house; Hell, all the schools, for that matter. Hadn't she read on the website that the Salem-Keizer School District was home to sixty-five schools?

Sixty-five overcrowded schools.

Thirty U.S. states held some sort of maximum students per classroom mandate. Not Oregon. The classrooms were as crowded as the neighborhoods allowed. It was one of the few things that had made her anxious about applying to teach in the state.

But it wasn't anxiety she felt now. Brooke picked up the carton of ice cream lying by her car and heaved it across the yard. Her sorrow, her confusion, and her fear all morphed into solid rage.

All those kids. How many were hurt? Dead?

Maddie.

Looking at Jen's house, Brooke tried to reassure herself that the little girl was fine, but she had to be sure. She decided to check in on them. Then she'd go to Candalaria to see how she could help.

Chapter Nine

The coastal rains fell steadily as the pewter clouds drained the atmospheric river above. Drenched, freezing, and terrified, Seth tried to catch his breath.

He took another step. His sneakers met the fertile mud and sent him sliding back down the path designated as a tsunami evacuation route.

"Evacuation route, my ass," he muttered.

He reached out with his hands catching on a root.

Two men who'd been steadily climbing behind him passed him as if pushing for first place in a relay.

"Can't you let up for one damn minute," Seth muttered to the weather. Each freezing raindrop hit his face like scorpion stings.

Using the roots, he heaved his body forward and took another step. He was grateful when he didn't slide. Like a football player ready to tackle, Seth kept his body crouched and forced his legs to carry him up the hillside.

A woman beside him slipped. She reached out, grabbed his arm for balance, and sent them both sliding.

Seth turned and saw her horrified face.

"Sorry! God, I'm sorry. I, I just keep sliding."

"Yeah." Seth glanced around and noticed that they weren't the only ones struggling to stay afoot. "Use the tree roots."

She nodded and began moving forward.

Seth kept pace with her and moved as fast as the hunt for the next root would allow.

He heard someone scream, slide, and then tumble, losing several dozen feet of battle in the process.

Seth was suddenly grateful there weren't thousands of people in front of him, sliding, crashing, making the journey for all of them impossible.

Had it been tourist season during the summer months, there would have been thousands, he knew. Instead, there were hundreds. Of course, Seth thought bitterly, in the summer, it probably wouldn't be raining, and the hillside wouldn't be a slippery, muddy mess.

Like spiders fleeing the hallways at the click of a light switch, people moved east in droves and fought for elevation.

Seeing families climb, Seth thought of his wife, Jen, and their daughter, Maddie. Would he ever see them again? Were they okay? Where had they been when the earth had ripped like a seven-hundred-mile zipper?

Why the hell did he have to be so God damn far away?

He fumed, letting images of his family smother the fear he felt for himself. Seth didn't have time for fear. He had to move, had to climb.

His feet slipped again on the moss and mud. As his body adjusted to the new landscape, his fingers automatically dug into the ground. He hoisted himself forward and up. Then again.

Both were key to his survival.

"Dude, where the hell is everyone going?"

Seth scrambled forward in the mud, barely glancing at the young man who'd come up beside him opposite the woman.

"Up," he managed.

"The hell for? You look like a bunch of lemmings." He skidded, caught the fronds of a fern, and hoisted up. "I asked for help down there," he said, motioning with his head toward the lower-elevation homes. "Got shoved out of the way. Twice. One guy tried to clock me when I grabbed his shirt to get him to stop."

Seth grunted as he hoisted himself up another notch. "There isn't time to stop."

"What? Look, the shaking is over, and I *need* help. No one on this messed-up hill will stop long enough to talk to me, dammit!"

Seth slowed for the first time since the shaking stopped and looked, quickly realizing the guy wasn't a man but a boy of about sixteen.

"Tsunami. I'm getting up the hill to escape the tsunami."

"Man, wait. What? No. No way. Where did you hear a tsunami's coming? I don't hear a siren."

"Look," Seth managed. "It's coming. And fast." He was suddenly grateful for all the news articles about the Cascadia Subduction Zone that he'd skimmed in the five years he'd lived in Salem.

They'd always made him roll his eyes. He'd never believed the earthquake would happen in his lifetime.

"We need to move. Now."

"But my friend. My friend and I are staying down in a rental. He got hurt in the shakin', bad." Despite his efforts, the teen's voice broke. "I need help moving him. Please! No one else will stop to help."

Seth's heart stumbled. He felt dread and stupidity slam into him in equal measure. Of course, some had been hurt. In his panic, it was as if that knowledge had eluded him. Reality came back with such force he felt ill.

Seth had seen the others running with him, and for reasons that seemed utterly crazy now, he had believed the whole town was there with him on that ridiculous hill.

Stomach rolling, Seth thought of those injured, of others who'd be physically unable to climb the terrain, even on dry, mud-free days. He thought of the unlucky few winter tourists like this boy who wouldn't even know a tsunami was coming, who wouldn't have any idea they needed to run.

He stopped climbing and looked at the town—something else panic hadn't initially allowed.

"Oh dear God."

Neighborhoods looked as if they'd been destroyed by aerial warfare.

Seth felt a rush of gratitude that he wasn't trapped in one of those buildings. Had he waited in the store for his burrito, hell only knew.

Seth had watched that store undulate. When the shaking had stopped, he hadn't looked back. He'd simply run.

He could see what was left of it now jutting out of liquified soil. Down the road, people climbed out of buildings and unfathomably entered others.

The boy shook Seth's shoulders, his voice rising above the screams of those climbing past, above the rain and wind. "Man? What the Hell, man? You okay?"

"Where is the house?" Seth snapped in reply.

"On Breakers Ave. Dude, he's hurt. Come on."

Right on the beach. He knew they didn't have time for even a short round trip to those rentals at running speed, let alone the time it would take to free the poor kid and then presumably carry him up the muddy hill that Seth and so many others were struggling to climb.

But he couldn't leave a child. How could any person abandon another like that?

Seth scanned the evacuation route heading east, or what was left of it.

He figured many locals knew the way. The problem was, he wasn't a local, and the evacuation path didn't resemble a path anymore.

Landslides had covered those paths and turned the once-manicured evacuation route into a feat for the strong and fast.

Panic, meanwhile, made even the strong and fast unsure.

All those climbing knew of the ferocity that was coming. Time was running out.

Seth shook his head.

"I'm sorry," he said and meant it. "There isn't time. Going back now is a death sentence."

"Bullshit. The ocean looks like it did this morning: rough but normal, and it's even," the boy said, throwing up his hands in frustration, "like low tide. Look how far out the ocean is. There ain't no tsunami coming."

It was then that Seth saw it. The kid was right about one thing. The ocean had receded impossibly far from shore. Seth's knees wanted to buckle. It took everything he had to keep from collapsing.

"Oh shit."

Seth watched as, for a breath, the receding water froze, then reversed direction. The first wave traveled from the underwater subduction zone across the open ocean at five hundred miles per hour like a jetliner across the skies, rising only inches. As the base of that wave reached the shallow shores of Oregon, it slowed to a mere forty-five miles an hour. Its height rose like a river cresting in a flash flood.

One hundred feet. The tsunami was predicted to climb to a hundred feet high in places. Seth remembered reading that once. He'd never expected to be anywhere near the coast when it did.

How high was he now? He tried to gauge and knew he wasn't high enough.

Seth's heart hammered as the first wave slammed into the first row of homes. It barreled through town, sweeping those who hadn't been strong enough, fast enough, who hadn't climbed high enough, out to sea.

Grabbing the arm of the boy, Seth pulled him east.

Chapter Ten

Brooke moved quickly down the gravel road toward Jen's place, wondering why Jen and Maddie hadn't come out of their house yet. In the short minutes since the earthquake, Ian had not only come out of his grandparents' home but had had time to yank Brooke off hers.

Knowing Jen, she was probably soothing Maddie, Brooke thought. God, Maddie. The shaking must have terrified the poor girl.

Brooke strained her ears, listening for the sound of Maddie's cry, but heard nothing from the house. It wasn't too far up the road. Four homes in total made up the small neighborhood. Each had been part of a single farm partitioned off over 150 years earlier. With the exception of Ian's grandparent's home, which sat on ten acres, the other homes sat on four-acre lots, putting Jen's place out of earshot.

Glancing over her shoulder toward Liberty Road, she cringed. From where she stood, with Ian's grandparents' house coming up on her right, the view over her shoulder should have been obstructed by her home.

Brooke's throat ached for that home her mother and grandmother had grown up in, the home she herself had planned to raise kids in someday.

Built in 1905, unlike most homes in the area, it had been adorned with full brick, making the gorgeous structure a historic landmark.

Now it was gone, along with the memories and dreams.

She turned away.

On her right, she approached George and Carol's brown home. Brooke paused for a moment, studying the house. Was it slightly tilted, or was that just her imagination?

Carol, a plump woman who loved to wear flower prints and knit fancy scarves for her Red Hatter group, ran out of the house, a look of shock on her face.

"Brooke! Oh, goodness child, you had me scared half to death. Why, I looked out the window not more than five minutes ago and saw your house. Oh, my dear, your poor house."

"I'm okay."

"You got out in time. I'm so glad."

Brooke shook her head. "I wasn't inside when the earthquake started."

Carol's hand flitted to her heart. "My stars. Come here, child, and give me a scrunch."

She walked straight over to Brooke, dressed in her gardening clothes with mud caked on the knees, and hugged Brooke the way a grandmother would. It felt good.

Carol pulled away, examined Brooke, lifting her arms to see the scrapes. "Oh, you poor thing. Let me get you some bandages for those cuts."

"Thanks, but I'm okay. I want to get over to see Jen and Maddie."

Brooke glanced over her shoulder toward Jen's house. Was it really taking this long to settle Maddie? It seemed strange Jen hadn't come out to check on everyone. Then again, Brooke imagined it would be scary for Maddie to see the brick home a tangled mess . . . but if Jen had seen it from the window, she would have run out the way Ian had.

She frowned. Clouds were rolling in. She'd wanted to get inside to the warmth of Jen's familiar home before the rains came.

Carol looked toward the house. "Yes, that would be good. Home all alone with a three-year-old after something like this. I was planning to head over there myself until I saw your home."

"Toilet's not flushin'. Just a heads up." Coming out of the house, Carol's husband, George, stopped and stared at Brooke, his seventy-year-old face breaking into a huge grin.

"Brooke. Are we glad to see you? Looked at the house. Didn't see how anyone could have survived it but had to go see. Would have been out earlier, but . . ." he stopped, scratched his head, then shot the hand up in the air, shaking it as he fought for words.

Brooke had never seen the older man look quite so confused and devastated. She said nothing, letting him finish.

"Well, we were in a bit of shock, I guess. First, we made sure the gas valve was off so the house didn't burn down. Hadn't looked outside at the other homes, you see. Just ran around ours trying to see what was what for damages, but then Carol looked out. Just got on my shoes to go, you know, see if you—."

"Gas,—" Brooke managed, a smile pulling at her lips despite the situation.

George was one of the most practical men she knew. Yet he managed to be so animated when he spoke. It was like watching a performance over at the local Pentacle Theater—one of Brooke's favorite activities in town—every time he got excited in a conversation.

"Oh yes.' Nodding enthusiastically, he gave her a brief one-armed hug. 'Been telling us about the dag-blasted earthquake for decades. Just kept harping until Carol and I finally started to listen."

"Seemed like it would never happen," Carol said.

"Well yeah, what with the thirty-seven percent chance in fifty years and all, but we got some provisions put away."

Carol smiled at her husband. "George anchored our house to the foundation himself."

He ran a hand over his face. "Still have multiple cracks in the drywall throughout the house, but it's stable. We also learned turning off the gas was one of the first things to do after the shaking, so I made sure we both knew how."

Brooke rubbed her hands over her chilled arms. "I'm glad you're both okay."

"You have a place to stay?" George asked. "We have a spare bedroom."

"Yes," Carol said, nodding. "You're welcome to it."

"Thanks, but I'm going to crash at Jen's."

"Of course! Of course, you are. That's good."

Carol touched the chain on her necklace as she glanced toward Jen's house. "You tell her and Maddie we'll stop by just before dinner time this evening with some food for the three of you."

"Okay."

"And let us know if you need anything before then," George added.

At a loss for something else to say, Brooke smiled. "I will. Thanks."

She turned and walked briskly toward Jen's.

Behind her, she heard George say, "Better get out all the supplies from the shed. Gonna need to cook. It'll be tricky to get set up after the rains come."

Chapter Eleven

Jennifer Monroy's house was closer to Ian's grandparents than to Brooke's nearest neighbors, George and Carol.

The only two-story home on the street, it felt massive after standing next to her flattened counterpart.

She made her way up the front porch, which sloped forward slightly, its posts fractured. She knocked, hardly letting a full minute pass before just turning the knob to go in. The door stuck. A solid push with her shoulder had it coming loose.

Brooke stared at the floor covered in items, some broken, some not.

"Jen? Maddie?" she called.

She listened but heard nothing. She wondered if Jen was rocking Maddie in their living room and had managed to get Maddie to sleep for a nap. That would explain why she wouldn't call back, not wanting to wake her daughter.

But the hairs on Brooke's neck danced. She ran nervous hands through her hair.

Trying to stay calm, Brooke scanned the littered floor. She didn't want to walk across the area barefoot, but her brand new interview shoes now resembled a lion's chew toy. Her fall to the driveway, the shaking, and the climbing had all taken a toll. What's more, her feet were killing her.

She shoveled through the mess toward the coat closet, opened it, and grabbed Jen's purple rain boots, grateful she and Jen wore the same size.

Slipping off the wobbly heals, sliding on the boots, Brooke listened again, hoping to hear Jen's soft voice reading a children's book to Maddie or singing a song, or the sound of the chair rocking, giving Brooke a clue where they might be.

The silence was as deafening to her now as the quake had been minutes earlier.

Screw naptime, she thought. Answer me, damn it. "Jen?"

When she still heard nothing, Brooke turned the corner into the family room and froze. She sucked in a sharp breath. Then her feet stumbled across the short distance to where Maddie had sat just the night before watching Home.

But Maddie wasn't there now.

"Oh, my God!"

Jen lay face down on the light blue carpet of the family room, arms outstretched toward the kitchen. The new sixty-inch TV lay smashed, half on her hip, half on the soft blue carpet. Over it, over Jen, lay the tall oak TV stand, one side crushing down on the back of Jen's neck.

Brooke whipped her cell phone out of her interview jacket's right pocket, dialed 911, and jumped over the part of the entertainment center that lay across Jen's calves. Feet falling into the space where the TV usually sat, Brooke took another step that put her next to Jen's face.

In her hand, the phone read Calling, then flashed No Service.

"No, Goddammit. Jen, hold on, I'm calling for help. Help's coming."

She dialed again, knelt, and had to fight the urge to throw up. The smell of urine filled the air, ammonia thick near the floor. A look of panic etched Jen's face, and for a moment, Brooke took the expression as proof of life.

"Jen, oh my God," she repeated. "I've got you. Hold on. It's going to be okay. Just hold on."

She glared at her phone, furious as it refused to connect. Typing 911 again, she hit the speaker function and dropped the phone on the carpet beside her, praying it would connect.

Positioning her body in front of the TV set, Brooke crouched, used her leg muscles, adrenaline providing strength. She strained. Inch by inch, she felt the oak lift off of Jen.

When Brooke stood, her fingers supported the top of the stand at waist level. The heavy oak dug into her fingers, made it impossible to rotate her hands so that her palms were under the stand rather than just her fingers.

She tried to bend again for leverage to hoist the entertainment center up, but it was all she could do to hold it in place. Sweat sprang out on her forehead.

"Jen. Jen, I can't lift it any higher. Can you move? Can you wiggle out? Hurry! I'm not sure how much longer I can hold it."

No answer came. In the silence, Brooke heard her own rapid breathing and the pounding of her own heart.

"No! No, God damn it! You're okay. You're fine. You just need a little help. You're unconscious. That's all. I can fix this."

Tears Brooke didn't even feel poured down her cheeks as she angled her body and tried to wedge her thigh under the stand. For a second, it worked.

She used the new support to work one hand under, then the other, to hoist it up, but sweat coated her palms. Her right hand slipped. The oak's edge crashed down on the back of Jen's leg. Brooke heard the sickening sound of bone breaking. "Oh God, I'm sorry. I'm so sorry."

But Jen didn't scream out in pain, didn't wake. She didn't cry out for help. Brooke heard nothing except the sound of her own ragged breath.

"No. Please, no."

She tried to read the display on her iPhone that lay faceup on powder blue carpet. Her eyes blurred with tears as she read Call Failed

Wiping what tears she could on her shoulder, Brooke tried to scoot the TV stand sideways. The idea of laying it back down on Jennifer's body ripped her heart. But the thick carpet gripped the edge of the wood at the base.

The only way she would be able to move the stand, she knew, would be to lay it flat and shove it with her feet. But of course, she wouldn't be able to lay it flat until she could move Jen.

Brooke suddenly and desperately wished her dad was there. She needed his help. She needed him. Because her best friend was dead.

"Jen." The word came out in a cracked whisper.

Tears flowed down her cheeks. She stood as minutes passed, unwilling to set the heavy wood back down onto her broken friend's body.

The weight bore down on her muscles. Her thighs and biceps shook with the strain, and she took a step to steady herself.

The heel of her rain boot pushed down on a plastic toy. "Somewhere Over the Rainbow" blared out of overused speakers.

"Maddie."

Fresh adrenaline brought a second wind.

"I'm sorry," she sobbed as she gently lowered the stand onto Jen.

Brooke crouched low to the ground again. Jen's face, still frozen in the same grotesque expression, stared back at her.

Noticing for the first time the awkward, unnatural angle of Jen's head to her body, Brooke choked back a sob. Her best friend was dead.

"I'll find her, Jen. I'll find Maddie."

Chapter Twelve

With the phone in her hand, Brooke called her dad while she dashed to the back patio, gasping for fresh air. Her body threatened to retch, and she had to blink several times to clear the tears. There wasn't time to fall apart. Not yet.

She put the phone on speaker and set the phone down on the deck's railing, trying him again when the first call failed.

She lifted her hands, pushing auburn hair back from her oval face. She kept her hands there, her face lifting to the blue sky.

"Where would Maddie go?"

It was the first time Brooke truly understood how different caring for a child outside of a classroom could be. She knew she'd always been a huge presence in the lives of her students. She made a difference in their lives and loved it, but there were still many aspects of her students' lives where her role as teacher didn't extend. Things like all-nighters, doctor's visits, and losing kids at the zoo fell squarely into parent territory.

It was one thing to hear the horror stories about the young child who got separated from his parents at a carnival or even at the grocery store. It was another thing entirely to experience it, especially after a natural disaster.

Brooke swallowed hard, breathed through her nose.

The last hour of her life had changed everything. She'd lost her home, her job opportunity, and with it, her hopes of putting down roots in Salem.

She'd lost her dog and now, her best friend. She couldn't take losing Maddie, too. But where was she? Was Maddie hurt? Lost?

Silence stung the air. Jen's silence. Could it be Maddie's silence too? A tear trekked down Brooke's cheek, instantly chilling in the cold weather. What if Maddie was somewhere outside? In the cold? Would she have a jacket? Did she know about her mom? If not, Brooke knew she needed to find Maddie before Maddie found Jen. But how?

It took everything she had to move the panic down, move away from the fight-or-flight response of the moment so she could think.

Where would Maddie go?

She dropped her hands, shook them as if the act might wake her from what felt like a nightmare.

"Where are you?" she breathed.

Brooke had no idea, but she knew from her child development classes in college that terrified kids Maddie's age tended to just take off running. Maddie could be anywhere.

She remembered the two of them playing a game of hide-and-seek. Maddie had hidden under the sink in the bathroom, and Brooke remembered asking her why she hadn't hidden under the bed.

"That's where monsters are," she'd said.

What if Maddie was scared? Brooke thought.

She turned and bolted back into the house, not daring to glance toward the family room. Bounding up the stairs, she flung open the vanity doors under the bathroom sink. Nothing.

"Maddie?"

Glass from the small bathroom mirror glinted on the floor, and Brooke did her best to avoid it as she stepped to the tub. The curtains moved easily with the swipe of her hand, but again, the space was empty.

"Maddie. Maddie. It's Auntie Brooke. Where are you?"

She heard nothing. The silence infuriated her. She clamped down on the fury and rounded the doorway on the left of the hallway, adjacent to the bathroom. "Maddie?"

Painted soft purple with stars across the roof and fairy stickers on the walls, the room felt empty without Maddie's presence. Brooke flipped the bed skirt up. She found a pair of pajama pants, two stuffed animals, and a candy wrapper. Moving toys away from the closet door, Brooke nearly let out a scream of frustration when she found the closet empty.

Brooke knew if Maddie was close, if she could hear her, Maddie would come out, would whimper—which meant she was looking in the wrong area.

"Crap!"

Running back downstairs, she checked in Jen's room. The closet there stood empty too. Brooke turned and saw it. On the bedroom floor next to Jen's craft desk was the porcelain princess fairy.

Brooke bent and lifted it, grateful the carpeted floor had saved the doll. Brooke stared at the doll's face—Maddie's face—and knew.

"The garden."

Setting the fairy on the bed, she flew out the back door, not stopping on the back patio to breathe this time.

Instead, she ran, her feet slogging, slipping through the slick grass. She went down hard on her knees once and cursed.

Shoving to her feet, she stumbled forward, leaping from the grassy manicured lawn closest to the house to the wild grasses and weeded area beyond. She ran.

Please be there.

The thought raced in her mind as if the words could conjure Maddie from thin air. That's when she heard it. Ten feet from the grove, the sounds of choked sobs and whimpers broke the silence.

To Brooke, at that moment, they were the best sounds in the world.

Maddie was alive.

Still unsure if Maddie was hurt, but not wanting to startle her, Brooke slowed her steps until she caught a glimpse of Maddie through the trees.

Brooke's relief flowed painfully through her, and she collapsed to her knees. Her hand went over her mouth as she fought for control, for calm. Maddie needed her to be calm, reassuring, but Brooke's body shook, and silent tears fell.

When she could stand, could breathe, she walked the remaining steps to the center of the grove.

Maddie sat on a log her father, Seth, had made into a bench. Her feet rested on its edge, her knees tucked up with her arms wrapped around them. Her head hung.

Brooke remembered all too well the day she'd lost her own mother. She'd been much older than Maddie, and still, the grief had been unlike anything she'd ever known. Crushing.

"Maddie," she whispered.

Maddie's head shot up in surprise. Her face showed relief at no longer being alone then crumpled, and the soft sobs from earlier became wails as she ran to Brooke.

Brooke scooped her up, feeling the little girls' feet brush her thighs. She felt a lump form in her throat and forced it down. Moving to sit on the log, she cradled Maddie in her arms.

Chapter Thirteen

Glancing toward the sky, Brooke sighed. The edge of a nimbostratus cloud, heavy with moisture, covered the entire skyscape to the northwest. The sun's warmth quickly diminished as the cloud moved beneath.

Brooke figured the temperature hovered around thirty-five now, and she scowled. Ante up, she thought with disgust. Even on a warm spring day, the moment would feel impossible.

Damn it. Damn it, damn it, damn it. Can't we get a break here?

It would be different if she were alone. The plans she would develop, the way she'd think through the next few hours, her ability to handle the next few hours; everything would be different. But she wasn't alone.

Still nestled on her lap, Maddie wore nothing but her long-sleeved glitter shirt and a pair of jeans. Her feet were bare. Her whole body shook.

Shivering herself, Brooke removed her interview jacket and wrapped it around Maddie. The material covered the girl from her shoulders to just under her toes.

At least that's a start, Brooke thought, and wondered what to do next.

We can't go inside with Jen there, but it's so cold out. It's going to get worse. Fast. Rains will be here soon and hypothermia's a very real risk at this point. So, what do I do?

How am I supposed to comfort a child who has just lost her mother? Brooke remembered being that child and still didn't have a clue.

God, did you see Jen dead? she wondered, glancing down at the top of Maddie's head, the girl's face pressed into Brooke's chest. Did you see her die? Were you there?

Brooke had so many questions. Questions she couldn't— wouldn't ask. Still, she wondered if Maddie understood what had caused the shaking that had killed her mother. Did three-year-olds know about and understand earthquakes? *Maybe to some degree in places like Japan or California where earthquakes happen frequently.* Brooke doubted toddlers in Oregon understood, though.

The shaking had been so strong. Even to Brooke, a thirty-two-year-old, the shock waves had gone on for what seemed like an eternity. How could a child of three understand that ferocity? Not knowing probably made the whole situation that much scarier for Maddie.

Sitting on the wooden bench in the tree grove for fairies, Maddie fought to regulate her breathing. In an unnerving cycle, she inhaled three quick breaths, then exhaled a single long one.

Her heart breaking for the little girl, Brooke was just starting to wonder if Maddie would fall asleep, exhausted from crying, when the sobs came again.

"Shhhh," Brooke whispered. She ran her hand up and down Maddie's back. "I've got you."

Grateful that she'd put on Jen's purple rain boots when she had first come into the house rather than her ruined heels, Brooke stood and began moving around the small fairy garden.

The wind whipped past her now exposed arms. In the distance, Brooke could see vertical lines descending from the darkest clouds. The rains were coming. She and Maddie would need shelter. Soon.

Not able to go back into the house, Brooke turned slowly, her eyes scanning the tree grove again. Could the trees themselves provide enough shelter for them to stay at least partially warm and dry?

The quake had shaken some already weak branches loose, and they now littered the ground. Many of the figurines lay broken among the debris—a battleground littered by fallen fairy soldiers.

A wind gust cut through her train of thought. No, Brooke decided, the grove won't cut it. We need to get inside.

Nap. If she could get Maddie to fall asleep. . . They would need the house for shelter. Not just for the night, either. They'd need it until Seth got back from the coast, and the only way Brooke could see to make it all work was to move Jen's body out of the house.

She wondered yet again if Maddie knew Jen was inside, then realized the little girl hadn't asked for her mom. Not once. Brooke held Maddie closer.

You poor baby. I'm so sorry.

Feeling helpless, she cradled Maddie, leaving the grove to walk the edge of the property.

Maddie's tears didn't stop.

Brooke's boots slogged through the mud. With each step, she wished she was in better physical shape. Her arms ached. She wasn't used to lifting, let alone carrying thirty pounds. The bruise on her hip didn't help matters. It sang with each step. Adrenaline fading, her head pounded. Her body shook.

Slowly, she made her way to the farthest corner of the property. There, she stopped walking and began to sway, wishing she could get Maddie's tears to stop.

She needed Maddie to nap. It was the only way.

Should I sing? It usually helped kids to calm down, right?

Worth a try, she decided. What song? "Hush Little Baby" came to mind, but Brooke had heard Jen sing it so many times. Would singing the song make Maddie think of Jen in a way that made her feel sadder?

"Somewhere Over the Rainbow" was Maddie's favorite song, but after stepping on the toy next to Jen's body, Brooke never wanted to hear that song again.

Then, she knew.

Rubbing Maddie's back, Brooke closed her eyes and began to sing the words she could remember from Rihanna's song in the movie *Home*.

"No. No, no, no, no," Maddie wailed, pounding tiny fists on Brooke's shoulders.

"Okay, baby. I'm sorry. Shhh. Um. Ummm. Let me try something else."

Trying to think of another song Maddie liked, she went with Shakira's "Try Everything."

This time, Maddie's cries softened. Under the jacket, her body began to relax. Slowly, her tears subsided. Her shaking softened, and she curled into Brooke, more cuddly than desperate, now.

So grateful the singing helped, Brooke felt a tear roll down her cheek. It landed in the corner of her mouth. She tasted its salt, felt the chill where the wind met the wet line, and she wiped it away with her shoulder.

She wanted so terribly to take Maddie's pain away. To take it all away, a bad dream, erased with that first waking yawn.

Taking a steadying breath, Brooke sang the verse again, and again Maddie's tension eased. "There, sweetie. There you go." She moved Maddie's soft curls away from her face.

"Again." The voice was so tiny, almost inaudible.

Brooke gazed at the tiny face, making sure she'd heard correctly. Had Maddie spoken? If she had, it was the first thing Maddie had said since Brooke had found her.

"What, sweetie?"

"Again. Sing it again, pwease."

Brooke sang and watched as Maddie's eyes began to droop, emotionally spent, exhaustion taking over.

As the dark, low-lying clouds rolled directly over them, Maddie slipped into sleep.

Chapter Fourteen

Brooke took a steadying breath.

Even if I can figure out where to lay Maddie down so I can do this, how the hell can I going to be able to do it at all?

Sure, she admitted, she'd been scared and in shock before. Maybe with a clear head, she'd have an easier time moving Jen, but the entertainment center had been so heavy.

Ian had mentioned that he would stop by at some point. She could go over early, ask for his and his family's help or ask George and Carol. But doing either would mean leaving Maddie alone.

What if she wakes up while I'm gone?

The few acres' walk there and back would take time. Maybe not a lot, but Brooke couldn't afford to lose any of it. And she'd have to tell the neighbors about Jen. She'd have to say the horrendous truth out loud, and Brooke wasn't ready to do that. She wasn't sure she ever would be.

Her throat constricted at the thought, her eyes burning with the threat of fresh tears. She'd just have to find a way to move Jen alone, and she couldn't afford doubt.

Looking around the yard, Brooke spotted the storage shed and made her way over. As she walked, Maddie's breath puffed out in warm pulses against her neck. Trying not to jostle her too much, Brooke worked to balance Maddie in one arm, then used her free hand to open the shed door as silently as possible.

It creaked. She cringed, but Maddie didn't wake.

Brooke reached for the light switch and flipped it. Nothing happened.

"Really?" she whispered. "You've got to kidding me."

She tried another switch. Still nothing.

"Great. Just great."

You can't afford doubt right now, no matter how shitty things are, she reminded herself. She glanced around at the disarray of boxes and totes, letting her eyes adjust to the dimly lit space. Some of the totes sported labels, and her eyes fell on one that read "Camping Gear."

Like with the house and fairy garden, the earthquake had left its mark here too. Stepping over and around the chaos on the floor while carrying Maddie in her arms, Brooke felt clumsy.

She moved slowly. Every time her foot found stability between chaos, she wondered if the nap would be over before she could put a solid nap plan in place. Worry lines creased her forehead. She couldn't fail. Not here. Not now.

Taking another deliberate breath, Brooke made her way to the camping box, hoping to find a sleeping bag.

A huge smile broke out on her exhausted face.

"Yes! Hell, yes."

It wasn't a sleeping bag in front of her. On the floor by the tote lay a folded-up portable crib.

Finally. A break.

She balanced Maddie in one arm again, reached down, and grabbed the handle, jerking the rectangle-shaped bed from its position.

Slinging it over her free shoulder, she reversed out of the shed with awkward movements, feeling like a robot in need of reprogramming.

Robot or not, she felt hope rising. The portable crib was precisely what she needed, what *they* needed.

Making her way to the grassy area of the yard closest to the house, Brooke rested one end of the crib in the grass and propped the other end up to rest on her hip.

Wind teasing the ends of her hair, she used her free shoulder to move what she could of her hair out of her face. Unstrapping the three Velcro pieces that secured the crib's trifold mattress around the structure of the pack 'n' play, Brooke let t fall open.

The winter grass provided a modest cushion, but the mattress still hit with a thud. Brooke bit her lower lip.

"Don't you wake on me," she whispered to Maddie.

She placed her hand on the back of Maddie's head for support, bent down, and laid Maddie on the mattress. Maddie moaned and rolled onto her belly, pulling her legs under her so that she reminded Brooke of a sleeping frog.

Letting out a breath she hadn't even realized she'd been holding, Brooke looked down at the little girl. The blazer she'd worn in the interview fell around Maddie, working temporarily as a lightweight blanket. She'd need something warmer.

Brooke shook out her exhausted arms, desperately wishing for a coffee break. She rolled her eyes. There would be no coffee breaks in her foreseeable future, she acknowledged. She needed to work fast.

Bending down, Brooke opened the sides of the pack 'n' play, snapping the sides into place, then lowering its floor into a secure position. She gave the equipment a few tugs to test for stability. Its legs stood firm, settling into the grass that lay a foot below the edge of the wooden balcony.

Seeing her plan falling into place, Brooke turned towards the mattress and the sleeping girl. Designed to fold into thirds, the mattress was thin but sturdy.

This better work. "Don't you wake on me," she repeated.

Brooke slowly rotated Maddie until the girl's body lined up along the middle section of the mattress. Gripping the two sides, she folded them up, cradling Maddie inside, and lifted the pad into the crib.

Leaving Maddie in the crib, Brooke returned to the shed, where she rummaged around until she found a large dark-blue sleeping bag. She unzipped it and shook it out. Curious, she sniffed, hoping the bag had been washed after the family's last camping trip. The scent of fabric softener, familiar and welcome, filled her nose.

Of course it's clean, Brooke thought, suddenly having a hard time picturing her tidy friend putting away a dirty sleeping bag.

She walked outside and looked up. "I could use your help here, Jen," she whispered.

Back at the crib, Brooke tucked the sleeping bag around Maddie.

Maddie would cry if she woke and wanted out, but at least the little girl wouldn't be able to walk into the house independently.

Brooke watched Maddie sleeping for a minute, shocked at how much the girl looked like her mother. The little face held serenity, like the calm Jen had carried so often in her day-to-day life.

Brooke willed her mind to hold the peaceful image, preparing herself for what she was about to do.

Chapter Fifteen

Brooke knew the scene this time. There were no surprises, but it was still a stunning, crushing blow to see Jen lying there, arms outstretched, face frozen in fear and in pain.

Brooke made her eyes focus on the TV stand. It occurred to her that the TV itself might not be helping things, and she decided to try to move it first.

Weighing in at fifty pounds, the TV was more awkward than it was heavy. Grabbing the narrower sides, she yanked up on the TV only to realize that one of its corners sat wedged under the entertainment center.

How am I supposed to do this?

Scanning the scene, she knew she would have to try to lift the stand again, this time with a clear head.

Brooke bent, positioned her hands, and heaved upward, but she could only gain two inches before having to set it back down.

"Shit!"

She kicked at the wood in frustration.

Taking four slow deep breaths, Brooke bunched her muscles and tried again, giving it everything she had. This time, she managed to lift it enough to straighten her knees, her fingers curled under the edges of the stand.

"Okay, Rambo, now what?"

She didn't want to try putting her knee under it again. Balancing the item like that had been too hard the last time. The sound of Jen's bone breaking, even now that Brooke understood Jen hadn't felt it, was *not* something Brooke cared to hear again.

Arms tiring, she set it back down as carefully as she could manage.

Glancing around the living room, she scowled. Nothing in the room measured the height she needed.

She checked on Maddie and then did a quick search through the house. It was in the upstairs bathroom that she found it: a sturdy, white plastic step stool just slightly shorter than the height she'd managed to lift the stand to on her first attempt.

She grabbed it, carried it downstairs, and positioned it beside her right foot. Again, she readied herself and hoisted the television stand.

Knees straight, fingers curled under the edge, she shifted her balance and scooted her toe out to push the stool under the TV stand. The no-skid bottom of each stool leg grabbed the plush carpet.

Brooke pushed harder. In response, the rubber feet of the stool dug into the plush carpet, sending the stool toppling sideways.

"Aaahh."

A tear slid down her cheek as she sat the stand back down.

Her forearms screamed with exhaustion. The morning's adrenaline had long since ebbed. Carrying Maddie around the yard, climbing up the pile of her ruined home, and setting up the crib had all weakened her. She shook her arms, trying to will strength back, and peaked outside again.

Maddie slept.

"Okay, Brooke. If this were a project you gave to your students, without the body under the entertainment center, of course . . ."

Jesus, this sucks.

If she'd been on her own, Brooke would happily have slept outside. But she had Maddie. Camping outside with a toddler sounded like it could be a blast in the summer if she planned the trip out first. In mid-February, in the wet and rainy Pacific Northwest with just above freezing temperatures . . .

No, thank you.

"Okay," she began again, the sound of her voice making her somehow feel less alone and more competent.

"I need to lift the shelf," she whispered. "I've done that, so that's something. Now I just need to slide the stupid stool that doesn't want to slide under it. How would I encourage my kids to solve a problem like this?"

Her hands moved to her biceps, rubbing up and down.

The grown-up-sized sleeping bag she'd placed over Maddie looked warm enough folded in the tight pack 'n' play.

With her interview jacket wrapped around Maddie as well, Brooke figured Maddie was warm and toasty. However, it left Brooke wearing only the thin blouse and dress pants she'd chosen to wear to the interview.

The air was cold on her exposed skin, a welcome sensation to counteract her workout-infused body.

She was dirty, sweaty, and figured she'd give ten bucks for a nice hot bath to soak away the day. Thinking of water, Brooke realized just how thirsty she was.

That was it. She just needed a glass of water. Then she'd figure the problem out.

Even the simple goal wasn't so simple. The kitchen was by far the most dangerous place in the house. Its floor lay littered with broken glass. Cabinet doors sat open, some swinging precariously on loose hinges. Medications and dishes made of plastic, tin, and other break-resistant material lay amidst the landmine. The refrigerator sat two feet away from the wall, having wiggled out of its slot between the wall and the cabinets. Behind it, the electric cord stretched, barely reaching the outlet.

As if taunting her, a broom handle poked out of the entry to a closet that sat at the opposite end of the kitchen. Across the minefield.

Brooke closed her eyes. She needed water, needed a break, needed to just go to sleep and begin again tomorrow.

Thinking of the time Jen had wanted to do the same thing when she'd been in labor, a quick and cynical laugh escaped. Labor could no more pause and restart at will than Brooke could nap in the middle of what she had to do.

She walked to the bathroom, pulled a thick, pale green towel off the rack, then went back to the kitchen. Laying the towel on the floor, she stepped on it with both boot-covered feet. She scooted it across the floor, glass clinking together as the makeshift bulldozer laid a path to the sink.

Brooke reached up, hoping for an unbroken cup that wasn't lying on the ground and found, pushed to the very back, a short coffee mug made of steel with a non-skid rubber bottom.

"Thank you."

Her fingers gripped the mug as if it was a precious diamond. She twisted the left sink handle. Nothing came out of the faucet. Frowning, she tried the hot water handle on the right— still nothing.

"We have some provisions. . ." George's words came back to her, and her jaw dropped.

"No water. You're kidding me, right? How the hell am I supposed to do what I need to do if I can't even fill a cup with water?"

Cursing, she gripped the cup, scooted around on her towel, and bulldozed her way to the fridge. Inside, the light was off. The gentle hum she had never really given much thought to didn't come.

Her mind raced. She remembered trying the lights in the house when she'd been looking for Maddie, remembered trying them again in the shed. Nothing.

How long, she wondered, would the electricity outage last?

No electricity was bad. It meant that even if she pulled this plan off somehow, the house, though dry and protected from the wind, would still get cold. Very cold.

Moreover, the food she was staring at wouldn't last more than a few more hours. Pressing her thumb and finger over the bridge of her nose, she closed her eyes. The electrical problem would have to wait.

She huffed out a breath. Bending, she touched the side of a carton of juice. It was still cold. Yanking it out, she poured a glass into her new favorite coffee mug and guzzled the orange juice down. It tasted like heaven.

Pouring a second glass, she put the juice back in the fridge and closed the door, hoping the food would stay cold long enough to make it until dinner.

Dinner. It was something else she would have to figure out. Brooke thought of the totally useless purchase of ice cream from that morning. If she'd known an earthquake was on its way, she'd have bought bottled water and soups, snack bars, and every other item she could have fit into her cart. The trip to Roth's, the interview, they felt like a lifetime ago.

Dinner time seemed like a lifetime away.

Cradling the juice in her hands, she pivoted toward the living room, then paused when the recycling bin caught her attention. The corner of the massive Sunday paper stuck out.

She snatched it, used the towel to scoot out of the kitchen, and did yet another check on Maddie. Less than half an hour had passed since laying her down, but it felt like an eternity. Brooke moved back to Jen, careful not to look directly at her. If she focused on the wood, on the TV, she could do what had to be done.

Hardening her emotions again, trying to go blank, she laid a page of the newspaper down on the thick carpet. Shifting, she picked up the stool, placed it on the newspaper, and positioned both next to her right foot as close to the center of the TV stand as possible.

With the toe of her boot, she practiced scooting the stool on the floor. After two successful scoots, she rolled her shoulders to loosen them.

"This better work, damn it."

She'd lift the stand and be able to slide the stool underneath. That would prop the edge of the entertainment center up enough that Brooke figured she'd be able to move Jen. Her stomach rolled at the thought of it, and she pushed it aside, deciding to deal with it when the time came. Not a moment sooner.

She flexed her fingers twice, rolled her shoulders one last time, and bent down.

Lifting as she had before, she stood, legs straight, back slanted, and carefully rebalanced for the stool scoot.

The earth jolted under her.

She lost her balance, and the TV stand crashed with a sickening thud. Brooke tumbled backward, a scream ripping from her throat, arms instinctively covering her head as she hit the ground.

Then, just as quickly as the aftershock had begun, it was over; a tiny fraction of time and force compared to the mainshock.

Still, Brooke's heart raced. It sat lodged in her throat. Adrenalin pumped through her, strong again. She couldn't hear anything but the blood rushing to her head. Her body shook. She tried to stand, but her legs refused to work. Of the fight, freeze, or flee responses, she'd frozen.

Brooke fought to calm herself, desperate to get to Maddie, knowing the little girl would be terrified and confused all alone in the crib.

Forcing herself to breathe, she sucked air in and pushed it out.

Again.

And again.

And again.

Finally, the ringing in her ears quieted. It was only then that Brooke realized how quiet everything else was. She couldn't hear Maddie. Why wasn't Maddie crying?

A new wave of terror struck. Surely the shaking would have woken even an exhausted child.

Images of her own home collapsing, of tree branches falling, flooded Brooke's mind. Maddie should be crying. Everything was quiet. Too quiet.

Brooke willed her legs to stand and ran.

Chapter Sixteen

Maddie was fine.

Brooke wasn't.

Her heart felt overloaded, as if it might just raise the white flag and up and quit on her. It slammed violently in her chest, a sharp contrast to the calm, sleeping child in front of her.

Maddie held still in her sleep, cuddled beneath the extra-large sleeping bag. The steady movement of Maddie's back rose and fell with each breath as she lay on her belly.

How? How did you sleep through the aftershock? Brooke wondered, though the answer hardly mattered. She wasn't going to be able to move Jen, which meant the house would be off-limits whether Maddie woke or not.

Not moving Jen also meant Brooke and Maddie needed a backup plan for housing.

She felt sick to her stomach, wondering what to do. Since she no longer planned to move Jen, Brooke knew she could just wait until Maddie woke. Then, the two of them could go stay at Ian's family's home or George and Carol's.

After watching her home crumble and then finding Jen dead inside an otherwise stable house, the aftershock had been a third, vicious strike to Brooke's sense of safety. She didn't want to sleep in *any* home that could bring death to her or Maddie.

Despite their warmth, buildings felt like potential death traps.

More, she wanted to be near Seth and Jen's house when Seth got home . . . only to find out he'd lost his wife—that Maddie had lost her mother. It was an impossible thing.

The image of Seth coming home and finding Jen's body had bile rising in Brooke's throat. She had to find a way to move Jen before he got back. Which should be anytime, she thought. News had spread by now. There was no way he hadn't heard about the earthquake.

She knew Seth. Jen and Maddie were his life. And it took, what, just under three hours to drive from Seaside to Salem? Granted, once he got close to Salem, some of the roads would be damaged.

Brooke checked the time on her phone. Barely 1:00 pm. Two hours and forty-five minutes since the earthquake. If he had to walk through parts of town, maybe it would take a few hours longer, she admitted, but had no way of knowing what the roads in town were like.

Brooke let her mind open to the sounds around her, listening for tires on gravel. She'd have to meet him out front, stop him from going in the house. But she didn't hear a car.

She thought of the neighbors again. They could help her move Jen to ensure Seth didn't come home to find her lying dead, but the clouds were too close.

Since they weren't going to shelter or sleep inside, they'd just have to find a way to make sleeping outside work. The problem was, Brooke didn't have much experience with camping.

Down in the Southwest, scorpions and tarantulas roamed the terrain Because they did, camping had always freaked her out.

It wasn't all that different in Oregon. Spiders were as common in Salem as monarch butterflies in Santa Barbara County's Ellwood Grove.

With over five hundred species of spiders in Oregon, she knew there were many she had yet to meet. Her least favorite was the ground-dwelling giant house spider. Though harmless, its body alone could reach nearly an inch in length with leg spans of up to three. They made her skin crawl.

At least there aren't any tarantulas in the valley. It was a small relief. However, she knew the Pacific Northwest Forest scorpions roamed the valley floor at night.

She remembered Jen telling her stories of how she and her family had taken black lights on camping trips to find the scorpions that hid in sleeping bags and shoes at night.

Brooke wondered if she'd be able to find a black light in Jen's shed.

Blacklight availability was just one of many concerns on Brooke's mind. It hardly rated because aside from the occasional black widow, most of the arachnids in the valley weren't poisonous or life-threatening.

Staying alive held immediate priority over the icky and creepy.

Brooke lifted her hands to the back of her neck, let her head fall gently back onto them as she stared up at the sky.

She needed to figure out how they were going to stay warm and dry throughout the night. For that, she needed to find Seth and Jen's family-sized tent that Jen had texted her pictures of the previous summer.

I can probably find it. I just hope I can figure out how to set the stupid thing up.

What if she couldn't figure it out? What if it had a rip? What if she got it up, and they still froze to death during the night?

Her arms, covered with tiny goosebumps, dropped back down to her sides.

"Shit, it's cold."

Brooke spoke in a whisper, barely audible, terrified that her language would somehow corrupt the three-year-old even in sleep.

Who the hell camps out with zero experience, she berated herself, in the dead of winter? *And even if I can somehow magically ensure we don't freeze, we need water.*

Brooke thought of the remaining juice in the fridge that she'd saved for Maddie. They would need water before long.

They'd need food, light, a way to cook, and probably a hundred other things.

The whole thing very nearly paralyzed her in panic. Swallowing, Brooke glanced at her surroundings.

It wasn't like she'd been dropped off in the middle of the South American jungle with nothing but a backpack to survive on, she reminded herself.

She was in Salem, Oregon, after all. She'd spent every summer in high school there and had taken several vacation weeks to Salem since. Her grandmother had grown up there. So had her mom. So it was familiar. It was home.

Her eyes zoomed in on the end of the gravel road, where the house she'd inherited from her grandmother less than two weeks earlier looked more like a failed game of dominos than stability.

Okay, she admitted, so home might not be the right word anymore, but it still wasn't a wild jungle. Possibilities surrounded her.

Supplies.

Leaving Maddie, she headed back toward the shed. Opening the shed door, she glanced at the disarray.

"Crap."

Brooke shook her head, hoping for a miracle, then rooted around, moving boxes, totes, and loose items until she stumbled upon a tote that read "Tarps."

She opened it and pulled out a large one. Eyeing the deck from the shed door, she wondered if setting up camp there would be best. The deck was flat. The house would provide shelter from any southerly winds.

And it was entirely too close to Maddie's lifeless mom.

"No, I've got to do whatever it takes to keep her far away from that."

The area surrounding the deck was covered in grass that, despite the winter months, grew green and lush. Manicured to its full potential, the yard was free of sharp rocks and sticks. Beyond it lay a more natural field thick with discomforts—items Brooke figured could rip the bottom of the tent.

The field had once been farmland, but despite Jen's love of gardening, she and Seth weren't farmers. In their attempt to be at least semi-environmentally conscious—the thought of Maddie growing up in a world irrevocably changed by the climate crisis freaked them out—they'd opted to keep the manicured grass area that needed to be watered small. The rest of the land, they left wild.

"Grass it is," Brooke mumbled, though she intended to set up camp at the edge of grass bordering the field that was the farthest from the house.

While the grass was lush, the winter rains made it sloshy so that her feet sank into the earth with every step. The tent needed to stay somewhat clean and dry, which was why she intended to use the tarp as the tent's front yard—a clean place to walk, change shoes, and, if necessary, dry off before coming in the tent.

To her surprise, the tarp spread easily. It smelled like tires and dirt and lay larger than Brooke had expected.

When she was satisfied with the location, she made her way back to the shed, rummaged, and found two tents, the large family tent from the photos and a small fairy play tent. She grabbed both, slinging the strap of each over separate shoulders.

With her hands free, she hefted the tote labeled "camping" and headed back outside.

Brooke was winded by the time she'd carried it and the tents back to the tarp, but she felt better.

They had a spot picked out to sleep. They had the tent. They had camping gear. Now she just had to figure out how to set it all up. She laid everything on the tarp. Her chilled fingers gripped the edge of the tote's lid and lifted it off. Inside, cooking equipment dominated the space.

She decided to go through the tote later, knowing she was miles away from being ready to cook dinner. *God. Dinner.* She didn't even know what was available, let alone how she would cook it without electricity, especially if she was right about the rain reaching them soon.

She hadn't even eaten lunch. Neither had Maddie, she realized. They'd need food, but that would have to wait until she was all set up.

"What else . . . ?"

Brooke's eyebrows furrowed as she tried to envision the night ahead. She would need diapers for Maddie, who still used the trainers for sleep . . . Which she wasn't wearing at the moment.

"Oh, crap. Please don't have an accident."

Maddie peeing in her pants would be disastrous.

Until the water came back on—hopefully soon—there would be no way to bathe Maddie or wash her clothes. Even if the water came back, with no electricity, those would be some very cold washes.

Maybe I should keep her in the trainers all day until Seth arrives. Just in case.

Determined not to screw things up, to make things as easy for Seth when he came home as she could manage, Brooke bolted inside. Breathing through her mouth to avoid taking in the smell of urine and death, she closed her mind to everything horrible in the house and focused on the task at hand.

She started by locking the front door. No point in making it easy for a neighbor to open it when Ian or the others came to check in. Brooke figured the locked door might give her more time to stop Seth from coming in too.

Satisfied, she turned, leaped over the fallen, shattered picture frames as she took the stairs at a jog, rounding the corner into Maddie's room.

Grabbing the mesh laundry basket from the closet, she dumped its contents and began filling the basket with clean clothes: socks, underwear, pants, shirts, sweaters, adorable pajama suits.

She grabbed the entire pack of pullups, both diaper wipe packages, and the changing pad wedged beside the bed. Brooke assumed it rarely got used these days. Wasn't that why Maddie's diapers were called pullups? Because she'd graduated to standing for changes? But just in case.

Brooke gathered blankets and a pillow from Maddie's bed and crammed them in the basket too.

Turning, she wondered what else to take. Toys and games filled the room, littered her floor.

It occurred to her that Maddie would need to stay occupied too. Remembering the earlier aftershock, she wanted to minimize the number of times she came into the house.

"Should I take stuffed animals?"

Several or just one, she wondered, staring at her options. It was overwhelming. Should she take the blocks or the singing robot? Or maybe the playdough? God, she couldn't take all of it, but what would bring Maddie the most peace? The best distraction?

Unable to decide, she grabbed what was closest to her; a stuffed bunny, a beautiful dark-skinned figurine wearing an Olympic gymnast suit, and a tub of pink, glittery playdough.

Everything loaded in the laundry basket, she carefully maneuvered her way back down the stairs.

Chapter Seventeen

Ian knocked on the chilled wood of the front door.

"Okay if I come in, ladies?"

The excitement of the afternoon surged through him. His grandparents had told him about the possibility of a mega-thrust earthquake every time he had visited them growing up.

"This ain't small stuff," his grandpa would say. Then after Ian turned fourteen, his grandpa had surprised him by swearing. "This ain't small shit, Ian. It's a one-in-three chance this thing's gonna happen in the next fifty years."

One-in-three in fifty years. That had been the narrative for what seemed like the whole of Ian's life.

Ian wasn't a gambler but had someone told him he had a one-in-three chance of winning a million in Powerball, he'd have bought the ticket.

Who the hell wouldn't?

One in three made for damn good odds, but it had always been the "in fifty years" piece that had had Ian waving it off, dismissing the danger.

Checking the time on his phone and noting the quickly dropping battery life, he shoved it back into his coat. He'd figure out how to charge it later. Ian found himself wondering if many people in town had things like backup phone chargers. How many had listened—had gotten prepared in advance with those odds?

Seriously, he thought, as he waited for Brooke or Jen to open the door, who plans with fifty-year outlooks in mind? Not Americans. If we did, retirement planning would look a whole lot different in this country.

Six months earlier, when he'd moved to Salem to start his contracting business, Ian had learned to build according to the local seismic codes. Doing so hadn't made the risk feel any more immediate.

However, Mother Nature had come that morning anyway in all her terrifying wonder. He'd survived. They all had. To Ian, it felt as though they'd conquered the devil himself. As the wind slipped silently by him, stinging the exposed skin on his face, he smiled.

"Ladies?" he hollered again, hearing nothing in response.

He tried the door but surprisingly found it locked. Jen never locked her doors during the day.

"Hey, Jen? Brooke? Maddie?"

Chapter Eighteen

Ian decided to go around the back of Jen and Seth's house to see if the patio door was unlocked.

He figured the girls were probably upstairs cleaning debris in and around Maddie's bedroom to ready it for the night ahead. Without any electricity, the early darkness would complicate the night ahead.

What he saw when he rounded the house confused him.

On the grass beside the deck, Maddie napped in a Pack-N-Play beneath a massive sleeping bag.

Brooke dumped out a large laundry bag onto a tarp at the far end of the grass lawn. He watched her move to rip the top off a large green tote, also sitting on the tarp next to what looked like a rolled-up tent, sleeping bags, and pillows.

Pillows?

The scene was so strange. Even Brooke's clothes baffled him. She wore the same fancy pants and collared shirt she'd worn climbing her ruined house—and rain boots.

Though it wasn't yet raining, he assumed they were better than the other shoes she'd had on, but he couldn't figure why she hadn't asked Jen to borrow some more comfortable clothes or even clean clothes?

A jacket, for Christ's sake?

He felt his irritation rising, wondering how she could be so careless. Again.

It was February nineteenth.

Still winter.

"Probably tell me she got too hot moving all this shit and took the jacket off," he muttered. Hands in his pockets, he made his way over to the girl he'd had feelings for, for more than a decade, wondering why she and Jen had chosen not to sleep in the house.

They damn well knew the rain was coming. Probably afraid of aftershocks, Ian decided.

One of the few who hadn't brushed off the risk, Jen had done some preparations for the possibility of an earthquake. She and Seth had hired Ian's contracting team to do seismic retrofitting on their home. He had to admire his work, as the house looked to be in great shape. They didn't need to worry enough to camp out, especially in this weather.

Maybe they just wanted to make sure.

Still, they shouldn't be walking around without jackets, he fumed, taking off his own as he passed by Maddie.

"Jesus, Brooke. Put this on, will you," he said, extending his jacket to her.

Brooke's eyes were unfocused when she spun in his direction. *Lost.* He watched her eyes slowly clear before she spoke. "I'm good."

"You're really gonna piss me off if you get sick."

Glancing nervously at Maddie, she said, "I'm sweating already. I've got to keep working."

Brooke Halliwell wasn't one to ask for help, a trait that had both impressed and irritated him in the past.

Her focus was more than just her usual independence, though. There was something else. Then Ian saw tears well in her eyes as she turned and began unrolling one of the tents from its bag.

"I'm sorry about Sparks," he began, bending to help unfold the tent corners.

Until that day, he had only ever seen her cry once. Once.

Her mom had died in a car crash when Brooke was only fourteen. It was the year her travels to Oregon had gone from quick summer trips with her parents to being dropped off at her grandmother's for entire summers while Brooke's dad fought fires around the western US.

Ian had only seen Brooke when his family trips to visit his grandparents had coincided with hers—a handful of times in those first thirteen years. They'd been casual acquaintances.

He'd held her anyways while she'd wept that summer years ago, grieving for her mom, missing her dad, missing home.

That had been the summer they'd genuinely become friends, though even then, he'd felt something deeper.

Ian watched his friend and his love interest of two decades pulling out the tent poles.

Brooke shook her head.

Ian paused. He'd been so ecstatic, riding the high of survival . . . and he was an idiot, he realized.

They'd survived, but she'd lost a great deal more than he had. "Look, It's a bummer about your house. I'm . . ." he felt so inadequate. "Sorry. Jen and I'll help you find another one if you're still planning on staying in Salem."

She shook her head again.

Not staying? he wondered. The possibility didn't sit well with him. A problem for later, he decided. He'd figure out a way to convince her to stay. For now, he just needed to convince her to get inside for the night.

"Jen's house is stable. It's not going to crash. You can take my word for it. Come on. I'll help you move this stuff back in, and—"

He reached down to scoop up a pile on the tarp to stuff into the laundry bag, cold slow wind creeping across his now exposed arms.

"Stop!" The word came out on a choked sob. "Please just stop."

Jaw dropping slightly, Ian looked over at Brooke. "It's going to be okay. The house, it'll hold."

She fell from her crouched position to her knees and, like Maddie earlier, began to sob.

Confused, at a loss, Ian draped his jacket over her hunched body and pulled her against him as he had so many years earlier.

"We can't. Go. In the house," Brooke managed, her sobs turning to heaved breaths as she fought for control.

"It's not going to fall. You can trust me on that."

"I know. But Jen's in there."

"Oookayyy." He wasn't following and wasn't sure what else to say. "Do you want me to go get Jen? Losing a dog's a hard thing. I can go in, do whatever she's working on so she can come out."

"No. She's…" her breath heaved again, came out too fast, rickety. "She's not coming out." Her voice broke again.

Ian pulled her against him, held her. She broke. The tears came out in retching sobs. She shook, fought for breath, and with her sorrow, he felt his own heart pound.

Brooke sniffled, pulled back.

He laid a hand on her cheek, wet from tears. "I'll be back." He stood. He had to see for himself, unwilling to believe, to accept.

Jen, the only one of them who'd actually grown up in Salem, had been his friend for as long as he could remember. Though Ian had never developed feelings for her the way he had for Brooke, Jen had been Ian's friend for years.

Maybe it wasn't too late. Maybe he could help her.

"Don't! Please, Ian."

By the sound in Brooke's voice, he already knew it was too late. More, he knew there was no way she would be out here if it were still possible to save her best friend. As a teacher, she'd had several first aid and CPR classes over the years.

Yet there was no way he'd ever forgive himself if he didn't make sure. What if Brooke was in shock and hadn't evaluated the situation correctly? What if she'd missed a weak pulse?

He had to try.

He climbed the single step up onto the deck and moved to the back door. It opened with ease, giving him more assurance that the house still stood strong.

Then the smell hit him.

It was pungent, acidic, unfamiliar. The rational part of his brain understood, but the emotional part, the stubborn part, kept his legs moving.

She lay on her stomach, her contorted neck and her right leg trapped underneath a massive oak TV stand. The scene confused him. The TV stand hadn't been there a week earlier when he'd had beers with Jen's husband, Seth. So why was Jen trapped under something that shouldn't even be there?

Running on automatic, Ian walked to where her head lay. The smell, even when he did his best not to breathe through his nose, assaulted his senses, causing his eyes to burn.

Though he tried not to, he noticed the wet stain on her pants.

He checked her pulse, checked her breathing, somehow hoping for another miracle in a day that had spared him and all the other neighbors, or so he'd thought. The stillness of her, the temperature of her much too cold body was like touching a doll.

It frightened him more than anything else he'd ever known. Why hadn't Brooke come to get him right away, or at all, for that matter?

Anger sparked. Hotly.

In a daze, he made his way to the patio, vomiting the contents of his stomach into the sleeping rose garden beneath the kitchen window.

Ian felt Brooke's hand on his back. "You should have gotten me." His tone came out horse, harsher than he'd meant, but he was so angry. At her. At fate. At the world.

She sat beside him, her voice a gentle contrast. "I had to find Maddie."

Maddie. Jesus.

He hadn't considered Maddie being anywhere but with Jen when the shaking had started, but he felt incredibly grateful that, apparently, the girl hadn't been. The emotions of the day rocked him. He was suddenly more tired than he'd thought possible. "Was she in her room?"

"No, she must have taken off running during the earthquake or right after. I'm not sure."

"How far did she go?"

"The trees," she explained, pointing to the grove.

"Does she know?"

Brooke shrugged. "I'm not sure. It took me an hour to calm her. She cried herself to sleep."

"I should have checked in sooner." And he was furious with himself that he hadn't.

He'd cared for his sea-sick-prone mother in the minutes following the quake as she'd recovered from the motion-sickness that the earthquake had induced.

Then he saw Brooke's home. Terror had been a cold blade through his belly. Learning she'd survived had sent him flying. He'd gone back to his grandparent's, cleaned up the breakage, and helped prepare for the next few weeks by finding flashlights, extra blankets, and canned food. He'd also helped empty the hot water tank into containers for drinking and had set out pans to collect rainwater.

Each task had felt to him like a necessary task on the critical path to survival. He'd done each while looking forward to spending an evening eating some of that food with Brooke Halliwell.

Ian hopped off the patio, made his way to the camping stuff, and tore off a run of toilet paper to wipe the vomit from his mouth.

"Do you have a place I can throw this?"

Brooke looked around and grabbed a plastic grocery bag that had held some of the camping supplies and gave it to him.

Tossing the toilet paper in, he sat on the tarp.

She remained standing, looking at the dense clouds in a darkening sky with both storm and night approaching.

"I need to hurry."

"I'm here. Anything. I mean it, Halliwell. You're not the best at asking for help. Always, 'I got it,'" he said.

"I don't—"

"Would you have come to get me? Tonight, I mean?"

She shrugged again. "I had Maddie. I couldn't leave her alone when she was napping. And there was so much to do here. Besides, you said you'd be by."

I did, he thought, feeling resentment stab. He wished, just once, Brooke would lean on him, Hell, on anyone other than herself for a change.

But that wasn't the Brooke he knew.

"Well, I'm here now. Why don't you come to stay at my place?"

She glared at him, and despite everything, he nearly smiled. Their attraction to each other had never been a secret between them or anyone else. The problem was, she'd never been willing to date someone who'd just fly out of her life weeks later. Two weeks. That was the most time they'd ever spent together at a time.

Ian held up his hands in surrender. "Not with me. I mean, you and Maddie can have my bed, but I'll sleep somewhere else."

"We can't."

"Because?"

"Because," she lowered herself to sit beside him, "I'm not ready to tell everyone about Jen, to put Maddie through that tonight, especially since I don't even know if Maddie knows that Jen's..." she trailed off, unable to complete the sentence. "Because I want to be here when Seth comes back. Because I don't feel safe in any building right now. I'm terrified of the aftershocks. Just because."

Thinking of Seth, Ian's gut squeezed against the anxiety that now clutched at him. *The coast. Seth had gone to do the whole sales pitch deal. Or the coast. Fuck.*

He pulled out his phone, saw the bars for service were gone. His grandpa had told them cell towers would be out for a long time. Not having a cell phone swamped Ian with a helplessness he didn't care for.

"It's supposed to storm tonight," he tried, shoving his phone back in his pants pocket.

"Better falling water than falling bricks."

He let out a long-suffering sigh. He'd need his family and George and Carol to convince her to bunk in a house. But with Maddie sleeping and night approaching, Ian figured the next morning would be the soonest he could convince Brooke to come by.

If sleeping outside for one night made her feel the safest, he'd damn well make sure she had everything she needed before he left.

Chapter Nineteen

Tuesday, February 20th, 2029 2:00 am

Brooke woke shivering. And wet.

She shot upright, surrounded by a half-inch of water on the floor of the tent.

"Oh, no, no, no, no, no. Shit!"

Though she'd wanted to position the tent on flat ground, she'd also wanted to be as far from the house and Jen as possible while remaining in the grass portion of the yard.

The edge of the grass yard sloped slightly. It hadn't seemed like a huge deal when she'd pitched the tent.

"I didn't know. How could I have known!"

She spat the words out in a whisper as she frantically began picking up her and Maddie's now-soaked possessions.

"Where am I supposed to put these?"

Where the tent sat highest on the grass, the rain had stitched through the bottom seems of the tent, dampening the material at the highest elevation, pooling in the lowest.

In the middle of winter, when no person in their right mind should be camping, she was now soaked too.

She took the soaked clothes, wedged them against the tent's seam where the water was leaking in, hoping to stop the flow.

She heard the pelting of raindrops on the tent, listened to the wind pull and push the material.

Brooke looked at Maddie, sleeping on the single cot that Brooke had managed to dig out the previous evening. There had to be more in the shed, Brooke knew, but she'd only found one before Maddie had woken, scared and confused, in the portable crib.

The thought of Maddie climbing out of the crib and wandering inside the house had terrified Brooke.

"I'm here," Brooke had hollered, making her way out of the shed to Maddie in record time.

Maddie had spoken little all evening and had clung to Brooke like a baby monkey on its mother's back. It hadn't been so bad, Brooke thought now. She had sung to the girl, getting small smiles from her occasionally, and had even enjoyed a protein bar and a can of vegetable lentil soup that Ian had brought over. Not that Maddie had eaten much.

Hopefully, I can get her to eat more in the morning.

Now, though, not having the second cot had complicated things. *Weren't tents supposed to keep you dry?* she fumed. Her muscles were tight, so cold it hurt to move.

Slowly, she picked up a bag filled with Jen's clothes— clothes Jen would never need again. Sickness rose in Brooke's throat. She swallowed it and pulled out items from the top of the pile.

She found a baby pink shirt with long sleeves and a pair of dry jeans. The warm nighttime-preferred sweatpants sat at the bottom of the cloth bag, wet.

"Jeans it is."

She stripped off the wet clothes that clung to her goosebump-covered skin. Using a T-shirt from the bag as a towel, she dried her skin as quickly as possible. Though the tent worked as a barrier to the wind whipping noisily across the fabric, it did little against the cold that sent thousands of painful pricks across her exposed skin.

She jerked the pants up to her waist and put on her shirt. Her body shivered, convulsed. Her stomach muscles clenched painfully.

"Shit, shit, shit, it's freezing," she muttered, searching for dry socks in the bag. She found two and pulled them on, her feet painfully cold as the material slid over them.

"Mom? Mommy?"

Brooke looked over to see Maddie rubbing her eyes in the darkness.

"Hi, Maddie," Brooke said, doing her best to keep her voice light. "It's me, Auntie Brooke."

Brooke threw the T-shirt towel onto the floor, using it as a floormat so her new socks wouldn't get too wet, and moved to sit on the cot with Maddie.

"Can't sleep?"

"Where's Mommy and Daddy?"

Brooke bit her bottom lip, unsure what to say. It had been an impossibly long day for them both. Impossibly hard.

She was cold, tired, and not altogether sure she could talk about Jen without falling apart. Maddie didn't need that. Besides, Seth should be the one to tell his daughter about Jen. Brooke didn't feel right taking on that responsibility. He'd be home soon.

"You and I are having an auntie time tonight, kiddo," she tried, hoping her tone sounded fun.

"Oh." Maddie cocked her head at Brooke. "Do we have to be in tent? I'm cold."

"You are, huh? Well," Brooke gathered the girl into her lap. "Let's warm you up."

Taking Maddie's small hands between her own, Brooke used the warmth of her breath to heat them. She alternated between blowing warm air and rubbing until Maddie's hands felt less like ice.

"Want a story?"

Brooke couldn't think of what else to do. They couldn't go inside. Distraction seemed like her only choice.

"I like stories. Can you laid down?"

Brooke smiled. "Lie."

"Humm?"

"Can you lie down?"

"Oh." Maddie's eyebrows furrowed. "Can you lie down?" she repeated, smiling at her grammatical achievement.

"Okay, kiddo, scoot over."

Grateful at least one of them had a dry sleeping bag, Brooke slid down into Maddie's with her.

The fit wasn't as tight as she would have thought.

Knowing Maddie often had co-slept with her parents when she was younger, Brooke wondered if Jen had bought the oversized sleeping bag for just that reason.

Maddie laid her head on Brooke's shoulder, placed her arm on Brooke's stomach.

"Auntie, you are shaking."

"It's cooold," Brooke said, trying to make her voice sound silly.

As she'd hoped, Maddie laughed. "Yep!"

Unable to make up a story in her current state of exhaustion, Brooke fell back on tradition and went with Cinderella.

"Once upon a time," Brooke began and did her best to stay focused on telling the story.

Her eyes, fully adjusted to the dark, could see their cardboard box of food, its bottom soaked. Like the paper packets of hot cereal, some of the contents would be unusable now, she knew. She bit back an oath.

Brooke hadn't known if the milk, eggs, or bacon would be usable by morning with the electricity out the previous day. Cold cereal eaten dry would have been an option had it not lain scattered amidst the kitchen floor chaos, making the packets of oatmeal the only breakfast option she'd managed to find the previous afternoon while Maddie had slept.

Hopefully, Seth would know what other items were salvageable when he got back from the coast. Brooke figured he'd be there before lunch at the latest.

A flash of panic moved through her. What if he'd come home already and she hadn't heard him? Had he found Jen?

No. He'd have come looking for Maddie as she had. They'd have heard him calling for his daughter. Would he come before dawn, she wondered, and wake them with his panicked cries?

Where was he? Seth should have been home well before dark.

His continued absence worried Brooke. *Hopefully, he's just catching a few hours down.* Maybe the roads weren't great outside of town either, and he had to walk farther than she'd guessed. She wished she could listen to the news to see how many cities had been devastated by the earthquake.

She found her phone in the pocket of the tent next to the cot, tried the internet, and got nothing. Knowing she'd try again another ten times before lunch, Brooke resolved herself to the tasks of the morning. She just had to keep Maddie safe and fed until Seth got home.

"Auntie?"

Brooke shook her head, realizing she'd zoned out. "Sorry, I was trying to remember what comes next in the story," she said.

"I know! Auntie Brooke, I know. Can I tell you the story? Pweese?"

"I think you'd better. I seem to be too old to remember."

Maddie giggled and told a toddler version of Cinderella while millions of people living west of the Cascade mountain range slept through their first homeless night.

Chapter Twenty

In the lingering haze between wake and sleep, memories flooded over Brooke, hammering like waves against Oregon's rocky shoreline.

The failed interview. The terrifying earthquake. Ian yanking her off her ruined home, trying to save Sparks. Jen's lifeless body. Maddie huddled, forever-changed in the fairy grove, just as Brooke had been forever-changed at fourteen.

Brooke wished the memories of the previous day were nothing more than night terrors, fading in the new daylight.

They would never fade.

The day ahead promised to be filled with trials of its own, leaving her anxious, edgy.

Beside her, Maddie lay bundled up, her hand coming out of the sleeping bag to lay on Brooke's face. Brooke focused on the feel of the tiny palm on her cheek, the slender fingers on the side of her nose. The simple human touch helped ground her, bringing her fully into the moment.

Brooke lowered the small hand to the pillow and rolled from lying on her back to her side. She gazed at the young face. Her honorary niece. It was a face she loved more than any on Earth, and yesterday that face had broken. Over and over.

Because the heart had.

Brooke scowled. She was exhausted.

After the day they'd endured, they desperately needed sleep—a solid eight down. What they'd gotten were a freezing, storm-filled mess and little sleep. The night had been a complete and utter failure.

"Tonight will be better, sweetie," she whispered to the still sleeping girl. "Today will be better."

Gently as she could manage, Brooke pulled her arm from under Maddie's pillow and rolled to her knees. Her hip and back felt like she'd been kicked by a mule. Brooke wasn't totally sure she could stand.

Moving into Downward Dog, she stretched her lower back out as best she could.

"Psst. Brooke. Open up."

Completely caught off guard, Brooke jumped, falling backward to land squarely on her butt. "Ian?!"

"Nah. It's the boogie man. Hurry, I'm freezin' out here."

Her fingers fumbled with the zipper of the tent. Ian peaked his head in first, spotted Maddie, and climbed in opposite the cot where she was sleeping, with a backpack slung over his shoulders.

The windstorm had passed, leaving behind a slow and steady rain.

Zipping the tent up, Brooke turned and saw Ian taking his plastic poncho off. He stuck it in the far back corner. He swiped at his forehead, where water dripped from his hair.

"Is it raining out there?" She teased.

"You really should be nice to me. I brought you something."

Brooke's eyebrows raised out of curiosity. She watched as he unloaded his bag and removed a tall thermos, two coffee mugs, and two spoons.

"You do like hot chocolate, right?"

"I . . ." She broke off, momentarily speechless.

"If you don't, I'm really not sure I can down the whole thermos by myself, but I'll try."

He'd brought her hot chocolate.

During Brooke's Junior year in high school, she and her dad had visited her grandmother for Christmas. Brooke and Jen had spent the week going for walks in the cold, with steaming cups of hot chocolate to warm them.

Ian and his younger brother had joined them a couple of times that week, desperate to get out of the house where grownups were taking holiday photos and singing carols.

Here they were, more than a dozen years later, in the cold. And Ian had remembered.

More, he'd somehow made the hot chocolate with no electricity while the rains fell. Then he'd braved that rain. To bring it to her.

She felt her heart turn to putty and cleared her throat. "I'm more of a coffee person at six in the morning," she confessed, trying not to sound as mushy as she felt.

"You grew up on me, Halliwell." He pulled off his wet gloves, tossed them into his jacket, and blew warm air into his hands a few times, loosening his cold, tight fingers before opening the lid of the thermos.

"Thank you."

"For telling you you've grown up?" There was a lightness in his tone.

Hers was more serious. "For coming over this morning."

"Shit. It was either hang out with my lovesick brother and his preggo wife, hang out with old or older people, or hang with you. You're saving me."

Brooke knew he was lying. "You love spending time with your family. And wait. Talk about burying the lead. Alex is married and about to be a dad?" Pure surprised delight filled her voice.

"Fawn's the wife. I think you'll like her. Speaking of, they want you and Maddie to come to dinner tonight."

"Alex and Fawn?"

"The whole family."

Brooke frowned and glanced at Maddie. "Do they know?"

"Yes. My mom wanted to come last night. Hell, they all did. They want you to come to dinner. So do I."

"I'll think about it."

"Turned us down last night."

"Last night, I had a lot to deal—"

"With," Ian finished for her. "I know. I get it, but you'll settle in by this evening. Besides, you gotta eat."

She sighed. "It'll be nice to spend some time with them tonight. Despite everything."

He handed her a steaming orange-and-black mug with the Oregon State University logo across it.

"Still diehard fans?" she asked, referring to his family.

He nodded. "Season passes, as always. I got to join in this year."

The excitement was clear in his voice.

"So it's true then." Brooke fought to keep the interest in her voice from being too hopeful, too obvious. "You've moved to Salem."

"Officially a transplant. You'll want to give that a minute," Ian said, referring to the cup she held to her lips. "It was boiling water when I poured it."

Brooke lowered the cup, choosing instead to let it warm her chilled hands. "Why?"

"Hot chocolate is usually best hot," he replied, a smile pulling at his lips as he poured his mug to half full.

Brooke watched as Ian pulled a corner of the sleeping bag that had fallen off the cot, sat on it, then focused on Brooke.

His steady gaze rattled her, the sensuality of it, but as always, his humor put her at ease. She needed that now.

"You know what I mean."

"Got tired of workin' behind a desk all day. About three years ago, I'd had enough. Studied. Got my contracting license."

"I didn't know that."

"Didn't tell anyone. Not for a long time. At first, I wasn't sure I'd go through with it. Wasn't sure I'd actually quit my job, start my own business. When I finally did, I wasn't sure the business wouldn't just go under."

"So your family didn't even know?"

Brooke took the first tentative sip of the hot chocolate. It burned slightly on the tip of her tongue, and she lowered the cup to give it another minute. "I can't see you not telling your dad. You two are so close."

"I did tell him when I got my first real client. A remodel of a hotel outside of town. It was an absolutely crazy first real job that I only landed because I was friends with the hotel manager."

He looked down at his drink, remembering the struggles. "At the time, I only had two guys working under me. There was no way the three of us could handle a job that size. I called my parents, told them the whole crazy story, and after their initial shock, my dad said he'd come out to help."

"Isn't he a pharmacist?"

Ian nodded. "He did Habitat for Humanity for a long time, so he took a sabbatical of sorts. Said it was just the kind of physical work he needed—that he was getting soft."

"Your dad?" Brooke asked, genuinely shocked. She'd always pictured his dad as burly and capable, just like his son.

Ian waved that off. "When dad got to town, we hired ten more guys, some subcontractors. He went back to his reg job. I did two other commercial jobs before my grandparents decided they wanted to do a remodel."

"And their grandson being in construction had nothing to do with that?"

Ian shrugged. "You could probably drink that now."

Brooke brought the mug up to her nose, savoring the sweet scent of chocolate. She took another tentative sip. It was still hot but no longer scalding. "It's good. Really good," she managed and meant it.

"Good." His gaze rested on hers.

The sensation felt surreal. They'd sat around drinking a beer or a soda together on more *nights* than Brooke could count. The early morning hour made it feel somehow more intimate.

"Is that why you're here then? To do the remodel?"

He nodded. "That, and my grandma had a fall last summer."

"I'm sorry. I hadn't heard. Is she doing better?"

"She is, mostly, or she pretends to be, but dad didn't like that she and my grandpa were alone up here. He still has a few years 'til retirement. He'd just taken the sabbatical to help me out with the hotel, and he has a pension with his company. It would be a big mistake for him to quit now, so I came. Perks of being self-employed."

"Will you stay? Permanently, I mean? Or will you go back when your dad retires?"

"I'm not sure. Before yesterday, I was working on getting a network going here. If I can make it work, I'll probably stay. It'd suck to start over a third time. Besides, a lot of reconstruction will need to be done now. New homes, new businesses."

"Wait," Brooke said. "Are you living with your grandparents?"

Ian choked on his hot chocolate, coughed, then laughed. "Like some guy in my parent's basement, only worse because I'm mooching off my grandparents?"

"No!" Mortified, she fumbled. "No, I didn't mean that at all! It's just that it sounds like you came here unsure if you'd stay, and I wondered if you'd stay at their house to help out while your grandma heals."

"Ah. No, I rented a house over in West Salem. I was thinking of asking the owners if they'd consider selling it to me, but Christ knows what condition it's in now."

"Are you going to check later today?"

"Nope. The bridges to West Salem are toast."

"You sound so sure."

Ian ran a hand over the back of his neck. "They were pretty much a guaranteed failure."

Brooke thought of her grandmother's home. If it was any indication, she was on the edge of a city that would need to be rebuilt one building—one heart—at a time.

Chapter Twenty-One

On the cot, Maddie stirred. "Mommy? Daddy?"

Brooke handed her mug to Ian and moved to Maddie. "Hi, honey. It's Auntie Brooke and Ian."

Maddie rubbed her eyes. "Mommy. Want mommy."

"Bet you're cold, Maddie," Brooke said, changing the subject.

Ian moved to sit beside Maddie on the cot, careful not to tip it with his weight. "It's freezing monkeys in here."

Maddie giggled.

"Don't worry. I brought," he bent conspiratorially to whisper in Maddie's ear, "hot chocolate."

"Eee!" she screamed, before Ian had had a chance to back up. "Really? You share wif mommy and daddy? Where's mommy and daddy?"

Brooke's heart sank. "It's just us right now."

Where the hell is Seth?

Ian pulled a small plastic cup from his bag, filled it with the rest of the hot chocolate, and handed it to Maddie.

He brought her a cup. Of course he had. Brooke knew she shouldn't have been surprised. What kind of man would show up to a tent with a woman and child and not have a cup for the child. But still. He'd made them hot chocolate. Knowing he'd done it for Maddie as much as for her had Brooke's heart taking another terrifying step toward goo.

Maddie handed her cup to Brooke, sat in her sleeping bag, and pulled it around her legs. She reached for her cup. "Very thank you, Ian."

"Yeah. You can bring that cup back at dinner. I've gotta go."

"Yummy, yumm, yumm," Maddie said, taking big gulps of her own.

"See you tonight," Ian told Brooke.

He wasn't letting her back out.

"Okay."

He grabbed his poncho, bunched it up, and threw it in the bag. "You need anything before then, come get me."

"We're fine."

Ian crouched, this time much closer to her than he had sat moments ago. "Stubborn," he corrected, brushing his thumb over her cheek. "Get. Me. Brooke."

His deep voice, his steady gaze, had her gulping.

"Sure," she managed and watched as he slipped out of the tent.

Chapter Twenty-Two

"Auntie, can I have breakfast now?"

Brooke shifted her attention from the entrance of the tent back to Maddie and smiled. "Of course you can, Maddie."

"Can I hab some cereal, pweese?"

"Humm."

Brooke suddenly felt her stomach drop. The previous evening, she'd been so focused on creating a shelter. Maybe, Brooke thought, she'd have been able to do it all in an hour flat on her own. With a just-turned-three-year-old girl who was scared and cold, who'd just lost her mom with her dad M.I.A., the tasks had taken on more challenges than Brooke could have imagined.

Breakfast hadn't even made it on her agenda.

It was a new day—Brooke hoped, a better day—but she had no idea what they were going to do for food, which sucked because the massive effort she'd put into the shelter had ultimately failed.

Brooke had *hoped* to be able to focus on new problems. Now she had the new crap and the old and had to fight to keep the scowl from her face.

Come on, Seth. Any minute now.

She thought of the refrigerator, all the food in it likely rotten by now without electricity. Keeping her voice as casual as possible, she said, "Well, we don't have milk, but I'm sure we can come up with something."

"But Auntie!" The whine told Brooke she'd better come up with something fast. Maddie hadn't slept well. A tired and hungry toddler would just be that much harder.

Brooke poked her head outside and let out a quiet sigh of relief. "Sun's coming out. Come on. Let's get up and see what we have for breakfast. You want to help me make it?"

"Sure!"

They crawled out. Brooke stood to her full height and lifted her arms above her head to stretch her lower back again.

"What this? What is it?"

Following Maddie's pointing finger, Brooke lifted an eyebrow. "I don't know. Let's see."

Bending beside a forest green tote she knew damn well hadn't been there the night before, Brooke lifted the lid. Inside, she found a note.

Hey, Maddie. I heard you like cereal. Didn't have milk. Hope it's okay. Ian.

Grateful almost as much for the smile that spread across her face as for the food, Brooke opened the grocery sack inside the tote and found ten tiny boxes of cereal, the kind generally found in hotel complimentary breakfast tables alongside pastries and fruit. It brought to mind images of blueberry muffins hot out of the stove and made her tummy growl.

God, she was starving.

Brooke read the note to Maddie and let the toddler choose her first box. Then Brooke chose one for herself. They moved back into the semi-warmth of the tent and ate breakfast right out of the box.

"Is cereal for all breakfasts today?"

All breakfasts? "Oh, all meals, you mean?"

Maddie nodded her head, hopeful.

"'Fraid not, kiddo. We're going to have to do healthy stuff."

"Like padcakes without the syrup?" Maddie asked, her face falling.

"Pancakes aren't healthy."

"Daddy say yes," she said defiantly. "When mommy's not home."

And just like that, Brooke realized, the fun cereal time was over. Maddie had just brought up food Seth served. . . when Jen wasn't home.

Brooke's fingers itched to grab for her cell phone. She'd tucked it into one of the pockets that lined the side of the tent, but now wasn't the time. Besides, her multiple attempts to reach Seth the night before hadn't worked. She hadn't been able to get service.

Reaching her arm around Maddie's shoulders, Brooke squeezed, kissing the top of Maddie's hair while the little girl ate her cereal one small piece at a time.

The smell of Maddie's baby shampoo was still strong enough to linger in the girl's golden bedhead curls.

We need a brush.

The thought, so absolutely ridiculous in comparison to all the things they *actually* needed, had a laugh bubbling out of her. Then, just as hastily as the laughter had teased, tears now threatened, a sudden awareness of how truly screwed they were.

How long until we can shower? she wondered.

Even that question seemed trivial.

They would need to go into the city to get groceries. Not that she wasn't grateful for the breakfast Ian had left—she was—but she didn't want to spend the week (or however long it took until things started getting back to normal) mooching off the neighbors.

If she could, she'd get enough food to make a meal for them as repayment for breakfast. There was still plenty of money in her account from her grandmother's estate.

Brooke bit her bottom lip. She would need some of that money to pay for rent now, seeing how she was now homeless. Goosebumps cruised across her skin. *Homeless.*

After her mom had died, her dad had spent six solid weeks in an internal debate about whether he should quit his job as a fireman before the fire season began.

Brooke had come down the stairs of their house late one evening, unable to sleep. She'd intended to ask him if he wanted to play a card game or something, but as she'd headed toward the kitchen, she'd heard him talking.

The late hour had puzzled her.

Who would be over this late, she'd wondered?

She'd peeked around the corner. He'd been talking to himself—something he'd done more frequently since her mom's passing. Lonely.

"Great. If I work, I can't parent all summer because I won't freaken' be here. If I parent, I can't do the damn fire season. We'll be living on the streets by August."

Brooke had watched her dad run his hands down his face. "All I've ever done is fight fires. How the hell else am I supposed to pull enough income? But damned if I'm going to let our little girl live on the streets."

He'd leaned back in his chair then, staring up at the ceiling with a look of defeat on his face that Brooke had never seen before.

Her heart had broken for him. She'd been terrified.

Homeless. We can't lose our house. No. No. I just lost my mom. She'd slipped silently back up to her room. And had wept.

The weeks following that night flowed with uncertainty until her mom's mom in Oregon had called and had saved them from the streets.

Now, Brooke wondered how to be that answer for Maddie until Seth came home and how to be that answer for herself in the following days and weeks. On the drive home from the interview, not having a job had been hard enough. Now she was stuck in the aftermath of an earthquake, caring for a toddler, homeless and grieving.

I'll fix it. Eventually, I'll find something to rent. As soon as Seth gets home to watch Maddie, I'll start looking. Even with my savings, can I rent an apartment in town without a job? Can I get a job without an apartment? She had so many questions, but she'd have to wait to figure out the housing.

For now, they needed food.

Chapter Twenty-Three

Brooke ran a hand through her hair, staring down the gravel road at her car's busted-out windows and very flat front tire. Debris flooded the driveway around the car.

She didn't have the keys to Jen's car and knew she'd have to go into the house eventually to search for them. Jen's body was still in the house. Finding keys would just have to wait until Maddie's nap, which was still hours away.

Brooke couldn't wait hours. She and Maddie needed to get food before lunch.

The neighbors could loan her a car, she supposed, but then they'd want to know why she was going to town.

Not wanting them to know mostly came down to money. Brooke and Maddie had already depended on the neighbors for two meals. She didn't know all that much about the neighbors' financial status, but George and Carol were retired. Ian's grandparents, Irene and Henry, were too.

Though Brooke didn't know who was staying with Irene and Henry, Ian had mentioned the house was packed. She doubted they had enough food to feed her and Maddie for long, and she didn't want them to have to spend their retirement income on providing more meals. So she and Maddie were going to take a walk to pick up some groceries.

"I get a ride in the princess pack-pack?" Maddie asked.

Brooke eyed the backpack child carrier. On it, she saw princesses dancing in luxurious ball gowns across the fabric.

"That's right."

"Why do I not sit in the strower with the camewope?"

The what? Brooke glanced down at the stroller beside her. The material was covered in cartoon animals partying on the beach.

"Maddie, do you mean this guy?" Brooke asked with a gentle chuckle, pointing.

"Umhu. He is da cutest camewope I ever sawed!"

"Oh, my gosh, Maddie, you are adorable. He is called a camel. Can you say camel?"

Maddie tried the word.

"Good! I think you are confusing the word with a cantaloupe. Cantaloupe is a fruit."

"I very like fruit."

"Yeah. It's pretty yummy."

Brooke figured she would always think of it as the camewope stroller but didn't want to confuse Maddie by using the phrase just now.

"You're not riding in the camel stroller because I need to use it to carry things. Besides, if you ride in the backpack, you get to be tall."

Not wanting the neighbors to know she was leaving to shop for groceries meant that Brooke would be taking Maddie to the store. Carrying Maddie would make the job harder.

Brooke shrugged. Even if money hadn't been an issue, she wouldn't have asked the neighbors to watch Maddie. The neighbors were trustworthy. They were awesome, but images of another aftershock hitting with Maddie in one of the homes terrified her.

Would an aftershock be enough to bring the other homes down? Maybe not. Maybe. Who knew?

As nonsensical as it was, Brooke just didn't want Maddie out of her sight until Seth got back. The fact that nearly an entire day had gone by without seeing him worried Brooke. She needed him to come home to his daughter, and Brooke still desperately wanted to be there when he did get home to stop him from going into the house.

She glanced toward Liberty Street. He wasn't there. She doubted he'd walked through the night, figuring he'd had to camp out somewhere.

If she made the round trip to the small grocery store quickly enough, she'd be back before lunch. Hopefully, she'd beat Seth home, and when he arrived, he'd see that he and his daughter had food. Brooke couldn't stand the idea of Seth coming home to learn he was a widower only to have to figure out how to get food for Maddie.

Brooke pulled out her phone and checked yet again to see if she could get a weather report, but the internet was still down. *No service, either*, she noted.

"When are they going to get that back up?" she grumbled under her breath. "Alright, kiddo. You ready?"

"Yippee!"

"I'll take that as a yes."

Brooke placed the child's backpack on the edge of the wooden patio. After hoisting the little girl into the carrier, Brooke stepped down to the grass. She squatted, her back to Maddie, and weaved Maddie's arms through the straps.

Bracing for the weight, knowing her bruised hip would protest, she reconsidered her choice not to take someone's car. *Am I a total idiot? Probably, but we need food. We're going.*

Brooke stood up. The carrier didn't absorb as much of Maddie's weight as Brooke had hoped.

With Maddie in the backpack, Brooke pushed the empty stroller she planned to use as a shopping cart around the side of the house to the road. The gravel beneath the wheels crunched. She slowed her pace, trying to quiet her journey. It didn't work. In the otherwise quiet morning, each turn of plastic wheel met the ground like iron thrown through an industrial wood chipper.

Lifting the stroller slightly so that the back two wheels didn't touch the ground, she cringed and desperately hoped no one would come out to investigate.

"I feel like a teen sneaking out of the house in the middle of the night," she muttered.

"What's that?!" Maddie's voice held fear and curiosity in equal measure.

Cringing at the volume of Maddie's voice, Brooke looked up at the tiny, horrified face above hers and the hand that pointed.

Following the direction of the finger, Brooke found herself staring at the ruined remains of her home. Not just bricks, Brooke noted. In her shock the day before, she'd seen only bricks.

The adrenaline had long passed. Standing at a distance with a clear head changed the image she knew she'd carry in her mind.

Twisted metal piping played among the bricks like a college art project. On top, debris appeared to have blown into the heap during the stormy night. Still wet from that storm, the mess that had once been her most-loved home covered her beloved dog Sparks.

A new wave of grief filled her. She longed to feel his weight laying on her feet while she graded papers. She even missed getting up early in the morning to let him out to pee.

Hell. How do I explain this—any of this—to a three-year-old?

"My home got hurt."

"That's your home? I'm sorwy auntie!"

"Thanks, honey." She took a deep breath. "It can be fixed. Don't worry."

Brooke knew "fixing" the home wasn't going to happen, but a new home could be built in its place. She still owned the land, Brooke reminded herself.

But Mr Neilson had turned her down for the job. Would she have to sell the land? Brooke wondered. She squeezed her eyes shut.

"Ready to help me pick out some groceries?" she asked Maddie.

"Oh, tay."

Brooke turned away from the mangled mess and headed north on Liberty.

Chapter Twenty-Four

She was wrong to have brought Maddie with her.

In terms of decisions, Brooke figured this one hit an all-time "so wrong." Before they'd begun the walk, Maddie's safety had been at the forefront of her mind—paramount. She hadn't considered much else.

She should have.

Many buildings on Liberty Road showed signs of trauma. Roads and sidewalks lay broken beneath plaster, glass, and shingles.

As she and Maddie approached the intersection at Kuebler Blvd, Brooke marveled at the tents and other less-official makeshift homes sprawled everywhere. Her heartbeat quickened.

She stopped walking and debated turning around.

"Hey, Earl!"

An old man standing in a yard to Brooke's left waved his hand wildly at an even older neighbor who'd just emerged from a tent. The older man scratched his butt and yawned, with his eyes dazed with sleep.

The younger neighbor hollered again. "Earl, did you hear? Got your HAM radio working yet?"

Earl turned and focused on his neighbor for the first time. "Not yet, Mick."

"They're saying most of the grocery stores are completely out of food. Heading to Roth's in ten. You should come before there's nothing left."

Brooke gaped at the two men.

"Be ready in five," Earl told Mick before diving back into the tent.

Out of food. How could the stores be nearly out of food? Already?! Less than a day had passed since the earthquake. *A mere twenty-one hours.*

She closed her eyes, biting her lips. Of course, they were almost out Her fingers began to rub around her temples, where a headache brewed.

Hadn't the stores run low on supplies quickly during storms? And this was so much worse.

Had she not been with a toddler, she'd have gone to the store before now, Brooke admitted. If she had been on her own, it might have been the first thing she'd have done, but the shock and grief of the previous day and the duties of caring for Maddie had postponed even the thought of grocery shopping.

Now what?

Brooke didn't want Maddie to see the destruction around them, but there was no time to turn around. They'd come so far already, and according to Mick and Earl, time was running out.

Besides Brooke hadn't seen any cars driving. The state of the roads made it foolish to try; that was something else Brooke hadn't realized before she and Maddie had set out on their journey. She hadn't understood that a trip to the store would only be manageable on foot or bike.

The primary facts of that morning hadn't changed, she decided. They needed food.

"Ooooh." Maddie, who'd been uncharacteristically quiet during the walk, squealed. "Doggie!"

Doggie?

Brooke turned her body slowly until she saw the fluffy yellow lab. It ran full-speed down the middle of the otherwise empty road, tongue hanging hilariously out of the side of his mouth. He skillfully avoided the road debris and looked as though he was tasting freedom for the first time.

A collar, bright blue, told Brooke he had an owner. As the dog passed them, Brooke wondered if his owner would ever find him. Were the shelters open? Doubtful. For now, she hoped the dog enjoyed his excursion.

At least someone is having fun.

"Aww, come back, doggie."

"I think he's... busy," Brooke tried.

"Doggie's are cute. They are da best in da suns and da moons."

That made Brooke smile. "I love dogs, too." She tried to keep her voice light, grateful something positive had lifted Maddie's mood.

"What other animals do you love, Maddie?"

"Kitties. Fwuffy kitties. And frogs, buterfwies, kuwawas..."

While Maddie listed off an impressive number of animals, Brooke refocused on their current situation.

The stores were almost out of food. At least, according to Mick and Earl. They could be wrong. Hell, she didn't even know what a HAM radio was, but the man seemed to have insider information.It could be misinformation, she admitted, but she and Maddie needed to hurry, just in case.

If the stores run out, how long would it take for them to restock?

She didn't have a clue. If she continued, Brooke knew the walk would further subject Maddie to the chaos around them. It wasn't ideal, but she hoped talking about animals—the little girl was still naming them off—would distract Maddie until they could reach Roth's grocery store.

Brooke picked up her pace, convinced moving toward town was the right choice.

She held on to that determination for another two blocks before she saw it. Her heart jumped, then plummeted.

She stopped the stroller and stared. The single-story building made of wood and brick hadn't collapsed completely, but Liberty Elementary School was in bad shape.

Citizens dressed in green vests and CERT-logoed hats stood outside. One man held what looked to Brooke like an expensive walkie-talkie.

"Need more help in there, Steve?" Brooke heard the man with the walkie-talkie ask. "Two more volunteers just arrived. Over."

"Found another child. Age ten. Broken arm. Possible broken leg. Cold and scared. Looks okay otherwise. I could use help carrying her out. Over."

"What's your location? Over."

"God. Is it Amanda?" A woman in her early forties asked the CERT man.

The terrified mom didn't appear to have slept all night.

This mother had worried about her daughter for nearly twenty-four hours, Brooke realized because the earthquake had struck in the late morning.

10:15 a.m.

During school hours.

Brooke had thought of Candalaria Elementary School after the earthquake. She'd even planned on going over to help out. Then, she'd forgotten all about helping when she'd found her best friend dead.

How many others had wanted to help but couldn't?

A tear slid down her cheek. Like coming out of a fog, out of her own bubble of circumstance and shock, the gravity of the destruction in town hit Brooke on a whole new level.

I should have been here yesterday to help.

Just as quickly as that idea came, Brooke dismissed it. No, she realized. She couldn't have come. She'd had Maddie, still had Maddie, leaving her a bystander on the sidewalk.

The woman ran around the north side of the building, away from the CERT members. Before Brooke could wonder why, the mom came back with another woman.

"They've found someone?"

"Is it Julie?" the new mom asked.

"I don't know," Brooke heard Amanda's mom say. The two women held hands and waited. Other parents and neighbors stood by.

Feeling helpless, Brooke thought of Candalaria. Had it collapsed? Sixty-five schools. That's what she'd read on the Salem-Keizer School District's website. The district was home to forty-two elementary, eleven middle, eight high, and four charter schools. Over forty thousand children. Children who had been in school when the shaking had started.

How many were trapped? How many parents stood like these women, outside waiting?

Which girl would be coming out? Was her leg broken? So much time had passed. Why hadn't they found the second girl yet?

Heartbroken, Brooke turned from the women, unsure of what to do. She wanted to help, wanted to throw herself into the building to find other kids, and knew she couldn't.

Hands in fists, she breathed, trying to think. As she inhaled, the stench of busted sewer lines and smoke filled her lungs, burning her nostrils. Lifting her eyes, Brooke looked beyond the immediate destruction, letting her vision expand. Another tear escaped. Her earlier assumption that the smoke was from campfires or barbeques had been wrong. She saw now. It billowed from burning buildings in the distance, burning homes.

Schools had fallen. Homes like hers had crumpled. Others had burned. Children were separated from caregivers.

The Salem that Brooke had always known and loved would never be the same.

Victims of their broken built environment, the community was scared, hurt, homeless, and grieving.

And Maddie sat perched above Brooke's shoulders in the backpack with front-row seats to it all.

Chapter Twenty-Five

Brooke turned from Liberty Elementary, from what her heart could no longer take. She walked two houses to the south, back towards home, then stopped.

Her legs, her hips, and her back throbbed. Moving carefully, she lowered herself to the sidewalk and gritted her teeth against the pain.

She got to her knees and then rotated around. While sitting on the wet, cold cement, she leaned back.

"Aah," Maddie screamed.

Although the backpack was only inches from the ground, the leaning motion made Maddie feel as though she was falling.

"I've got you," Brooke assured.

Unconvinced, Maddie gripped Brooke's hair like a rider gripping the reins on a horse while Brooke lowered the metal feet of the backpack to the ground.

Feeling Maddie's weight transfer to the sidewalk, Brooke let out a short whimper of relief and admitted to herself that she'd needed to do the stroller earlier.

Shoulda, coulda, woulda. Hindsight, she fumed.

Brooke had wanted to get to the store with Maddie in the pack and the stroller ready to load with groceries.

She reached her hands up and gently patted Maddie's fingers that were still wrapped in Brooke's hair. "Sweetie, can you let go, please?"

"Sowwy, Auntie Brooke."

Maddie let go, allowing Brooke to work her arms out of the straps. She stretched her back, then arched it and winced. What she wouldn't give for a hot bath.

"Why you put me down?" Maddie asked.

"Change of plans, kiddo."

Maddie tilted her head. "Pwans? We not get food? I'm hungry."

Brooke debated what to say. If the men had been right, Roth's was nearly out of food. Nearly didn't mean the store had nothing. She and Maddie could go, grab what they could, but Brooke couldn't justify exposing Maddie to the destruction around them.

A raindrop fell, wet on Brooke's cheek. *The perfect scapegoat.*

"I'd hoped we could get to the store before the rain came."

Maddie held up her hand, lifted her face to the clouds. "It's raining. Auntie, look, I can catch drops with my mowf."

"I can see that. Pretty cool."

Brooke pushed her thumb down to unlock the belt around Maddie. Then, standing, she placed her hands under Maddie's arms and lifted the three-year-old out of the backpack.

Panting from the effort, Brooke looked down. "You know, kid, you might have outgrown that thing."

Maddie pouted. "No. Why I am getting out?"

"Time to ride in the camelope."

"Ooh! Yippie!"

Maddie wiggled her slender body under the stroller's attached food tray and sat in the still-dry seat. Brooke looked at the sky. They wouldn't stay dry for long, she thought, as she secured Maddie's seatbelt.

Light gray clouds covered the sky now.

"Here we go." Brooke forced herself to keep her words light, not letting her disappointment, her panic about not being able to buy food come through in her tone.

"Big hug first?"

Smiling now, Brooke squeezed under the stroller's canopy and gave Maddie the biggest hug the awkward space allowed.

Maddie giggled. "Not that big."

Brooke turned to place the now empty backpack on her shoulders, its metal frame too large to fit in the stroller.

After securing its straps around her waist, she took a step north, feeling panic well up inside. They needed food. When Seth got home, he'd need a way to feed his daughter. Hell, she needed a way to feed his daughter until he got back. What were they going to do?

Glancing back toward the injured elementary school, Brooke promised herself she'd figure out another way to get food. She'd find one that didn't involve traumatizing Maddie any more than she probably already had, she thought in disgust.

Christ.

She heard people waking up to face their new reality. Like her, they would need to eat and there wouldn't be enough at the stores to feed the city.

Chapter Twenty-Six

The rain, no longer a gentle mist, continued to strengthen. Large drops slid like toboggans down the slick, dark green material of Brooke's raincoat to land squarely on the ass of her jeans.

In the stroller, Maddie sang her twentieth rendition of "She'll Be Coming Round the Mountain." Glancing down, Brooke could see her through a small skylight in the animal print canopy. Maddie sat dry under its reach, cuddled in a small throw blanket for extra warmth.

Good thing she's not still in the backpack, Brooke mused.

She tugged at the hem of her raincoat, willing the material to stretch farther, cover more of her pants. The attempt failed. Again.

It was pointless, anyway. Brooke's pants were thoroughly saturated. Even the denim tucked deep below the height of the purple rainboots she wore didn't stand a chance.

Gravity at its finest.

Not that she should complain, Brooke reminded herself. The jacket helped. Without it, her torso would be just as wet. Just as cold.

She thought of Ian.

He'd left her and Maddie the breakfast tote that morning. Brooke had found the jacket tucked Beside the bag of food and a few bottles of water.

More than those necessary-to-life contents, the single tote had provided Brooke hope amid an impossible situation. That hope had pushed her to believe that she could start this new day successfully.

Like buying groceries for herself and Maddie. *And hadn't that gone swimmingly?*

Eyebrows creasing in self-irritation, Brooke stopped pushing the stroller to wipe the rain from her forehead, her eyes.

She was freezing. Her stomach muscles clenched spasmodically against the chill. Exposed to the elements, Brooke's fingers could barely grip the stroller anymore, and she wished she had some waterproof gloves to go with the coat.

Why not throw in wishes for a complete waterproof outfit and a warm fire to stand beside?

You can do this. You're almost there. Just a little farther. You can make it to the tent, dry off, and warm up. Just a little more now.

She pushed forward the last half block before turning right off Liberty. And there they were. Brooke gaped at the scene in front of George and Carol's home.

Their slightly earthquake-damaged single-story home was set back from a large and, thanks to Carol's love of gardening, well-manicured grass-covered front lawn.

An off-white ten by twenty caravan canopy that hadn't been there that morning provided a massive umbrella over that front lawn, sheltering those hanging out beneath.

Hanging out. It was the only phrase that fit, Brooke thought. The group looked as though they were getting ready for a regular summer barbeque, complete with lawn chairs, blue ice coolers, and food.

Across the yard beyond the cover of the canopy, bowls, buckets, and cooking pots strewn about collected rainwater.

It wasn't just another everyday summer barbeque.

But the group had a fire going in the front yard, in the middle of winter, beneath a canopy that held back the pouring rain.

A fire.

Brooke's legs moved toward the answered wish, the warmth, before she'd consciously registered the decision to walk.

"Oh, look." Carol simultaneously waved and pointed so the others could follow the direction of her excitement. "There are Maddie and Brooke. Hello, you two."

Ian, a look on his face Brooke couldn't read, ran out from under the canopy with an umbrella. Opening it up, he made his way to them and held it above Brooke as she continued toward George and Carol's yard.

"Thanks," she said.

"Where have you been?"

Brooke's expression of gratitude for his chivalrous umbrella move quickly changed, her eyebrows rising in surprise. "On a walk."

"For two flippin' hours?" He fought to keep his voice a whisper so that Maddie wouldn't hear. Brooke, however, heard just fine.

Two hours? She stopped walking briefly to glance at her phone. Damn near, she noted.

"I had a... chore," she said lamely.

"A chore." He let out a slow breath and ran a hand over the back of his neck. "Look, Halliwill, I can't remember a time where I couldn't just pick up a phone to call someone. Damn if I'm not frustrated the phones aren't working."

She shrugged. "I get it."

"Not being able to call when I'm worried about someone is worse. I *care* about you."

"I was fine. I can—"

"Let me guess," he cut in. "Handle yourself?"

"Halliwell, I didn't know where you'd gone, when you'd be back—hell, *if* you'd be back. I sat around wondering if you'd left to find a shelter."

"I..."

She had hoped no one would notice their absence and had expected to return with food to share. Now guilt filled her.

Brooke remembered the warming center; the stench, the sounds of sickness, the filth. If that was what a shelter looked like with electricity, running water, and working sewer systems before a massive earthquake, she thought, there was no way in hell she would ever consider taking Maddie to one in the current post-disaster state of things.

Shivering from a mix of fear and chill, she shook her head vehemently.

"I told you to come get me. Whatever you needed. Why didn't you? Christ, Brooke, where'd you go?"

She debated how to respond. She felt so stupid for having gone for groceries with Maddie, knowing she'd severely underestimated how bad things currently were in town. She'd exposed a three-year-old girl to its horrors when she could have left Maddie with him. With them.

That she'd gone without taking another adult with her, not traveling in pairs, he wouldn't understand that choice.

Ian was and had always been a protector. He took care of others around him. So did she. However, unlike her, he worked best in a team and had no qualms about asking for help and depending on others.

She did.

Carol stood, walked to the edge of the canopy closest to Ian, Maddie, and Brooke. "You three going to come in out of the rain or what?"

Chapter Twenty-Seven

The Pendleton blanket wrapped around Brooke laid heavy over a dry jacket. Beneath, she wore a complete change of clothes, given to her by Ian's mom, Laura Russick.

Just slightly shorter than Mrs. Russick, the clothing fit well enough, Brooke thought as she looked at Laura and her husband Bill, who were readying a new pot of water for lunch. They were good people, good parents to Ian and his brother Alex.

Every summer during Brooke's stay with her grandma, Laura, Bill, and their boys would visit Salem for their annual two-week summer vacation, staying with Bill's parents.

Brooke remembered looking forward to those summers with Jen. She'd looked forward to those two weeks with Ian and Alex, too, though Alex had often been the odd kid out at three years younger than them.

At every visit, Laura had treated Brooke as family. This afternoon was no exception. Brooke felt incredibly grateful.

Maddie left Ian, who'd been showing her how to tie fancy knots, and climbed onto Brooke's lap.

Comfortable around the neighbors she'd grown up around, Maddie had spent the past hour slowly exploring the group's activities but in short bursts. In the absence of her parents, of Jen in particular, Maddie frequently returned to Brooke's arms for comfort.

Brooke watched the fire dance, thinking of how strange the sight was in the middle of the day. Her dad fought fires for a living. The smell reminded her of him. Brooke wished she could call him, tell him about all that had happened since the earthquake. She wanted him to be there with them.

The smoke floating toward her reminded her of how the residents of the warming center had smelled—soot and urine.

Was this what they had all done when the warming center had shoved them out into the cold at 6:30 a.m. sharp that Sunday morning? Had they found dry wood somewhere and lit a fire for warmth?

To her, sitting around a fire in the middle of the day, surrounded by homes, felt surreal. Since her dad had spent his summers fighting fires, Brooke and her mom hadn't gone camping much. They'd preferred the vacations that included hotel rooms and breakfast bars, but Brooke imagined even a camper would find the surroundings strange.

It wasn't all that different from a barbecue, she supposed. She wished her day was that simple: a barbecue, a football game on a big-screen TV, and a warm, safe house. Instead, their situation was closer to being shoved back in time to the 1800s.

Maddie nuzzled into Brooke's chest. "You are da best auntie in the suns and da moons."

Snapping back to the moment, Brooke smiled down at Maddie. "Aww, thanks. You are the best too. Did Ian show you the double overhand knot?" Brooke asked her, wondering how long Ian would stay mad at her for leaving that morning.

Maddie nodded but said nothing. The girl who'd sung in the stroller wasn't singing now. In fact, she was barely talking.

Thinking of Jen, Brooke thought, her stomach twisting. Desperate to distract Maddie, she went on. "I bet you're hungry. I'm starving."

Maddie laid her head on Brooke's cheek, pulled small feet up onto Brooke's thigh, and said nothing.

Shit. Where are you, Seth? Maddie needs her dad right now. Hurry home.

Though no one said anything in front of Maddie, Brooke knew that news of Jen's death had passed from person to person. The air was filled with sadness, yet every adult did their best to hide it in front of Maddie.

Brooke pulled her phone out, checked yet again to see if any of her text messages to her dad had gone through. Running a frustrated hand through her hair at the lack of notifications on her lock screen, she wished a text would come in from him.

"So, Brooke, I hear you're applying to teach here in Salem. Any hooks yet?" The question came from Fawn Russick. Fawn, Ian's very pregnant sister-in-law, looked as calm as if she had just walked out of her resort in Maui. Given her state, the situation, and everyone else being on edge, Brooke fumbled.

"I—yes, I interviewed for a job yesterday."

When everyone shot her looks of confusion, she clarified, "It was an early morning interview." *Before the earthquake.* She didn't say it—didn't want Maddie thinking about it.

"You serious?" Alex, Fawn's husband, turned from where he was pouring a cup and a half of boiling water to a freeze-dried Mountain House lasagna meal. "Girl!" He turned to his brother. "You hear that, Ian? Brooke's settling in."

The water sloshed in the pan as Alex jerked mid-pour. His joking tone and casual demeanor that he'd been trying so hard to keep relaxed, dropped away. "Shit," he looked at Maddie, then at his pregnant wife. "Shoot. Sorry." Then he looked back at Brooke. "I. Your house. I. I wasn't thinking. It's been such a long day, and I'm exhausted. I'm so sorry."

"Don't worry about it, Alex. Besides, I am going to settle here."

"Still?"

With a serious tone, Ian turned from the tent pole he was repairing to look at her.

"That was the plan forty-eight hours ago." She nearly told the group that she hadn't gotten the job but didn't want to add to Maddie's distress.

"Besides," she gently ran her hand over Maddie's golden hair and pasted a smile on her face, hoping the correct tone would follow. "I've got this adorable girl to play with. Who would want to go anywhere else?"

If only it were that easy, she thought. She felt Maddie relax against her a fraction. *Good.*

From the corner of her eye, she saw Ian watching her and weighing her answer. It made her want to squirm.

She did want to stay in Salem, but her life was nothing like it had been forty-eight hours earlier, and they both knew it. When she'd woken the previous day, she'd had a house, a job opportunity, a dog, and a best friend living next door.

She'd lost all four.

She thought of Liberty Elementary and wondered if Candalaria had suffered the same fate. God, she hoped not. All those kids.

It made the idea of job hunting—critically important before—seem shallow. Still, the thoughts swirled. Things would be very different now. Getting a job would be easier in a city outside of a disaster zone. Easy made sense. A part of her wondered if she'd consider things "easy" when Seth came home to Maddie and things settled down.

She turned back to Ian's sister-in-law. "I'm sure the job will call soon, and I'll rent a place in town." Brooke's eyes moved down toward the top of Maddie's head. She acknowledged that her words sounded idiotic, but they were necessary to reassure.

Fawn smiled at her. "That's good. Maybe now Ian will finally take you out on a date."

"Oh, nice." Ian put his fingertips to his closed eyes, his lips curving up in an embarrassed grin. "That was smooth, Fawn."

She laughed, resting a hand on her rounded belly. "Sorry, hun, but I've been hearing about Brooke Halliwell since the first time your brother had me over for a family dinner."

Ian looked at Brooke, waving a section of the tent pole. "Not true." He handed the section to his dad, who was doing his level best not to laugh. "The second dinner, maybe. But not the first."

Ian was joking, his mood naturally lightening with the change in topic.

"What's a date?" Maddie asked.

"It's . . . going for coffee," Brooke said, so grateful the conversation had Maddie talking.

"Dinner," Ian corrected.

Brooke tilted her head in amusement.

"Oh," Maddie said. "Then can I have a date, pweese? I'm starving."

Everyone laughed.

"Maddie, you are an angel." Ian's grandma, Irene Russick—decked out in an OSU Beaver's jacket—beamed at the little girl. "Would you like to help me serve the food?"

Maddie hopped out of Brooke's lap. "Yes! I very wove to help."

Irene and her husband Henry worked to dump hot, rehydrated lasagna onto paper plates and pass them out, while Maddie brought plastic forks to everyone.

Brooke felt guilt grip her. She was about to be served lunch because she'd turned around at Liberty Elementary School and had never bought the groceries she'd intended to buy.

If it weren't for the generosity of these neighbors, she wouldn't be eating, wouldn't have eaten all day, for that matter. For someone as independent as she was, the realization terrified her.

George came around the corner carrying a case of beer.

Brooke let out a sigh. She could use one right about now.

Alex, clearly in agreement, grinned. "Are you serious right now? That's awesome. I didn't think I'd see a beer for the next month."

Chapter Twenty-Eight

"I got it!" George thumped a triumphant sideways fist on the cooler beside him. "Must have had a bad battery earlier."

The sounds of radio static and wavering voices boomed out of a small electronic device in his hand. It was dark out now. The afternoon had flown by as Brooke had done her best to clean the tent. She'd laid Maddie down for a nap and had tried to figure out how to make their next night better than the first.

She and Maddie had eaten dinner with the group again beneath the canopy, and Brooke's guilt for not being able to contribute to the meals had grown.

Now they all huddled around the flicker of the night's fire, warming themselves before heading off to bed.

Standing beside George, Ian's grandfather, Henry waved enthusiastically. "Come now. Everyone sit down and scoot in."

"Maddie, hop down for a sec, okay?"

The little face turned into a pout. "I want cuddles."

It made Brooke smile. "Me too. It's just for a second. Promise."

Eyebrows knitted, Maddie lowered herself off Brooke's lap.

"Thanks." Brooke scooted her chair closer to the fire pit.

The other adults followed suit, except for Fawn, who stayed farther back, not wanting to breathe too much of the smoke while pregnant.

Brooke glanced at Fawn's huge belly. One of those slender girls who didn't look pregnant until she turned sideways, Fawn looked like a pregnant pixie. In the glow of the fire, Fawn's face seemed peaceful, which baffled Brooke. She found herself wondering how tough post-earthquake life was for a pregnant woman.

Hopefully, things will start looking up soon. She turned her attention back to the device George held.

At about eight inches long, the oval red-and-black gadget read WeatherX. On one side, there were buttons marked AM, FM, and WB, and on the other, a sliding switch read options for Torch, Off, Lantern, and Siren.

Though it looked unimportant on an average day, the device had been a large conversation piece during dinner. Like a crystal ball, those sitting around Brooke swore it held all the answers.

Though she felt skeptical, the blazing bright white of its lantern brought her momentary comfort. With electricity out, she had quickly realized how flashlights like this one offered her control over light where little else could anymore. At least for now.

Maddie wiggled back into her lap to listen as George tuned the NOAA Weather frequency.

"Tonight, partly cloudy. Slight chance of a drizzle. Lows thirty to thirty-five. East wind five to ten mph shifting to the southeast after midnight."

"At least the weather report still comes through," Bill commented.

Glancing back, Alex rose from his chair, moved from the heat of the fire to sit by his wife. "FM's a bust. Which sucks. Could use some music right about now."

"What does sucks mean?" Maddie asked.

Fawn slapped her husband's knee when he laughed. "You have two weeks, tops, to break that cursin' habit of yours."

"Stinks," Brooke cut in. "Alex just meant it's sad that the normal songs don't work right now." She turned to Fawn. "You're really due that soon?"

Fawn nodded, and though her body language was still calm, Brooke now saw the concern in her eyes.

What would Salem be like in two weeks, Brooke wondered? It couldn't be easy to deliver a baby right after a major disaster, no matter what their crystal ball had in store.

"Might get, well," George corrected, "should be able to get something on AM."

He went back to fiddling with the dials and quickly found a station.

They all sat back, bellies full, and listened.

"That's right." A female voice flowed through the small speakers. "The USGS has confirmed the earthquake, which struck at 10:15 a.m. on February nineteenth as a magnitude 9.2. It traveled over six hundred miles, starting offshore of Cape Mendocino, California, all the way up to Vancouver Island in British Columbia, affecting millions."

A 9.2. Not just Salem. Oh my God. Brooke felt her breathing quicken.

"Folks, if you're just tuning in, you're listening to OPB. I'm Shawn Lager."

"And I'm Joann Jefferies."

"Man, oh man. What a thing. Our hearts go out to each and every one of you. We are reporting around the clock, as best we can, on the devastating earthquake and tsunami."

Tsunami? Brooke's eyebrows grew together. *As in gigantic waves?* She closed her eyes, focusing on the radio announcer's solemn, baritone voice, trying to stave off panic.

"However, many of our staff have been unable to make it in."

"Yes," Joann added. "Like you, they are caring for friends and family. Information from our remaining team members continues to come, and we . . . hang on, it looks like we've just made contact with one of our coastal reporters."

"This is Nancy Owens, reporting from Seaside, Oregon. How's the sound quality?"

Brooke's stomach plummeted.

Seaside. Seth.

"We can hear you," Shawn confirmed. "What can you tell us?"

"The situation is not good. I'm standing in the hills east of the city. It's . . . it is just unlike anything I have ever seen."

Brooke held her breath, held the little girl who sat in her lap, afraid to move, to hope.

"The shaking was incredibly strong in Seaside. Much of the land succumbed to what's called liquefaction. The water beneath the soil rose, turning the ground into a liquid, similar to quicksand."

Brooke felt her heart kick into sonic speed. She glanced around and found Ian watching her.

"Breathe," he mouthed. His eyes were kind and but the concern in them matched what she felt.

"How scary," Brooke heard Joann say before Nancy's voice came back on.

"Yes, as you can imagine, buildings didn't hold up very well. Worse, I'm told by local authorities that many of the evacuation routes were covered by landslides. And it's. . .well, Seaside is very low in elevation, so the evacuation zones are incredibly far from the majority of homes and businesses. Three miles, in some cases. Many of those homes were cut off from the evacuation routes due to downed bridges over the Necanicum River. And the tsunami waves—I'm told the first one came only fifteen minutes after the shaking stopped."

"Waves? There were more than one?" Shawn asked.

"Yes. For most people, the image that comes to mind is just one enormous wave coming through; however, a tsunami is a series of waves that are more like rising tides spilling into the city with incredible force and height. The second was the largest, reaching seventy feet high in places."

There was a moment of shocked silence on the radio.

"I'm not sure I could have evacuated anywhere after that shaking," Joann said. "I became nauseated from the continuous ground movement, as I've heard many others did. And fifteen minutes is not long to recover, let alone move fast."

"And what of those who were disabled or hospitalized? What about the young children, the elderly? Nancy, can you tell us of the survivors?"

"Information is coming slowly, as you can imagine. At the moment, I'm sorry to report—" Nancy's voice cracked, and there was a pause, "that I don't know of any."

"Any?"

"No, but as I said, we don't have all of the information. Those who got out of there made it to the hills. It will take time and manpower to find them. Most are sheltering in whatever they can find. It's cold, and the rains have been falling consistently all day."

"Has the water from the tsunami receded? Can the survivors make it back to town?"

"The waters have receded, but I'm told emergency managers don't expect Seaside to return to its state of normalcy for at least a decade. The waves inundated the entire city. Boats are sitting on what's left of homes. There. . . there's just nothing left. Nothing to return to."

Brooke swallowed hard as George quickly switched off the radio. They'd all wanted to know how things around the region were looking. They'd wanted to hear reports about expectations for the Willamette Valley.

Silence filled the air. Brooke had never fully considered the possibility that, like Jen, Seth might never come home.

She thought about the conversation she and Jen had had just days earlier. Seth had been out of town for a job. In Seaside. Had he been swept away?

Maddie sneezed.

Momentarily panicked that Maddie was crying, that Maddie had understood the implications of what was just said, Brooke gently but quickly spun the little girl on her lap so that they faced each other.

Not in tears, Maddie looked at her, quizzical. "Listen to music now?"

Relief flowed around the group, each person realizing Maddie was unaware of the significance of what they'd just heard.

But *they* each understood.

Her heart breaking for Maddie, Brooke gathered the little girl close, wondering if Maddie had just become her daughter.

Chapter Twenty-Nine

Wednesday, February 21, 2029 at 12:15 pm

Brooke forced the end of the shovel into the soil, the sound of it sliding into the ground sharply contrasting with the chirping of birds.

Closing her eyes, Brooke breathed in the scent of rain on soil and used it to steady herself.

The night had been long—so incredibly long. Thanks to the weather report, she'd known there was little chance of rain, but with temps predicted to be in the low thirties, she'd caved.

Henry and Irene, Ian's grandparents, already had such a full house with what Brooke had learned was a late-in-the-game baby shower.

Instead, Brooke had accepted the invite for her and Maddie to crash on the living room couches at George and Carol's.

Going inside had unnerved her. Though George had mentioned the cracks in the drywall, seeing them made her stomach uneasy. Stable. He'd told her the house was stable. Still, the cracks worried her.

But the couches, long and a bit lumpy, had been far better than the tent floor of the previous night. Despite the comfort, she was overwhelmed with worries of aftershocks, concerns about Seth, anxiety of possibly being a new mom, and grief. She'd tossed and turned most of the night.

Brooke hadn't wanted to close her eyes, afraid of what the nightmares might bring, so she'd spent the final hours problem-solving.

She and Maddie needed a stable, permanent home. Trying to make it over the Cascade Mountain range to Eastern Oregon, where apparently the earthquake's impact would be far less damaging, wasn't an option. Brooke still couldn't believe how large of an area the earthquake had covered.

The previous evening, Bill had pulled her aside. Most bridges in the state were down, and roads were impassable by car. Redmond, he'd informed her, was most likely her best option . . .a hundred and thirty miles away.

As she dug, Brooke wondered if she could make it to Redmond had she been on her own in the warm summer months. Could she carry enough food and water to walk that far?

But it wasn't summer. In mid-February, snow blanketed the pass. Impossibly cold nights and brutally strong wind greeted all who would try.

And she wasn't on her own. She had a three-year-old now.

The tent wasn't going to cut it. Neither were two lumpy couches.

Brooke glanced at the two-story structure Maddie called home, then back at the shovel jammed in the soil.

With effort, Brooke hefted the shovel up, dumping its contents into a heap off to the side.

It was just past noon. Maddie slept in the now-dried-out tent, taking what Brooke hoped would be a nice, long nap. Brooke needed the time.

She and Maddie had to stay in Salem, and for now, had to shelter in place. They needed Jen and Seth's house to do it. Brooke knew she needed to get in the house to access any remaining food in the cupboards. Maddie needed new clothes, and Brooke wanted Maddie back in the comfort of her room.

Making those things happen, however, meant accomplishing a nightmare.

Chapter Thirty

Ian heard the shovel moving through earth. He paused, his hand inches from the metal latch of the side-yard gate.

Fuck.

On any other day, that sound would have made him wonder what Jen was planting. When he'd officially moved to town the previous summer, he'd seen her garden evolve.

Hell, he thought, he'd helped it evolve when, during his second week in town, Jen had hired him to build her eight custom flower beds.

It hadn't taken him long, but he'd taken his time. They'd turned out pretty damn good, he admitted. In fact, he'd been riding that pride when he'd shown up with the final raised bed, ready to snag Seth for some basketball.

Jen had pulled into the drive right behind him, so he and Seth had helped her unload six boxes of bulbs from Schreiner's Iris Gardens before heading out to The Hoop, a local indoor basketball gym.

It had been a good day—a simple day.

Ian remembered setting down the boxes of bulbs. With a huge grin on Jen's beautiful, young face, she'd hugged him, kissing her husband. She'd been so stoked.

His grin faded as memory took a back seat to the very here-and-now sound of shovel hitting dirt again. Ian's hands balled into fists.

Two days ago, he'd gotten sick. He'd vomited right into those custom-made flower beds for the very same reason that today, he knew two things with absolution: Jen wasn't the one wielding the shovel, and the shovel sure as hell wasn't being used for gardening.

Ian cursed Brooke for what she'd begun on her own. When would the damn woman learn to ask for help?

He turned the latch, slick with rain, and swung open the gate.

Chapter Thirty-One

Brooke heard the gate open. She pivoted.

Ian Russick, in all his rugged charm, walked towards her, but not with his usual swagger. He—stalked, she decided. It was the only word she could think of to describe his gait.

"You're kiddin me, right?"

Quickly lifting an open hand, she moved it downward, signaling for him to lower his voice. "About?"

Ian glanced around. "She is the tent?"

"Maddie's been down for about twenty. Hopefully, she'll stay down for another hour." Brooke looked at her as-of-yet pitiful hole and scowled. "Or so."

"So, just on your own?"

His tone matched the attitude he'd walked toward her with—hard.

Okay, so I get that you're mad. Care to tell me why?

Whoever said women's moods were all over the map had only gotten half the equation, Brooke decided. Men could be equally frustrating.

In just seventy-two hours, Ian had gone from being a frustrated hero on the mound of her ruined house to a sweet and flirtatious hero at breakfast the next morning. Then he shifted to mad when she'd gone AWOL. And yes, she understood his point there, but then he did another one-eighty on her and had been fun and flirty again at dinner.

The fun and flirtiness had naturally changed when they'd heard the reports about the coastline, Seaside. Ian and Seth had been friends. She couldn't blame him for being worried, except he didn't seem concerned now, nor did he look fun and flirtatious.

He looked pissed.

Not understanding why, Brooke shrugged. "Yeah, I—Look, Ian, I have to do this. I may not have a lot of time, so whatever's up, spill it."

Standing a good three feet from her, he didn't say anything and just watched her.

She tried not to squirm under his steady gaze. "If it's about Seth, I'm sure he's fine," she said, not believing her own words. "He's probably helping those who need it on his way here. He'll be here."

"I hope you're right about Seth, but that's not why I'm here." Walking to her, he cupped her chin in his hand. "At the risk of sounding like a damn broken record, you should have called."

She raised an eyebrow. "These damn things," she said, pulling her cell phone out of her back pocket while keeping her eyes on his. "don't exactly work right now, remember?"

"I, well . . Shit, no. For a second there, I did forget."

"I get it. I forget too. Habit."

He nodded. "You still should have come to get me, Brooke."

He grabbed the shovel's handle above her chilled fingers.

She let go of the shovel he then held, pivoted away from him, and rubbed the palm of her hand on her forehead as she tried to ease her brewing headache.

"And what?" she asked. "Hey, Maddie, let's go see if I can help us dig a grave for your mother. I couldn't go to you or anyone for this. I couldn't let her hear, let her see, or let her wonder what I was up to. If I had gone to get you, Maddie would have been so excited that you were over that she probably wouldn't have taken a nap."

Staring down at the hole and the shovel, she took a slow breath. She'd been so young when her mom's car accident had happened. That incident had shaken her belief in counting on others. She'd watched as her dad—who'd counted on her mom as much as her mom had counted on him—had suddenly found himself without her.

Her mom had been loving and incredibly dependable. But even the most reliable person couldn't be there for you if they died. It was one of the most gut-wrenching lessons she'd learned.

After the accident, she'd been slow to let anyone but her dad, her grandmother, and Jen into her heart. They had slowly helped her expand that circle, but she still was resistant to most.

A tear slid down her cheek. In less than a month, she'd lost two of the people in her life she'd allowed herself to count on without qualification. Losing them caused that growth to slide backward. She could feel it all but slide away. She wanted to be stronger, to lean on others the way they had all wanted her to, but she was scared.

Brooke looked at Ian Russick. He, too, had been a part of the stability she'd felt with the neighbors on her grandmother's secluded street, but he'd stayed for such a short time each summer.

Yet he'd never let her down, she thought now. Like the others on this small street, Ian Russick had never let her down.

Had the way Brooke had known she could count on him, on these neighbors, been why she'd always felt like Salem was her true home, she wondered now. Had she been drawn there simply because her time in Salem had allowed her to believe, to trust, to lean, however slightly?

A part of her wanted to hate Salem for planting that trust only to rip so much of it from her chest. How could she count on Ian or the rest of them, she thought, staring at the half-dug grave.

"Brooke?" Ian laid a hand on her shoulder.

Shaking her head to clear it, she took the shovel from him, shoved it in for another scoop.

Without a word, Ian moved to the back shed. He found a second shovel lying in the mud. Using the side of his denim jeans, he cleaned off the area he planned to hold for a better grip.

The side of Brooke's pants looked just like his. Strange how such a small thing could make her feel so connected to him.

He sauntered back to her, almost casual but for the haunted look in his eyes. She knew he didn't want to dig, didn't want to do what had to be done any more than she did. But like the others on this small road on the south side of town, he was there for her. Brooke wondered if she'd be able to ever accept what they all offered.

"Thank you."

"For?"

"What you're about to do."

"What we're about to do," he corrected.

Chapter Thirty-Two

Wednesday, February 21, 2029, 1:00 pm

Seth loaded supplies into the Red Cross bag. "Here, Isaac."

The boy who'd climbed the evacuation hill, who'd beaten the odds and reached the high ground with him, glowered.

Seth had finally learned his name as they'd sat helpless on top of the hill for hours on Monday, watching wave after devastating wave pummel Neskowin.

Cars had floated. Homes had ripped apart, their severed limbs surrounded by the small objects that had filled them just minutes earlier. Seth had seen trees, detached decks, and stop signs joining in like obstacles in a pinball game.

And as if chosen to play the cursed game, people had been tossed in the waves, hitting pin after pin.

Seth's feelings of inadequacy had swamped him with rage. Beside him, Isaac wept for the horror of it all and for the friend he'd lost—just one of the thousands.

They'd joined others and had spent all day Tuesday looking for survivors. Aside from a small group who'd taken refuge on another hill, they'd found only corpses.

Seth had been bombarded with one haunting image after another. The short winter day had felt like an eternity.

A part of Seth wanted to spend another day looking. Maybe they'd missed someone. But the group had made the call. They didn't have another day to spare.

Isaac took the bag. He slung it over his shoulder and stared down at his feet. Seth took in a deep sympathetic breath. It was a hell of a thing. He imagined Isaac would replay the tsunami in nightmares. They all would.

The tsunami danger, at least, had passed, but what they faced now held equal lethality.

Standing near a fifteen-foot shed that one of the residents called a cache, three women passed out supplies.

"Now listen up," one of the women said. "Neskowin residents have stocked this full of emergency supplies over the past four years, keeping inventory and rotating expired goods when necessary. We are going to try to get you what you'll need."

Living on the coast, they'd taken the threat more seriously than most of the people Seth knew in the Willamette Valley. He would be forever grateful.

Each person beside him held an American Red Cross bag filled with protein bars, bottled waters, disposable ponchos, emergency blankets, flashlights, matches, hand sanitizer, wet wipes, and mini first aid boxes that Seth figured couldn't handle much more than the inevitable blisters on their feet.

He couldn't fathom the amount of time, coordination, and money that had gone into ensuring each and every item he now carried. Humbled beyond measure, his hands rubbed at the back of his neck.

"This would sure be easier in the summer."

"Maybe." A retired dentist in his late sixties handed Seth a bag of mixed nuts to add to his already packed bag. "Problem with summer is we'd never have had enough supplies to pass out. The Cache only holds so much, and we don't get that much funding for it from the state. Out of pocket, mostly." He shrugged. "Anyways, fewer people in winter, so we just might make it."

"Make it where?" Isaac asked.

"The Valley."

"Your bullshittin'. Why so far?"

Seth met Isaac's eyes, "We can't stay on the coast. Help is several weeks out."

The dentist, decked out in steel-toed, waterproof boots and a high-quality poncho, nodded. "Staying any longer, especially this time o' year, is like inviting the Grim Reaper on a date." He ran a finger across his cork-screw mustache. "Of course, the walk won't be a picnic either."

That didn't surprise Seth. "How far is it? Sixty miles?"

Isaac swore.

The dentist nodded. "Thereabouts. The average adult can walk three, maybe four miles an hour. It would take a minimum of two days to walk at that speed for ten hours each day. Of course, few could do that. We have some elderly like myself, some small kids, some disabled, and some injured. We'll need to move slow and take frequent breaks."

"Can we even travel on the roads?"

He nodded at Isaac. "In parts. Bridges will be down. Frankly, I'm not sure what to expect there. May have to manage our way through rivers. In the dead of winter, no less, so we'll have to be mindful there. Sleeping in this is enough of a hypothermic nightmare as it is, though the emergency blankets should help. Landslides could be a real problem for us."

Seth wiped the rain from his forehead. "More?"

"Yes. With the ground unstable and the rains coming down like this, we'll have more landslides, and we'll already be maneuvering our way around landslides that occurred in the shaking."

"What's next, manticores and wraiths?" Sarcasm and fury filled Isaac's voice.

"I almost wish it could be that simple," the dentist told them as a couple motioned for everyone to follow.

Seth took his first step toward the valley that lay over the coastal mountain range, sent the dentist a confused look.

"You can battle that sort of enemy. Fight back some. Mother nature's more ruthless."

Chapter Thirty-Three

Laura Russick knocked on the side yard gate. "Hey, you two, how does some Mac and Cheese sound?"

Brooke sat by the tent, trying to get clean socks on Maddie.

"Mac and Cheese?" One sock still half on, Maddie leaped out of Brooke's lap.

Caught off guard by the girl's speed, Brooke tried to grab Maddie's shirt to stop her, missed.

"Madelyn Lee Monroy, stop right there."

Maddie froze, then turned to face Brooke. "No."

"You need shoes. It's freezing."

"No. I want to eat." And with that, she took off running again.

Watching the tiny feet hit the cold, muddy earth, Brooke moaned and dropped her forehead to the palm of her hand.

Maddie's sock would be toast, which meant Brooke needed to find dry ones. On a typical day, Brooke wouldn't have cared, but no electricity and no running water turned the simple chore of laundry into a whole new ballgame.

Especially with a girl in diapers.

They were running low. If Maddie ran out before they could pick up more, Brooke worried Maddie might have accidents. Changing diapers outdoors in the February cold, with no opportunities to bath or shower Maddie, was challenging enough.

The choice between using diaper wipes judiciously to avoid running out and using extra to ensure sanitation was a daily conundrum. Brooke usually opted for the latter, which meant the wipes were running low.

And now, she thought in disgust, she was scolding Maddie over socks Guilt swamped her. Tears started welling, and she watched as Maddie ran the final steps toward Ian's mom as the woman entered the backyard, a large bowl balanced on her right hand.

Wiping furiously at her eyes—Maddie didn't need to see her cry on top of everything—Brooke took the toddler-free moment to go in the tent and search through the bag of remaining clean clothes. Initially packed to the nines, precious little lay in the bag now.

She sifted through what was there and stuck her hand desperately into pant legs, hoping to find socks hiding. When that failed, she patted down the last few shirts, wondering if socks lay between the folds, but again found nothing.

Shit.

Looking around, she stared at the pile of dirty clothing the two had accumulated. Thanks to the February winter weather, the clothes weren't just one-day-of-use dirty. Some of Maddie's clothes were completely caked in mud. Brooke's stank to high heaven, too, sweaty from the many gut-wrenching moments the three days had brought to them. Too many moments.

Brooke considered her options. The previous night had changed everything, and she knew the "just until Seth got home" planning she'd been doing was gone.

She had to come up with some long-term solutions. For Maddie. For herself. For their future together.

She stuck her head out of the tent and saw Laura and Maddie sitting up in the camping chairs.

The camping chairs had no table to surround, and clouds threatened yet another rainy day. Brooke knew she needed to get into the house. Every long-term goal for her, for Maddie, depended on it.

Then, maybe, she could collect rainwater to wash the clothes and hang them in the bathroom to dry. Clothing was just one issue, shelter from the cold another. She had to get in.

It made the remaining tasks of the day all the more paramount, giving her little excuse to put off the tasks that made bile rise in her throat just at the thought of them.

Wishing she could just fall apart, Brooke stripped off socks she'd put on just that morning—her last pair. The intense hour and a half of digging that morning had left them sweaty. Still, they were mostly dry and the best available. She slid her rainboots over bare feet and exited the tent.

"Auntie Brooke, wook. Wook. My favorite. I very wove this." Maddie pointed to the large bowl Laura carried.

"Fun. Come here, kiddo."

She went to Maddie's chair, crouched down to grab Maddie's soaked and muddy feet. "You can eat as soon as you have shoes on."

Brooke slid her size eight-and-a-half socks on the toddler. Their height rose to Maddie's knees, so Brooke tucked them under the pants and slid the boots over them. It would have to do.

Laura set down the second bowl she'd brought over for Brooke, motioned for Brooke to follow.

Brooke eyed the bowl for a moment, her stomach growling, her mouth watering in response. She found herself wondering how on earth Laura had managed to make a meal, even one as simple as mac and cheese, without milk and butter, without electricity.

She pushed aside thoughts of eating for the moment. They walked just far enough away that they could speak without being overheard by Maddie while she ate.

"What's wrong?"

Brooke looked into Laura's compassionate eyes.

Am I that obvious?

"I'm failing." The words came out in a whoosh before she could stop them.

"Failing how?"

"Jen's gone. Maybe... probably," she amended. "Seth too. Maddie can't go in her own home, and in the dead of winter, I have her camping outdoors in the aftermath of a *major* disaster. And I just scolded her over stupid socks."

A tear did fall now, and she wanted to curse.

Laura raised an eyebrow. "If that was you scolding, you've nothing to feel guilty about. Oh, honey, I remember the toddler days. They are somethin' else and can be brutally hard. Some of my favorite years with Ian and Alex, though."

The idea of Ian as a toddler made Brooke smile just a little. "I bet they were handfuls."

"They were. Crayons on walls, toilet paper strewn throughout the house, and good lord, the messes they made when they ate."

She smiled wistfully as they both glanced over at Maddie.

"Trust me, scolding comes with the territory, even on days when you wish you didn't have to. You're going to be a great mother to her."

Brooke's small smile vanished.

"This isn't the way I'd envisioned becoming a mom. My heart is breaking for her. All the time." Her voice broke. "I know what it's like to lose a mom. I can't imagine what it would have been like if I'd lost my dad in that car accident too."

Brooke looked down at her hands, remembering how powerless the hands had felt and how vulnerable she had felt when her dad had pulled her out early from her eighth-grade math class that day.

Laura sat quietly for a moment before speaking. "There's a part of me that desperately wishes we'd just had Bill's parents come to us for the baby shower. It's scary being here through all of this, but with his mom's recent fall, she wasn't supposed to travel. And Fawn, she couldn't fly, but she insisted on one last pre-baby travel adventure. If this earthquake had to have happened when my boys, Fawn, and the baby were here, I'm glad Bill and I were with them. I bet your dad is worried."

"He'd know what to do. I don't. I think I do, and then every time I try to move forward, I can't. I'm screwing everything up."

Laura shook her head. "First, I'll repeat. You are going to be a great mom to Maddie if Seth doesn't make it home, so stop fretting. As for the rest...."

Brooke looked at her.

"You are a very capable woman, Brooke. And you are very independent."

"I'm usually better at the whole *on my own* thing."

Laura placed a comforting hand over Brooke's. "Don't you see, though? You aren't the problem here. You are still very capable—something I highly admire, by the way. But this isn't a time for independence. This disaster is too big. It's too damn hard for any one person. The only way through this is by leaning on each other."

Chapter Thirty-Four

Brooke felt the last of Maddie's wakeful energy relax into sleep. Shifting, she moved Maddie onto the cot.

After Maddie had finished her mac and cheese, she and Brooke had played tag in the grass, had a mini dance party while Brooke did her best to sing, and they'd served pretend tea. The tea party had reminded Maddie of Jen.

Tears had come—Maddie wanted to see her mom and did not fully understand why she couldn't. Eventually, those tears had led to Maddie going down for an unexpected second nap.

Running a hand through her now-oily hair, Brooke rose. She didn't want to waste the opportunity to get something done. A second nap during the day was rare for Maddie. Brooke figured there was just enough light left for what she had to do.

Standing as tall as the tent allowed, she unzipped the door, stepped out, and saw Ian, Alex, Bill, and Laura coming through the side gate into the backyard.

Shit. What are you all doing here?

Ian pointed at the tent and mouthed, "Sleeping?"

Brooke nodded.

The four Russicks looked like soldiers ready for battle, she thought, their faces hard, determined. A mom, a dad, and two grown brothers, standing as one.

Alex got to her first. "Let's do this."

Brooke's eyebrows furrowed in confusion.

He rolled his eyes at her but kept his voice low. "Dude, Brooke. My brother here tells me you two spent this morning digging. Then my mom tells us Maddie's been cryin' for, like, ages. She was going to come to see if she could help, but then it got quiet. Pretty obvious what you were planning to do if Maddie fell asleep. Did you really think we'd let you go it alone?"

Laura nodded. "It's time you lean on us a little."

"I . . ." Brooke fumbled as realization struck. They were there to help get Jen out of the house, to help bury her. "I couldn't ask you—can't ask you to . . ."

Bill held up a hand to stop Brooke midsentence. "We've known that girl pretty much since she was born."

Laura nodded. "Jen had just turned eight months when we came to visit that summer. We watched her grow, year after year, into the kind and beautiful woman she became."

"She's family. Like you," Alex said, surprising Brooke.

"This whole neighborhood is like family," Ian said, keeping his eyes on hers. "We look out for each other."

"The older gang is back at the house with Fawn," Bill put in. "In her state, she can't help, and we, well, the five of us should be able to manage things."

Brooke's throat felt as though it had closed, the lump in it swelling with emotions. She had to dig her nails into her palms, using pain to distract, to hold back the grief for why they were there. Unable to speak, she nodded.

Laura opened a bag she carried and pulled out a large, folded sheet of aluminum foil. Unfolding the material like a practiced seamstress, she laid it flat at the tent door. It glistened in the sunlight that peaked through a break in the clouds.

"This should make some noise and alert us if Maddie wakes while we're inside. I hope." She shook her head. "Lord, help us. Let's just get this done."

They walked to the backdoor together.

Brooke lifted the neckline of her sweater over her nose the instant the door opened. The sour stench made her eyes water as if she'd been sprayed by a skunk. She squeezed her eyes shut, opened them. It took three repeats to clear them, and still they burned.

"Oh, you poor child." Laura moved past her husband, her boys, past Brooke, and knelt beside Jen. "You poor baby. I'm so sorry." She brushed a hand over Jen's exposed cheek, moving hair that fell across her eyes. "We're here. I'm sorry we didn't come sooner. We're here."

Bill came, stepping over an aloe plant that had crashed off the entertainment center in the earthquake, and put a hand on his wife's shoulder. "Are you sure . . . ?"

"Yes," Laura replied. "Brooke and Maddie, they need this home. Jen deserves to be laid to rest, Bill. And Maddie needs to be able to say goodbye to her mother. None of that is possible if we don't do this."

"If Seth comes back, he can't see this," Ian added.

"When," Laura corrected. She looked at Brooke. "We can't lose all hope on that just yet."

Though Laura's voice shook, Brooke heard the steel behind it, the determination.

Bill let out a long breath, rubbed a hand over the back of his neck, surveying the scene. "Let me think a minute."

His hand moved from his neck to rub the stubble of his three-day beard. It matched the length of both his sons' beards, and Brooke wondered how long their beards would grow during the next few months.

She'd never seen them with facial hair. Seeing the three of them looking rugged left her shaken.

No running water. No showers.

For how long, she wondered. Brooke remembered Jen telling her about a semi-long power outage from 2021 when an ice storm had made the city look like the victim of a hurricane. Jen hadn't had power for four straight days.

154

The earthquake had clearly done more damage than any ice storm could. It had also impacted a much larger region. So how long would the electricity be out? Surely the city would have the water back on soon. Within the week at most, she hoped. Even a week felt like an eternity.

"Alright, Ian and I, we'll lift the entertainment center straight up. Nowhere to set it on the ground. Alex, can you move the TV out from under it then?"

Alex nodded. "More awkward than heavy, I'd guess."

"Then, Laura . . . " Bill's voice trailed off.

"Brooke and I will help Jen," she finished for him. "We can lift her, can't we," she said to Brooke, straightening her shoulders.

"We've got Jen," Brooke confirmed, though she was surprised she could breathe, let alone talk with her heart wedged in her throat.

She watched as Ian rubbed his hands on his jeans, looked at his dad. "On three."

Though twenty-five years older than Ian, Bill had three decades of construction under his belt from his volunteer work with Habitat for Humanity. Bill was fit and knew how to move heavy things safely. Together, they bent, preparing to lift from the legs.

"Wait." Brooke held up a hand.

"You need a minute?" Ian asked her, concern evident in his voice.

"No. Well, kind of. Just, I'll be back."

Without explaining, she moved past them, past Jen, into the kitchen. When she returned, she held a dustpan. Quickly, Brooke began to shovel all that lay behind the base of the stand. Cleaning the broken clutter from the room would have to wait, so she shoved it all into a pile off to the side, leaving the carpet bare.

Understanding, Bill smiled. "That' a girl!" He looked at Ian. "One, two, three."

Brooke heard them grunt as they hoisted the stand. Rather than just lifting it high enough to get the TV and Jen out from under, they were able to stand the piece of furniture back in place now.

The wood was splintered on one side, damaged like her life, Brooke thought miserably.

"That was smart, Brooke." Laura shook her head.

"Seeing her like this," Brooke managed, "I didn't do very well trying to get her out when . . . when I found her." Memories of her missteps with the stool digging into the carpet and the sound of a bone breaking flooded her.

Ian's gaze met hers. "You ready for this?"

"No. Let's do it anyway."

Alex moved to the right side of Jen, with Ian moving to her left. They grabbed the sides of the flatscreen TV, lifted, and side-stepped until they made it past her body.

"We can move Jen," Alex said, setting the broken TV down on one of the living room couches, its screen facing the ceiling.

Laura looked at Brooke.

Brooke shook her head. "I need to do this."

Laura gave her a quick, hard hug. "We do."

She moved to Jen's feet. "Alex, sweetie, do me a favor. Go outside. Sit by the tent. Make sure that if Maddie wakes, she doesn't come outside that tent, doesn't see."

"On it."

As Alex headed out the backdoor, Brooke stared at her friend's broken body and felt herself die a little more inside. The sensation shocked her. She'd known Jen was dead.

For three days now, she'd known, but there was something about seeing Jen lying there without the TV, without the stand, exposed. It made Jen look so vulnerable.

The scene had been complex, messy, confusing. Now the space held only Jen, making her death all the more real. Rigor mortis left her bloated.

I'm here. I've got you.

She took a steadying breath, placed her hands under Jen's armpits. Her body was cold, so cold. Brooke's breath hitched.

She and Laura lifted her. Even with Laura's help, the job was much more challenging than Brooke had anticipated. Ian and Bill moved in from the sides and placed their hands beneath the small of Jen's back to take the extra weight while Laura fought to steady Jen's broken leg.

Advancing slowly around corners, they carried Jen to the door. Brooke peeked out. Alex, on patrol by the tent, gave her a thumbs up.

"Let's go," she mouthed to the others.

The four of them maneuvered through the patio door, weaving to let each person through. They made their way down the patio steps onto the grass and over to the hole that Brooke and Ian had dug.

Though the hole was long enough and wide enough for Jen's slender body, Brooke and Ian had only managed to dig down about two feet before Maddie had woken. They'd run out of time.

Standing beside the shallow grave, Brooke knew they would have to cover it with rocks after filling in the dirt. Eventually, they could have her moved to a proper grave with a casket.

Together, they lowered Jen's body. Then with silent tears, they let the first scoops of dirt fall from their shovels to cover her.

Chapter Thirty-Five

"I... Codswallop, I'd need a calculator," George told the group.

Alex dug in his jacket pocket. "Phone has one." He pulled it out, touched the screen. "Seven percent," he said, shaking his head in disgust. "Damn thing's gonna die. What numbers am I runnin'?"

"Let's see," George said. "That'd be Carol and me, Fawn and Alex, Ian and Brooke."

Brooke blushed at George listing her and Ian the way he had, like they were a couple, then shrugged it off, too exhausted to care all that much.

The fire in the center of their circle danced. Brooke watched it, feeling its familiarity with the previous night's. The simple new routine brought her some peace. She was grateful. They needed peace in their hearts, she knew, and rest.

She'd helped dig a grave and helped carry her friend to that spot. Brooke could practically hear the shovel scooping. The smell of dirt mixed with horrid decay lingered. Her own treacherous eyes, a camera she couldn't control, had captured an image of that first shovel of wet dirt dropping onto the body. She dreaded the nightmare that would surely follow.

It had been a horrible experience.

We should have stopped there, Brooke thought, half pleading with the universe for a do-over. But of course, that wasn't going to happen.

"Maddie," Brooke had said, cradling the girl on her lap. "I need to talk to you about your mom."

Maddie squirmed. "Mommy's mad at me."

"What?"

"I watch Home again. I not mean to be bad, but mommy washed the dishes. I not hear it. I loudered the volume. Mommy teached me how, but it gots too much loud. She pushed me weally hard. It not okay to push! I got scared. I ranned."

Brooke's stomach had squeezed then, the vice-like intensity so strong she'd wondered if she might vomit.

Maddie had been missing her mother. That had been obvious, but Brooke hadn't known how much the three-year-old understood why Jen was gone. She'd assumed Maddie had thought her mom was hurt and that Jen was away, healing.

Guilt tangled messily with grief.

Letting Maddie believe Jen had just been hurt was as wrong as Maddie thinking her mom had spent the past three days so furious at her daughter that Jen had all but abandoned her.

The image of Jen's body positioned under the TV stand, arms outstretched above her head, made horrible sense now.

Brooke could picture the moment perfectly. Maddie, standing to change the volume on the TV. The room, starting to shake, the heavy, unsecured oak entertainment center toppling over. Jen shoving her daughter out of the way, taking the impact herself.

Brooke remembered finding Maddie on the bench, scooping her up and trying to calm her by singing the song from Home. She squeezed her eyes shut. No wonder Maddie had screamed then. *Could I have picked a worse song?*

Jen had died saving her daughter.

So Brooke had told Maddie that her mother was a hero: a hero who would never be coming home.

Confused and devastated, Maddie had curled into a ball, screaming for her mother.

What a day. Lost in the dance of the flames now, Brooke bit her lips. She'd heard someone say once that grief was just love with nowhere to go. She and Maddie were unquestionably lost.

She felt stripped raw, sore everywhere.

Reaching onto the foldout table beside her, Brooke grabbed a Pepsi. The twelve pack had been one of many items she'd gathered from Jen's house that evening.

The house still needed to be cleaned, glass swept up, spills mopped, furniture righted, but those were chores for another day.

That mess and even Brooke's own wobbly, tired legs hadn't stopped her from grabbing what food she could from the cabinets, however.

Though it wasn't really her food, Brooke felt more at ease being able to contribute what she'd gathered toward the evening's group dinner.

For once, she thought, rolling her eyes.

Depending on others made her edgy, like waiting for the other shoe to drop but not knowing when. Contributing to the meal gave her what she quietly admitted was a false sense of independence. She could pretend she could do it all on her own.

Had the neighbors not been around, maybe she could have found food, water, and shelter. It was humbling to realize how much she and Maddie had needed them. Time and again.

She popped the lid on the Pepsi, heard the satisfying fizz of carbonation.

The chill of the night made the equally chilled drink less than ideal, she supposed, yet Brooke needed it, needed the comfort of sugar and caffeine. Taking a slow and satisfying sip, she listened to George finish naming off those in the group.

"Maddie, Irene, and Henry, and then Laura and Bill… Hey, where is Bill, anyway?" he asked.

"He went inside to nap on the couch." Fawn yawned. "Can't say I blame him."

Brooked nodded. "How's the baby today?"

Fawn patted her tummy. "Been kicking me all day, and these Braxton Hicks contractions are pretty strong. It's like doing crunch after crunch every few minutes."

"Braxton Hicks?" Brooke asked.

"They're like practice contractions," Fawn explained. "They usually don't hurt much, but they are getting stronger this week. My abs are wiped out, even when the rest of me is just sitting still."

"Stress isn't good for the baby. Should you be inside resting?" her husband asked.

"No. I don't think I'd be comfortable lying down right now. I think I'll walk. Maddie, would you like to join me? We can stay close to the fire, so it's not too dark."

"Okay!"

Maddie had moved past the meltdown. Brooke was incredibly grateful for a child's ability to be in the moment. Hopping down from her chair, Maddie ran to Fawn's side and began to do little twirls as she walked beside Fawn.

"So, what numbers am I running?" Alex asked again, watching his wife stroll around George and Carol's front yard, where they'd set up dinner again under the canopy.

"Well, that's eleven people," George said, "times, let's see. They say fourteen days, but this is the end of day three, so eleven more days. One gallon of water, per person, per day."

"So, just eleven times eleven: one-twenty-one," Alex said, not bothering with the calculator.

George nodded.

Brooke looked from one to the other: "One-twenty-one what?"

"We need one hundred and twenty-one gallons of water between us for the next eleven days," George explained.

Brooke wanted to swear.

Is it really going to take the city eleven more days to get the water turned back on?

APPARENTLY, THE EMOTIONAL FATIGUE OF THE DAY WASN'T OVER, SHE CONCEDED, FEELING HER STOMACH TIGHTEN.

Ian moved Maddie's now-empty chair in front of him and propped his feet on it. "I'm fucking beat," he said, letting his head rest on the back of his plastic lawn chair.

"Ian Joseph Russick!" His mom admonished: "Language!"

He winced. "Sorry. Still, maybe we should go over all this in the morning. This has been one hell of a day."

Laura nodded. "It has, and we can, but I'm feeling very nervous about where we are with things. As tired as I am, I'd really feel better with some sort of plan. I'm not sleeping well."

Irene, Ian's Grandma, pulled orange and black hand-knitted gloves from her pockets and slid them on. "Well then, how bad is the situation?"

"It depends on the item we're discussing," Laura said. "That amount of water, for example, is meant to cover drinking, washing, and hygiene. It's one gallon of water per person per day."

"Guess we'll just have to spend a good chunk of the next two weeks drunk as skunks and save the water for hygiene."

Henry rolled his eyes at his youngest grandson: "You're drinking our last beer."

Alex's face fell so fast that Brooke nearly laughed. He looked like his baseball team had just lost the World Series.

"Staying hydrated is just one of many considerations right now," Laura added. "Any unused food from the fridge or freezer, we lost days ago. We need to ration whatever food we have left, plus batteries for the flashlights."

"Cell phone flashlights will help some, for as long as they last." Alex glared at the skinny red battery line. "Hell, just scratch that. Tonight's probably the end of this one for the foreseeable future."

Brooke pulled hers out. Twelve percent.

"And we can't overlook the kindling for cooking," Laura continued, "and firewood for staying warm. I took inventory of the various supplies this morning. For the life of me, I can't see us stretching them that far. Five days more, maybe, but not eleven."

Brooke's eyebrows furrowed. Two weeks for electricity, too, then? Thinking of the four days Jen had gone without it after the ice storm, Brooke supposed two weeks sounded about right, but the thought of going without electricity or water for eleven more days seemed like an eternity.

"I'll make another pass through the house in the morning," Brooke said. "It's possible there are some canned goods in the attic or something. I can gather things like batteries too. If you give me a list, I will gather everything I can."

"That's great, Brooke. I'll feel better knowing what we have," Laura confessed.

"We have enough food for breakfast, right?" Ian pressed.

Laura nodded.

"Then I still say we conk out for the night. We can lay the supplies out in the yard tomorrow. Brooke can add what she finds. We will figure out a plan then. My brain's a complete sludge right now."

"Nothing new there," Alex teased.

Ian tossed his empty beer can at his little brother. It hit him square in the chest. Alex laughed, just as the earth heaved violently under them all.

Chapter Thirty-Six

Brooke's chair undulated. She felt like she was sitting on a giant trampoline while sumo wrestlers jumped around her.

The soda can she gripped in her hand jerked. Soda sloshed from the opening. Cold and sticky liquid spilled onto her jacket and pants. Dropping the can, she gripped the arms of the chair.

No. No. No. Not again.

She scanned for Maddie and saw her and Fawn on their hands and knees in the grass. Had Fawn fallen? Brooke had witnessed her wobble on more than one occasion in her late stage of pregnancy.

God, the baby.

And Maddie.

The grinding plates had stolen Maddie's family. If anyone had a right to feel terror at that moment, it was the three-year-old currently huddled like a turtle under attack.

Brooke lunged herself out of the chair to go to them and heard someone screaming. The rocking knocked her to her knees as she looked over her shoulder. George and Carol's home swayed.

Images of her own home flashed. Not waiting for the inevitable collapse, she crawled as fast as she could manage on the vibrating earth and then used her body to shelter Maddie and Fawn.

Brooke could hear nothing but the roaring. Terror was as tangible as the feel of Maddie's back pressed against her belly. Brooke closed her eyes and braced for impact; a flying board or roof shingle—Hell only knew.

She screamed. The sound ripped from her chest; its volume drowned out by the tortuous, compressing earth.

Closing her eyes, she held onto Maddie and Fawn until the earthquake stopped. Her heart pumped so rapidly that even kneeling, she swayed, lightheaded.

"Maddie, Fawn?" she managed.

"I'm. . .I'm okay, I think," Fawn said but didn't move from her spot.

Sweat poured down Brooke's back. Her body shook violently. She sat back on her heels, forced her lungs to take deeper gulps of the crisp air, trying to make her exhales longer than her inhales. Panic clawed at her.

Maddie, feeling Brooke's body move away from hers, scrambled onto Brooke's legs and began to sob.

"Shhh," Brooke crooned. She rolled sideways so that she sat flat on the wet ground and readjusted Maddie into her lap.

"Are you—can you please get Laura?" Fawn asked.

"Um." Brooke had no idea if she could stand, let alone help.

The shaking, so similar to what had stolen Jen, Sparks, her own home, and possibly Seth, too, had fear radiating through her. She couldn't get her heart to slow.

What did the shaking cost me this time? Who did it take?

Her nausea escalated. Brooke closed her eyes and took in slow, deep breaths, forcing the gag reflex down.

She felt Maddie's small hand on her back. "Auntie Brooke, are you okay?"

Nodding, Brooke waited until the worst of the nausea had passed before opening her eyes. She turned her attention back to Fawn. "Laura?"

"Yes, but oh, Brooke, are you going to be alright?"

"I'm . . . Yeah, I'm good."

Turning to search for Laura, Brooke's heart leaped into her throat.

The front of Carol and George's house where the porch had been minutes earlier lay caved in, its contents having spewed enough dust and wind to extinguish the fire. Darkness consumed the yard but for the streams of light coming from two flashlights.

Brooke heard George calling out, his voice hard as if being strict would somehow net a better response. He shouted, "Bill! Egads, man, holler back so we can find you."

Henry, voice more panic than command, pleaded, "My son. Oh, Christ Jesus. Bill?"

Brooke stood. The butt and knees of her jeans were soaked from the grass.

"Are you okay?" she asked Fawn.

"I think so." Reaching a hand up to grab Brooke's, Fawn maneuvered her body to stand. She had tears running down her cheeks. "I fell down. I didn't land on my stomach, but I crashed down pretty hard. The baby. Do you think the baby's okay?"

It unnerved Brooke to see Fawn, who was usually so composed, rattled.

"Yes, of course."

Brooke tried yelling for Laura from across the yard, but the commotion by the house was too loud.

Fawn laid her hands on her huge belly. "I'm not sure I can walk just yet. My lower back is killing me."

Brooke kept her voice calm, confident. "The baby will be fine. You both will." *This earthquake isn't taking anyone else I care about.* "I'll go find her. Maddie, stay here until I get back."

Maddie grabbed Brooke's leg.

"Maddie, can you please stay with me so that I'm not alone?"

Fawn's words were pleading. Maddie stilled, and her desire to help and please adults kicked in. She let go of Brooke, going heroically to Fawn.

166

Brooke ran the short distance toward the house, moving toward the duo of lights. In their glow, she noticed that large parts of the house, possibly entire rooms within the structure, still stood. Most of the damage she could see resulted from the small patio, which had caved in, completely obstructing the front entrance.

"Dad. God damn it!" Alex kicked at a board by his feet that lay wedged under a mass of debris. His attempt to dislodge it failed. "No!"

"I think I hear him. Dad, hold on! You hold on. We're coming in." Ian threw himself up onto the heap at his feet, tearing at loose pieces as if he could simply tunnel into the mess.

Brooke grabbed his arm to pull him off the pile.

"What are you doing?" he asked, his voice harsh and desperate.

His contractor's build tensed with adrenaline, and it took everything in Brooke's power to slow him down. She let go of Ian's arm and stepped in front of him.

"You can't. Fools rush in, remember?"

Eyes she could barely see in the depth of darkness focused and cleared; panic was replaced by helpless anger. "Damnit."

Alex came running around the side of the house. "Back door's not budging. Something's wedged behind it good 'n' tight."

"Maybe with more people?" Laura suggested. Tears ran down her face.

"No." Alex shoved his hands into his front pockets. "Gonna need to—"

"Laura, I hate to do this, but Fawn needs you," Brooke interrupted.

"She okay?" Alex asked. The color drained from his face. "Is my baby okay?"

Laura went to her youngest son and placed a hand on his cheek. "I'm sure she's fine. I'll go see how I can help. You stay here. Your dad needs you."

"I … ugh." Alex ran frustrated hands through his hair.

"What were you saying about the back door?" Brooke prompted him, knowing they needed to hurry.

Alex lowered his hands and shoved them into his coat pockets. "We could go through a window, but far as I could see, it's a damn obstacle course in there. We're going to need a lot of light to maneuver around the crap and help find a way to get him out. Where are the other flashlights?"

"Inside.'

Ian looked at his grandpa. "Inside?"

"We used these two," Henry said, gesturing to the dim dollar-store flashlights that his wife Irene and their neighbor of over forty years, Carol, held, "to see what we were doin' when we started the fire. The chairs were already set up, so we just didn't need that much light. With Bill napping on the couch ..."

He shrugged, scratched his head. "I placed the basket of flashlights we've collected just inside the front door. Figured that way, we could grab one if we needed it for a bathroom run, but otherwise, the flashlights wouldn't get wet out in the rain."

"We're under a canopy," Alex pointed out.

Henry nodded at his grandson. "True, but rain comes down sideways in Oregon sometimes. Wanted to be extra safe. Had to be."

George went to stand by his friend. "Keeping the electronics inside was a smart move."

"Yeah, until the front of the house caved in. The hell was dad in this house for anyway? Why didn't he go home to sleep?"

Knowing Alex was referring to Bill's parents' house as "home," Brooke felt her stomach sink. "I suggested he stay here instead."

Everyone turned to look at her. Brooke bit her top lip. "Bill said he didn't want to go down for the night because he wanted to help clean up later, put out the fire. He was tired and sore from…."

Brooke trailed off, not willing to mention Jen. "We're all tired, but he was determined to come help clean up when we were all ready to turn in. It was so dark out already. He just wanted a quick rest. It seemed ridiculous to have him go so far down the road for the nap."

She looked at Ian's grandparents' home. Though the structure stood deep in darkness, the house appeared to hold steady.

He would have been safe in there. I should have let him just go home. "I didn't know."

Ian, mimicking his brother's earlier move, kicked at a wooden board on the ground. "Great. Just fucking great. Are you kidding me right now?"

"Ian!" his mom admonished.

"I didn't mean Brooke," Ian told his mother. "Sorry," he said to Brooke. "No one could have known. This whole situation is just so damn infuriating."

From inside, Bill's cries of pain pulsed.

"The hell with it. We need to get in. Now," Ian told them. "What's the best window to use?"

They split up, Henry and Alex going with Irene as she led with her flashlight. Her hand shook, the light wobbling, but still, she led the way.

Her son was in the house, trapped, hurt, scared. Brooke was overwhelmed by the woman's courage.

Brooke watched them walk around the left side of the home, then caught up with Ian. He walked beside George, the three of them following Carol, who, like Irene, led the way with the help of a junky dollar store flashlight.

Their feet moved quickly over the lawn. Their hearts moved faster.

Chapter Thirty-Seven

Brooke fel her purple boots squish into the wet grass. The Willamette Valley wind whipped past her cheeks.

Every s ep she took sounded like suction cups being pulled from mirrors. She heard the labored breathing of her teammates. heard her own heartbeat, a steady throbbing in her head, and she heard Bill's voice, pained and fading.

She tripped over a garden stone, caught herself, and pulled out her phone.

Ian placed his hand over it, pushed it down without breaking stride. "Save it. We'll need all the light we can get once we find a way in."

Shrugging, Brooke pocketed the phone again. Then her eyebrow rose when he took her hand, held it as they walked.

His stride was longer than hers. Determined to save his dad, Ian moved over decorative lawn gnomes, pavers, and rosemary plants without skipping a beat.

"There. That's gotta do it." He pointed to an East-facing window three feet off the ground. A large crack pierced the two-by-four pane.

Carol shinned her light at the window, its reflection a small sun in the night. Ian dropped Brooke's hand and reached for the flashlight.

Letting him have it, Carol stood back with her husband, awaiting instructions. Ian then approached the window. At six-foot-one, he had no problem looking through the glass to scan the room. Then he took a couple of steps back.

Watching him and anticipating his next move, Brooke moved beside the older couple.

She wasn't at all surprised when Ian pocketed the flashlight and grabbed one of the small pavers from the garden.

He looked at Carol. "Sorry."

Then without waiting for a reaction, he hurled it through the glass of one of the few windows on the block that hadn't given way to shakes.

"God. Whhh. Whhhh. Ehhhhh."

The pain that had radiated from the other broken windows now soared toward Brooke. It shot like an arrow to her heart.

"Bill." It was a whisper and all she could manage.

He wasn't her family, but she'd known him for as long as she'd known his sons. So she couldn't stand the sound of his cries. She felt sure her heart was about to flatten like her broken home.

The pure awe of Mother Nature's wrath coursed through her like an electric shock.

They couldn't lose anyone else.

Ian yelled into the darkness. "Dad, I'm coming in. Hang on."

Alex came bolting around the back of the house. "Heard the glass break. Find a good one?"

Ian nodded. "This window's low enough. We should be able to hoist him out."

"Gotta find him first."

"Here." Brooke ripped off her jacket, wadded it into a ball, and used it to break off the largest of the remaining shards of glass protruding from the windowsill.

"Thanks." Ian handed her the flashlight.

He then laid Brooke's coat, with embedded glass shards, over the windowsill as a barrier between the smaller leftover shards protruding from the frame and his hands. He vaulted inside, Alex close behind.

Standing on opposite sides of the window, Brooke handed Ian back the flashlight, watched its beam as he and Alex moved through the house toward the sounds of their dad.

Brooke moved to the window. Using both hands and her sturdy boots, she scaled the short wall and jumped to the floor of George and Carol's bedroom.

"Dad. We're here."

"Yeah, Dad. We've got you."

Following the voices, Brooke pulled her phone out of the back pocket of her jeans, used her phone's light to make her way through the mess on the floor.

She found them in the center of what minutes earlier had been the living room. The couch sat in the center of the room. Brooke knew it was there to minimize the chill at night. She moved it there, farthest from the windows, when she'd slept there with Maddie the night before.

It had been a smart move. Without electricity, searching out pockets of moderate warmth had become the entire group's new norm.

But that choice had cost Bill a great deal.

He lay on the floor beside the couch now, a structural beam lying directly over his leg, pinning him. His face was white with pain.

Brooke wondered for a second time that night if she'd throw up. She'd been the one to suggest he sleep in the house. She'd placed Bill in harm's way.

Guilt was a tangible weight on her chest. "Hey, Bill. We're going to get you out of here, okay."

Eyes pleading with her to do just that, he blew out a breath as his two sons grabbed a side of the beam. When they lifted, Bill gripped the arm of the couch. His eyes rolled back in his head, and he passed out.

The two brothers eased the beam onto the floor.

"Dad!"

Ian wiped sweaty palms on his jeans. "He'll be okay. Brooke, grab him under the armpits. I need you to help carry him just . . ." He closed his eyes, cursed. "Just like you did with Jen. I'd do it, but with the break, it's going to take two of us down here."

She looked at the leg, marveled at how much it had resembled Jen's. The difference was that Jen hadn't felt the break.

She swallowed hard. "I got it."

She took Ian's flashlight, laid it on the edge of a nearby coffee table, and did her best to aim the light toward their exit. Then, praying they could move Bill before he woke, she moved into position.

Ian lifted, cradling his dad's upper legs with one arm, the lower back with another. Alex led the way out of the room while supporting the portion of the broken leg to ensure minimal damage.

"Ian, Brooke, Alex, you kids find him?"

"We got him, Grandpa," Alex told him. "He's hurt. We're gonna need a doctor."

"I'll get the truck. Oh my God, my poor baby." Irene's voice faded as she ran toward the driveway.

They worked as a team. Ian, Alex, and Brooke lifted Bill to the height of the windowsill. It was painstaking work, and they were exhausted, muscles fatigued from a day that had demanded more than their fair share.

From outside, Henry and George held up a piece of plywood they'd grabbed from the back of Ian's truck. Ian and Alex slowly moved Bill's legs through the window. Then Henry and George laid Bill's legs onto the board as carefully as they could manage, using it to provide basic support for the broken leg.

Alex and Ian climbed carefully out of the window, moving around the plywood so they could help pull the rest of Bill's body through.

Sweat poured down Brooke's back, holding Bill's upper body weight, while the others prepared to pass him through the opening.

"Something wrong with the back door?" George asked.

Alex grunted. "Your fridge slid up against it, somehow wedged itself between the damn wall and the cabinets, and I think the door jam's messed up too. I couldn't budge the door."

"Brooke, I want you to step as close to the window as possible," Ian said.

She moved forward, careful not to let Bill's back scrape against the window frame.

The group made two lines on either side of Bill and slowly brought him safely through. Ian, Carol, and Henry stood on one side, Alex and George on the other.

Brooke shook out her tired arms and began climbing out the window just as Irene came running toward them.

"Truck's running; we can— Oh my dear boy, oh my God." She ran to Bill.

"He's just passed out," her husband assured her. "Need to load him up."

"And go where?" she demanded anxiously. "You know as well as I do that the Salem Hospital is most likely in a tangled heap. Those buildings weren't designed to handle that kind of shaking." Tears flowed down her face.

"We'll find someone, even if we have to find a veterinarian, Mom. We'll find someone who can help."

Irene sniffled loudly and nodded. "Where's Laura? She'll want to come."

"She's probably still with Fawn."

Alex looked at Brooke. "Still? That's not good. Mom'd be here if she could. Here, Grandma, can you help here? I need to . . ."

"Go." Irene and Brooke moved in, Irene supporting her son's all-but-lifeless body while her grandson went to check on his wife. She grunted under the weight, heaved out a breath, then steadied as Brooke helped support Bill's lower back.

"Henry?" Irene asked.

"Bill's going to be just fine. Let's get him in the truck."

Chapter Thirty-Eight

"I just think your dad should stay and rest until we can find a doctor."

Ian spared a single glance at Brooke, unsure of how to respond. To give himself a minute, he cleared more items from the bed of the truck.

Everyone was exhausted, but there was just no way to move a nearly two-hundred-pound man into a seating position while minimizing damage to the leg. They'd have to lay him down in the back of the truck.

"Resting didn't go so well for him last time," he said shortly.

Standing in the driveway, Brooke laid her arms on the side of the truck and placed her chin on them, her attention moving from the task at hand to him.

"Your grandparents' house looks sturdy."

"You thought the same about George's?"

Brooke's head snapped back as if she'd been slapped. She said nothing.

Ian lowered a toolbox from the very back of the bed onto the driveway. "I'm not blaming you for what happened."

"Could have fooled me," she said, straightening.

He looked at her. Just behind where Brooke stood, Ian's neighbors tended to his dad in the front yard. A few of them worked to carry a twin mattress from a spare bedroom at Seth and Jen's house.

As soon as Ian cleared his junk, they'd tie down the mattress in the bed of the truck, secure his dad to that, with two other people riding in the back, ensuring he didn't roll around. As plans went, Ian had to admit it sounded pretty shitty. He didn't know what else to do.

His hands stung in the chill. For the first time since he'd started the new career path, he wished to hell he wasn't a contractor.

Why the hell did he have to own so many God-damned tools?

"You couldn't have known," he repeated. "I didn't. You're a teacher. Based on your interactions with Maddie, I'd guess you're a great one."

"Thanks."

He ignored the irritation in her voice. "Probably make a dino mom someday, but you're no contractor."

"No."

Now she sounded more confused than angry. Ian took a deep breath. "I am. I saw that house. I should have known it wasn't safe."

"You didn't tell him to sleep in there," she pointed out.

He nodded. "True, but I didn't tell George and Carol to find a new place to stay either. That could have just as easily been them inside when the shaking began. Worse, if that couch had been a foot to the left, we'd be having another funeral this week."

"Humm." She hopped into the bed of the truck with him and started gathering small tools that had spilled from one of the toolbox drawers during the shaking.

She'd been right there with him, Ian admitted to himself, helping him ready the truck for his dad, even though, apparently, she thought doing so wasn't the right call.

He looked at her now. Brooke Halliwell had a hard time trusting the dependability of others. Her dad and Jen had been two of the few she'd fully let in. He planned to get added to that list.

Despite her hesitancy to depend on others, however, she had always been incredibly dependable.

Even when fatigue ruled.

In the darkness, he could see the bags under her eyes. It amazed him how, even with all that the day had brought and continued to deliver, he could still look at her and feel his heart boomerang.

He wiped his hands on his jeans to clean them, feeling the grime caked to them from the countless times he'd wiped them that same way all day.

Pulling the shirt out from under his new jacket that Alex had run home to grab—Brooke had a new one on too—Ian wiped his hands off as best he could before taking her hand. "Humm?"

She shrugged. "Maybe you're right, but no one did die. Your dad has years of experience with building. He trusted that the house was safe. Otherwise, he'd have told George and Carol to find a new place. He felt safe going in, even with his Habitat for Humanity experience. This isn't on you."

She took his other hand, looked into his eyes. "I still say you should wait to load your dad into the truck."

"He needs a doctor. His leg…" Ian felt his stomach clench. He'd been in contracting a while now. Injuries were par for the course, but his was different. Seeing a parent in pain, knowing the medical system was just as screwed as the patients, Ian had never felt more helpless. No cell service, no electricity, potentially no morphine…

"Yes." Brooke pulled her hands away, rolled from a squat to sit, her feet dangling off the bed. "But you didn't see the town."

"I can imagine."

She shook her head. "The roads, they're untouched in places, crumpled in others. Glass and bricks flow into it like mini landslides. There are downed powerlines, tree branches, broken down cars."

Ian arched his lower back. It hurt like hell. His whole body felt like he'd climbed a mountain.

He imagined most of his neighbors were pretty sore. Glancing over at the group on the lawn, he saw Maddie in the middle. She sat looking at the photos he had on his phone. Giving her the phone had been the only thing he'd come up with to keep the little girl occupied while the rest of them worked.

He felt more than a little unnerved at how adept the toddler was with the touchscreen technology. Still, since the internet and phones were down, Ian supposed she couldn't cause much trouble with it.

Like the others, he'd been judicious about his phone usage, saving battery power, but three days of no chargers meant his phone would be dead by morning. At least in its final hours, it entertained Maddie. He needed all adult hands on deck until they got his dad loaded into the truck.

"The truck can handle it."

He hoped.

Brooke shrugged. "Maybe. But how long do you think it will take to find a doctor? It's late, and there are no streetlights, no annoying advertisement signs on buildings, no porch lights. We can't call anyone, have no idea if clinics are open. Even doctors have to sleep, so if you manage to find an office that's still functional, there's no guarantee you'll find anyone working."

"What are you thinking?"

"Go on a scouting mission first."

He considered her for a minute. "Scouting?"

"You always could put a smile on my son's face."

Ian turned to his mom, approaching from the lawn. Realizing he was smiling, Ian shook his head. Damned if his mother wasn't right. He reached a hand up, placed it on Brooke's cheek. "Thanks."

"For?" Brooke asked.

"Talking me down. And the smile." He jumped out of the truck, hugged his mom. "How's Dad doing?"

"He's awake. If we don't move him, he might stay that way. I'm worried he'll pass out again when we move him. He's in a lot of pain."

"We're not going to drive him around," Ian told her. "At least not yet."

"But why?"

Ian looked at Brooke. "I'm going on a scouting mission. I'll find a doctor, then come for Dad. It could take a while. No point putting Dad through the pain of a bumpy ride until we have a destination. Besides, I have some friends I can check with to see if they know of a doctor who can help. Might even be able to get a doc to come here."

Laura turned to Brooke and smiled. "I think that sounds smart."

"Mom, why don't we go over really quick? Join the others. I wanna go over this new plan with them."

"That's something else we need to talk about."

Ian and Brooke exchanged glances and waited silently for the news.

"It looks like Fawn is in labor."

Brooke hopped down from the truck. "Wait, what?"

Ian scratched his head. "What do you mean by *looks like*?"

"She's having contractions. Real ones. They aren't rhythmic yet, meaning they aren't evenly spaced. Sometimes, labor stalls out before they become rhythmic. We're keeping her as calm as possible, hoping to stall them, given the chaos of the moment, but I think this is it."

Brooke gaped. "I thought she wasn't due for a couple more weeks."

"She's thirty-eight weeks today," Laura confirmed. "Probably, it's close to when her body would have naturally gone into labor, but the stress of this latest earthquake appears to have triggered it. Lucky, remarkable, really, the girl didn't go into labor during the first quake. Fawn is strong."

Laura looked from Fawn, who stood, leaning her hands on a tree trunk, to Brooke. "I like knowing that both my boys found strong women."

Brooke's mouth dropped open a second time.

"Jesus, Mom," Ian said in mock embarrassment. "Don't scare the woman off. She's just starting to warm up to the idea."

Brooke stared at him.

Now, Ian chuckled. "In fact, I'm countin' on it."

His chuckle turned into a full-blown laugh at the expression on Brooke's face: a mix of nerves, pleasure, and embarrassment.

Feeling better, he kissed both women on the cheek, then quickly headed off to update those he thought of as his team.

Chapter Thirty-Nine

The two homes on the south side of their road, Brooke's and now George and Carol's, were no longer habitable.

Mother Nature's wrath had left the eleven neighbors—with a twelfth on the way—only two homes standing.

They'd decided to split up, dividing into three care units. As the girl's new guardian, Brooke had naturally paired with Maddie.

Maddie had wanted to sleep in her own room. No one had blamed her. After all, wanting Maddie to have the safety and stability of her home had been one of the reasons they'd all worked so hard, so Maddie and Brooke were staying in the large two-story home.

Henry and Irene's home was much smaller, but no one wanted to add to Maddie's week of hell.

The group naturally did not want to expose Maddie to the moans and possible screams of a woman delivering a baby, not to mention the blood.

Trying to create the best possible birthing room, Carol had ushered Fawn and her husband to Irene and Henry's master suite, praying there were no complications.

Since no one had wanted Bill's pain to disturb the toddler either, Irene, unwilling to leave her son's side, had set up to care for Bill in the house's second-largest bedroom.

She and George planned to take shifts caring for him until Ian and Henry returned with news of a doctor.

Laura, feeling torn, had opted to be the go-between, splitting her time caring for her daughter-in-law and her husband.

So, Brooke and Maddie had the large house all to themselves.

The day had moved fast. It had been scary, sad, and often loud and busy with people.

In Maddie's room, Brooke marveled at the quiet and the calm. Watching Maddie sleep, Brooke couldn't help but realize how out of place the moment felt. Salem was hardly recognizable, she thought, its infrastructure a mess.

Maddie's family was forever broken.

Yet, Maddie's room felt normal, as if the space had been immune to the devastation. Brooke sat in the rocking chair next to the bed, soaking in the illusion. It was a welcome lie.

In it, Brooke could pretend that Jen and Sparks were alive. Seth was alive and home. She could pretend the town thrived, Bill's leg wasn't broken, and Fawn was in labor at Salem Hospital. Brooke could pretend her home stood strong and that she'd gotten the job at Candalaria Elementary.

They were illusions of continuity, of putting down roots. The reality was too painful. And she was too tired. Watching Maddie's chest rise and fall beneath the fairy covers, Brooke let the illusions play in her mind as she drifted off to sleep.

Chapter Forty

Brooke heard a knock at the door. Dressed in sweatpants, a mismatched sweater, and thick socks, she answered it . . . and immediately regretted not brushing her hair first.

No question, they were all experiencing some of the least posh-and-pampered days of their lives. With no running water, they hadn't showered. There hadn't been enough water to sponge bathe, so some rain-soaked towels had been Brooke's only wipe-downs since the earthquake.

But there was no excuse not to have her hair brushed. She wanted to curse.

"Oh, hey." She swept her hair to one side, hoping somehow the act made it appear less tangled. Right.

Ian stuck his thumbs into the front pockets of his jeans, grinned at her. "I like this look."

"Oh, shut up."

"No, I'm serious. It's cute."

Beyond mortified, Brooke glared.

Ian chuckled. "I need you and Maddie to pack. Changes of clothes, toothbrushes, that sort of thing."

"Why?" she asked, her embarrassment quickly replaced with bafflement, which then cleared. "You found a doctor?"

"Better. We're heading to a shelter. Fawn had the baby. 'Bout three a.m."

Brooke grinned. "Really? How is . . . Wait, boy or girl?"

"Girl. Savanna. She's adorable and doin' fine. Fawn too."

"Wow." Brooke laid a hand on the door jamb. "You're a brother. A dad."

Ian ran a hand through his dark hair, shaking his head in equal disbelief.

The warming center flashed in Brooke's mind. The smell had been epic. She remembered the sounds of hacking coughs and vomit purging. She remembered all too well the state of the bathrooms. The forty people in that room, just one week ago, had been some of Salem, Oregon's poorest residents. They'd made up a minority.

Now, how many people were homeless? Of those who still had a home, how many, Brooke wondered, had no food or water? No one in Salem had bathed in a week. With no running water, people were dirty, hungry, cold, and undoubtedly sick.

No way was she about to expose the girl to that. They could hold out for another week or so until the power came back on and the water flowed again. Ian wouldn't like that answer, she knew.

Evading, she asked, "Would you like some coffee?"

A look of longing crossed Ian's face, so deep that it was Brooke who chuckled now. "I hear ya. I managed to get a small fire going out back this morning and found a drip filter setup in a small box in the attic."

She looked up. The blue sky was a nice change of pace from the solid cloud cover of the past few days.

"Yes. Hell yes. But I'll have to make it fast."

"Water just finished boiling."

She waved her hand, signaling for him to follow. They went to the back patio. Brooke pulled a blue camping mug from a tote, filling it three-fourths of the way.

"Sides are hot, but it's all I have at the moment."

"I think I love you."

She laughed, rolling her eyes, and refilled her cup. Its bitter smell reminded her of the night Jen and Maddie had shown her the fairy garden—the last time she'd seen Jen alive. Fresh pain flooded her. She missed Jen so much, yet she was grateful the smell of the coffee had brought back the precious memory.

"Want to sit?" she asked.

Ian held up a finger and moaned as he drank. "Oh. Good. God. Alright," he said after a minute. "Back to business. I'd like to sit, but I can't. We're all packed. Henry needed to grab a few things, but we're heading out soon. I want you and Maddie to come."

"You found a doctor for Bill, I take it? At the shelter? How late were you out?"

"Sun was coming up when we pulled in. hell of a long night, but worth it. A friend of mine knew of a shelter near Life Source Natural Grocers. Got lucky there. It's nearly a full week before the city thought they'd have any up and running."

"That will help a lot of people like me who have lost homes. I'm sorry you don't know how yours is doing. That's got to be hard."

"Auntie Brooke?"

Brooke turned toward the sounds of Maddie crying, calling for her. Standing, Brooke went into the house. "You're awake? Hi sweetie. I'm here. Aw, what's wrong?"

"I want, I want, I want mommy." She stomped her foot on the kitchen floor. "Want my daddy. Where's my daddy?"

Brooke pulled her in for a hug.

"Hey, kid." Ian moved into the living room and looked at Brooke.

Maddie sniffled.

Brooke met Ian's gaze and considered going with him to the shelter. It embarrassed her that she wanted to be by his side, that that feeling was so complete she nearly gave in. She didn't want him to go.

He raised his eyebrow, gestured with his head toward the door.

Setting Maddie on her hip as she stood, Brooke shook her head. "I've seen Salem's emergency shelters under the best of conditions. There was no time to plan for this."

She thought of the lack of supplies that had saddened her at the warming center, and she remembered how the city had struggled to find even seven volunteers to help out.

The shelters would be disastrous.

"How many of you are going?" Brooke asked Ian.

"Everyone. They'll have food, water. Fawn and the baby can get looked over by the doctor too, just in case."

"Baby?"

Ian smiled at Maddie. "Fawn had a baby."

Maddie's tears dried up. "I very wove babies. They are happy in my heart."

Ian moved in, rustled Maddie's blond curls, then, with his tone lighter than the expression in his eyes, told Brooke, "I don't know when we'll be back."

"I figured you'd take everyone there, come back in the evenings. This sounds . . . more permanent," Brooke decided.

Ian looked at Maddie. "Can you go grab your favorite toy?"

"Sure!" Maddie squirmed until Brooke set her down and ran upstairs.

"Brooke, we're nearly out of supplies. If you guys don't come now, you'll end up needing to meet us there anyway."

"How low? I thought we had at least five days left."

"We were supposed to inventory it this morning, but George had taken point on organizing supplies. Since we were all eatin' meals in his and Carol's front yard, I haven't been in their house since we got my dad out, but I think most of the stock was in their living room."

"Oh, crap."

"My mom's been beating herself up all morning about it. She convinced George to put most of it there, so it would be easy to grab. We're assuming the stuff's toast now."

Brooke bit her lip. "I want to keep Maddie in her comfort zone as long as possible. She's been through enough. Besides, I found some extra food in the garage. It should be enough for at least a few days and maybe a week." She shrugged. "I'll keep her here until we run out. Then we'll head over."

It was a lie. She hadn't found extra food and was banking on finding some at George and Carols. Brooke was determined to find a way to survive at home with Maddie until the electricity and water came back online, the roads were cleared, and the grocery stores restocked. One more week. Ten days at most, she figured. It'd be challenging, but it'd be better than staying in a shelter.

Besides, Brooke thought, Bill wouldn't be the only injured person in the shelter. Maddie didn't need the trauma of seeing the injured and the suffering.

Ian sighed. "Don't take too long. If it's not filled already, the shelter will fill up fast, especially since other shelters haven't had a chance to open yet. J.T., the friend I talked to last night, says most shelters won't open for another week or more."

"Okay."

Even more reason not to go to the shelter. Chaos.

"Don't do that."

"What?"

He scowled at her. "That, 'I got this' thing."

She smiled innocently at him, "But I do *got* this."

"I'm serious."

Brooke sighed. "It's not ego, Ian. I'm not going to the shelter until I'm out of options. And for now, at least, I've got this."

"Moments like this are easier with a team, Brooke."

She moved her hair behind her ear. "I'm getting more comfortable being part of this group, depending on this group."

"Me too I hope."

"Yes, actually, and I'm not too proud to admit that I've needed you guys through a lot of this. I'm not ready to leave yet, Ian, but I promise to come if it becomes too much. I'm bummed you guys have to go. I just hate shelters."

"I want to stay with Ian," Maddie said, and nearly had Brooke giving in.

Ian's steady gaze didn't help. Her heart skidded. Damn him. She took a slow breath.

"We're going to see him very soon," Brooke said, not taking her eyes off Ian. She would hold her ground for now.

Resigned, Ian kissed Brooke on the cheek, as he had the day before. "See you," he said, his tone more *insistent* than casual, and headed out.

Maddie, a stuffed elephant in her hand, came over, lifted her arms for Brooke. Brooke picked her up again.

You've lost so much. I won't let you lose your home, your bedroom, your familiar place, too. Besides, things will start getting back to normal soon.

Brooke watched Ian walk to the driveway, climb in the driver's seat of the pickup truck that had just pulled up. Henry, who'd driven it over, hopped out and climbed into the bed of the truck to help George support Bill as he lay on a mattress. Behind the truck, Irene drove George's SUV, Carol sitting in the passenger seat with Fawn, Alex, and the new baby in the back.

Holding Maddie, Brooke waived as they drove away.

Chapter Forty-One

The following two days went by with the speed of a very pissed-off bumblebee. Every pan, pot, bucket, or bin that could hold water waited for rain, but precious little had fallen since the neighbor's departure.

Running between collection sites at every sprinkle or short downpour might have provided them with enough water had it not been for all the exertion required to care for Maddie.

Getting a toddler to drink water on a routine basis when she wanted juice or milk had had Brooke working her ass off just to keep Maddie hydrated before quenching her own thirst.

On their third day without the neighbors now, Brooke's lips were painfully chapped, and a persistent headache threatened to slow her down.

She checked the faucets on what became an obsessive routine, each time more furious than the last when the twist of a knob provided no relief.

Food was a similar story. While she'd lied to Ian about finding extra food in the garage, she'd gotten incredibly lucky later that morning digging through the attic. Buried in Seth's old Army stuff, she'd found MREs, Meals, Ready-to-Eat, in a small, white grocery bag.

They hadn't tasted great, but they'd been loaded with calories. More, they hadn't required any cooking.

Like the water, though, getting a three-year-old to eat MREs hadn't helped her headache. Brooke figured the act would have been impossible unless that child was starving. In those first two days, Maddie had only eaten when she'd hit that point.

Just the thought of the power struggles made Brooke scowl, but she had an even bigger problem now. Her scowl threw darts at the pretty popcorn clouds much too high and far apart to offer hope.

Brooke marched back into the house and stopped in front of the kitchen sink. Beside the sink, in tall plastic cups that had survived their fall from the cabinets during the shaking, was the last of their drinking water. Probably eight ounces each, Brooke figured, hoping a storm of massive proportions would roll in by lunchtime.

She looked out the small window above the sink, saw the gorgeous sprawl of a sunny sky. *Great.*

She closed her eyes, hoping to hear activity in the pipes of the walls that would fulfill the wish denied to her from the sky.

She flexed her fingers, then ran her hands down her face. "You can do this."

Hands shaking, she reached out and turned the faucet. Nothing fell. She wrinkled her nose against the stench of food trapped and rotting in the garbage disposal. Knowing she couldn't turn on the water for something as simple as flushing it down or power the electricity to grind it away left her feeling lost.

The headache, a nasty combination of dehydration, caffeine withdrawal, and stress, began to pound against the new flood of adrenalin.

She was consumed with fury at the universe for providing enough rain to flood her tent that first night after the earthquake, only to withhold it when she and Maddie needed it most.

What if the City of Salem couldn't get the water back on for a few more days? After all, it hadn't been a full two weeks yet. And they were near the outskirts of town. Would it take longer for them to get it back? Could she and Maddie wait for rain?

Moving back outside to watch Maddie try to find worms in the grass, Brooke thought of her options, desperately wishing she could check the weather.

The emergency radio, which could have provided a weather report, lay buried in George and Carol's bedroom, along with the bulk of the remaining flashlights and possibly some food and water.

Fear of the building had kept her from going in. Brooke knew it could be dangerous. Every time she'd considered risking it, she'd worried as she did now.

What if I get hurt or trapped? Maddie would be all alone then, and no one would even know.

She felt habitually for the phone in her back pocket and wondered yet again why she didn't just set it down somewhere. Its battery, which she'd been so careful to save, had finally given out the previous evening. With its death, she could no longer tell time, plunging their situation to a new low.

She'd never known a life without a clock. Though not crucial to her survival, not knowing the time made Brooke feel more vulnerable.

Rock and a hard place, Brooke decided. She was either going to have to take Maddie to the shelter, hoping they still had room, or she'd have to risk checking for supplies at George and Carol's.

Watching Maddie play—using an Elmo-like voice while talking with her stuffed animals as she showed them her worm collection—Brooke knew she'd do whatever it took to keep Maddie in her familiar home.

She looked up at the sky one last time. "Rain, damn it," she whispered. "Give us something."

Chapter Forty-Two

Brooke walked over, took Maddie's hand, and guided her through the gate toward the front yard.

"Auntie Brooke, where are we going?"

They stood together, Maddie looking at Brooke in anticipation, Brooke looking at the caved-in entry to George and Carol's house.

Now how in the hell am I going to look through that with Maddie? She can't go in there.

"Can you find worms with your stuffies in the front yard?"

"No. No more worms."

"No worms, huh? Well…" She took Maddie back inside, gathered up a few toys and books that she hoped would entertain the girl for more than five minutes, and threw them in a bag. Then she grabbed the highchair from the kitchen and carried it, a bike helmet, and the bag to the front yard of George and Carol's house.

"Maddie, I need you to play for a minute while I check something out. Can you do that?"

"I want cereal."

"I know, baby; me too. I'm going to see if I can find some. Okay?"

"Can I have chocolate?"

"Cereal?"

"Uh-huh."

Brooke knew there was no way she'd find anything like that in the pile. Whatever 'fun' food the group had was long gone.

"I'll see what I can find."

"Yea!"

Brooke wiggled Maddie into the highchair, secured the straps, and laid out the toys on the plastic tray. "I'll be right back."

Brooke then kept her movements nonchalant as she rounded the building, but once she was out of Maddie's sight, she ran. She put the bike helmet on, hoping it would protect her head if something fell on her.

Going through the same window they had rescued Ian's dad from, she made her way gingerly over toppled furniture, trinkets, and glass to where the front door had once been—to where the group's supplies had been when the second aftershock hit.

She hadn't taken much time to look around the area when they'd rescued Bill. Anything that hadn't been relevant to getting him out hadn't registered, she realized now. Plus, it had been dark.

Now, with the danger over and the sunlight emanating through broken windows, Brooke realized why Ian hadn't bothered to check the supplies. It was possible, she assumed, that some edible item lay beneath the destruction, but most were surely smashed, broken open, spilled, or spoiled.

It would take painstaking time and luck to dig through the debris safely. She scanned the area, wondering where to start, when a flash of red caught her attention. There, just beside the couch, lay the small emergency radio.

Please still have batteries.

The sound of a shrill scream broke her concentration.

Maddie.

Grabbing the radio, Brooke went running over the fallen furniture, through the window, and around to the front of the house. All the toys and books Brooke had gathered for Maddie lay on the grass below the high chair, clearly thrown off by the now angry toddler.

She was fine, Brooke realized, but she was crying and scared, alone in the middle of the yard. Brooke cursed herself and fought to unhook the buckle of the high chair so she could cradle her new daughter.

"I'm sorry. Shhhh. I'm here. I'm sorry you got scared."

I'm scared too.

Chapter Forty-Three

Brooke held Maddie until the girl calmed.

"Did you find chocolate cereal?"

Brooke frowned, hating that she had to give the girl any more disappointment. "No, but I found this."

She lifted the AM/FM radio. "I'm hoping it might tell me where we can go for some cereal."

Brooke hesitated. She needed to turn it on and try to find a radio station to check for rain. If she learned a storm was coming, she'd feel better. If she could hydrate, digging out food might not seem so impossible either, she decided.

She could look for food during Maddie's nap. They'd be okay. But they needed the rain.

"Do you want to listen to the radio?"

"I push da buttons?"

"Sure."

Brooke showed her the on switch then sat down in the driveway to listen. If the sky was going to refuse her water, at least she and Maddie could soak up some of the sun's warmth.

Turning the dial through the static, she found the AM Oregon Public Broadcasting station they'd listened to the night they'd learned about the tsunami. She'd wanted the weather, but curiosity got the best of her, and she paused to listen.

"We can't stress enough how important it is to do a thorough job washing your hands through this," Brooke heard a woman say.

"That was Florence Lake, the head of Oregon's Department of Health and Human Services. I'm Shawn Lager."

"And I'm Joann Jefferies. Up next, we have Walter Randow, the director of Oregon's Department of Emergency Management. Good morning, Director. We know how busy you are. Thank you for taking the time to speak with us today."

"Thank you for having me."

"We've just heard some of the struggles throughout the region relating to sanitation," Brooke heard Shawn say. "What can you tell our listeners about the recovery efforts so far?"

Director Randow cleared his throat. "Prior to the event, DOGAMI, alongside the American Red Cross, the Oregon Seismic Safety Policy Advisory Commission, and the Federal Emergency Management Agency conducted assessments for our Oregon Resilience Report."

Brooke felt her stomach jitter. "Hey, Maddie, why don't you do some summersaults in the grass?"

"No. I want to listen!"

Not wanting to argue and risk missing vital information, Brooke simply closed her eyes and hoped the news didn't scare Maddie. Besides, the sound of the radio had the toddler sitting still.

"What did the assessments find?" Joann asked.

"They looked at the infrastructure in the Pacific Northwest likely to be impacted by an earthquake like the one we unfortunately just had. Based on those assessments and the size of the earthquake, we believe it will take up to thirteen months to get water flowing again, both for drinking and sanitation."

"Thirteen months. That's like, what, four hundred days?" Shawn asked.

"In the Willamette Valley, yes," Director Randow confirmed. "We expect it could take more than a decade for coastal communities."

Brooke felt her hands go clammy. *Four. Hundred. Days.* She felt as though someone had just slammed a fist into her face. Why had her neighbors, who'd seemed to know what to expect, talked about supplies on a two-week timeframe?

"Some other infrastructure will take longer, some less time. In the Valley, we expect electricity to be back up and running in about three months. Natural gas may be back within six weeks. But healthcare facilities will most likely take a couple of years to get back to normal functionality, and we expect top-priority highways to take close to a year and a half to repair."

"It sounds like we have a long road ahead of us," Joann said.

"Yes. With the stronger shaking and the devastating tsunami along the coast, restoration for all those categories will take much longer. We are working hard to bring in help from outside agencies to get shelters open as fast as possible for all locations impacted."

"How long until the shelters in the valley have access to water?" Joann asked.

"Shelters, including water distribution centers, should be up and running in a few days."

"So," Shawn said, "about two weeks exactly from the day of the earthquake."

"Yes. The goal had been to have the distribution centers and shelters running two weeks after the earthquake hit. It was the shortest amount of time possible to accomplish the task, given the region's state. I'm happy to report that the planning and exercises done in preparation for Cascadia were key. Because of them, because of the many people working so hard through this, we are hopeful we will make that deadline."

"Two weeks is still a long time for those who weren't prepared," Joann added.

Brooke heard the director sigh.

"Yes. We worked hard to motivate the region to get Two-Weeks-Ready. In many ways, I think the campaign was a success, but there wasn't enough time to build full community involvement. We believe roughly eight percent of the population had supplies to last that long."

"And the other ninety-two percent?"

"They're struggling—suffering. We're getting to as many people as we can and will continue to do so. Our hearts go out to everyone going through this horrendous disaster. If you can hold out just a few more days, help is on the way."

Two weeks.

Brooke shut off the radio. Her neighbors had planned on going to the shelters all along. At the very least, they had known they would have to wait two weeks for supplies to be available.

She hadn't understood—hadn't asked the right questions. Suddenly, her habits of constantly checking for running water, hitting light switches, and stomaching MREs until things got back to normal felt foolish. She felt foolish.

We could be in that shelter now, Brooke thought. What if they were full now? She'd have to battle ninety-two percent of the population who were as desperate as she was for what she assumed would be scarce supplies. The eight percent who'd been ready would be looking for shelter or supplies soon enough, too. Few, if any, would have enough water for four hundred days.

Fear that she wouldn't be able to find a shelter with room for them swamped her, but she knew now it was pointless to stay in the neighborhood. Life wouldn't be back to normal for a long time. She needed help. They needed help.

"Come on, Maddie. Let's get some water."

"I want milk."

"I know, kiddo. I don't have any just now."

Trying to keep her voice light, Brooke guided Maddie inside and got the two plastic cups still sitting by the sink. She sat to help Maddie drink hers. They couldn't afford any spills. As soon as the water touched the little girl's lips, she began to drink, finishing it fast enough to tell Brooke just how thirsty the girl had been.

Knowing she was about to seek refuge from the city she had hoped to serve, Brooke brought the precious final reserves of water to her lips and drank.

Chapter Forty-Four

Brooke marveled at the sensation of her foot on the gas pedal. Only a week had passed since the earthquake. Seven days without driving wasn't all that long, but it felt like years.

Brooke supposed going without heat, phones, and fresh drinking water flowing from faucets had all taken their toll. So had the lack of electricity, showers, and flushing toilets during that frigid February week.

Being in a running car made her feel as though she'd just time traveled from 1850 back to the age of technology. It felt good.

She'd never driven Jen's car. The small Geo Prism maneuvered easier around turns than her own and thankfully had a car seat for Maddie.

"Auntie Brooke?"

"Yeah?"

"Where we are going?"

Brooke glanced in the rearview mirror at Maddie and debated with herself on how to answer. *We're going to try to find Ian and the others.* No, Maddie wouldn't like hearing they were missing.

I'm going to find us a place to stay for a few days. Maddie had just gotten settled into her room again.

We ran out of food and water and are desperately hoping someone in town can care for us for a while.

Shit, Brooke thought. The truth didn't feel suitable for a three-year-old.

"I have a few errands to run today."

"What's that?"

"Things I need to drive around to do."

"I have music?"

Brooke considered. She knew from the handheld radio that she was unlikely to get any music stations on FM to come in and didn't want any news reports to scare Maddie. Shrugging, she hit the CD player. Raffi's voice came gently out of the worn speakers.

Maddie squealed. Strapped in the toddler seat, she did her best to wiggle and dance in a way that reminded Brooke how uninhibited toddlers were. No one would tell them what was or wasn't dancing.

Grateful for Maddie's distraction, Brooke put her focus fully back on the road. The small size of the car made it possible to weave around some of the debris on the road. She had to drive over debris in some places, going slow and hoping nothing would pop the car's tires.

Liberty Elementary School sat just around the next turn. Her guilt flooded her, fresh as the day she'd walked away from the volunteers, the parents, the kids.

Had they gotten all the kids out? she wondered. If she had left Maddie with Ian that day, Brooke knew she would have stopped to help. Would her presence have made a difference?

She steeled herself as the school came into view. The building looked much like it had the last time she'd seen it, yet this time, no groups stood outside. Instead, in their place was a single wooden cross in the soil.

No. Oh God, no.

She tried to hold back tears, but a choked sob escaped. Hearing it over the music, Maddie stopped dancing. "You are sad, Auntie Brooke?" She sounded scared, worried.

Brooke shook her head, hoped it looked convincing.

"You have da hiccups?"

The confusion in Maddie's tiny, sweet voice nearly broke Brooke. She shook her head again, driving past the school, forcing herself to breathe.

If she had helped that day, could she have saved that life? Could she have been the person who made the difference? Brooke imagined it took a team to find and save those trapped. . . . But what if she could have saved someone? Did the cross belong to a teacher? A parent? A staff member? A child?

It was a question she knew would haunt her forever.

She hit the next button on the CD player, hoping a new song would distract Maddie. When it worked, Brooke nearly let out another sob, this time in relief. Scaring Maddie wasn't on the day's agenda.

Forcing herself to breathe, Brooke focused on the drive.

She and her neighbors had so much open land near her street that there had been plenty of room to set up garbage and human waste areas.

In the heart of the city, space was severely limited. Garbage bags lined the curbs, but many had been torn open. Home to opossums, skunks, raccoons, deer, and rats, Salem had just become a free-for-all—its quantity of garbage far exceeding that of the city's plastic garbage bins.

How much worse would it get when the residents ran out of garbage bags?

Finally past the elementary school, Brooke felt like a driver in Mario Cart as she continued to weave around debris through a part of town she hadn't seen since the earthquake. Seeing the new damage was jarring.

"Again, again," Maddie said.

Brooke looked over her shoulder at Maddie. "Huh?"

Maddie wiggled, her little hands shaking in the air. "Again, Pweese. I very love it."

"The song? Oh, sure." Brooke reset the song, loving Raffi in that moment.

A woman came out of a tent made from sheets, watched Brooke and Maddie drive past. Brooke wondered if the woman wanted her to stop.

The area of Liberty street they drove on was zoned commercial; businesses run out of previous residential homes. Now, those buildings, complete with yards, looked more like strange campgrounds. There were tents in some spaces, sleeping bags or blankets stretched out on top of cardboard in others. Tarps were strewn haphazardly to provide cover.

Where the buildings looked sturdier, window openings hid behind misshaped pieces of plywood. Brooke figured the plywood had been nailed to stop looters or bad weather, or both. She wondered if the buildings housed people. There was no telling the state of the inside, she knew.

Were these campers the owners of those businesses? Had their homes fallen? Did being on Liberty make them feel safer, assuming they'd be the first to receive help when it came? How many, like this woman, were hoping Brooke was there to help?

Chapter Forty-Five

Brooke drove until Liberty began to curve where it connected with Commercial Street, the main artery in South Salem. She had planned to make a right, but cars sat in a line around that curve, parked at what would have been a red light. Like the other infrastructure requiring electrical power, the traffic signal sat dead, offering no advice to drivers.

That didn't seem to matter, Brooke mused, since all the cars snaking halfway into the intersection sat abandoned.

The once yellow-and-white gas station to her left could have provided a sneaky path through the tangle, but it had problems of its own. Victim to a fire after the earthquake, the entire west side of the station sported melted plastic and charred wood. Abandoned cars clogged the entrance to the east pumps.

Shit.

Brooke looked down at her own gas gauge. With so much going on, she hadn't thought much about gasoline. Jen's tank registered just above empty, its yellow light screaming at her. Without electricity, pumps would sit idle.

She thought of the OPB report from that morning. No electricity in Salem for three to four months. *More than a hundred days.*

And she'd only made it through seven.

Brooke cringed. She doubted the shelters in town had several days' worth of food and water for families to take to their homes. That meant, if she could even find a shelter with room, she and Maddie would essentially be staying in said homeless shelter for the foreseeable future.

"We there?" Maddie asked as Brooke sat with the car idling.

"Um, not quite yet." Brooke glared at her dashboard, wishing she could just give it a good kick, but she didn't want to alarm Maddie. *I hope we find a shelter before we run out of gas.*

She looked around. The Office Depot parking lot across from the gas station was filled with tents, looking like a city-sanctioned homeless shelter. Its presence triggered chills that flowed through Brooke. If shelters were truly up and established, why would so many people make camps outside?

It wasn't a good sign.

But if there weren't shelters, why hadn't her neighbors returned? Ian had told her he'd found one. If it was full, there had to be more. Right?

She shrugged, desperately wishing she could make a single phone call, wishing she had a map. Had the parking lot been empty, Brooke could have used it to detour around the abandoned cars to get to Commercial.

Glancing in the only other direction available, she looked at the second Roth's grocery store on the street. Like the first one miles back, its windows were boarded up. Large concrete barriers lined the parking lot entrances. Signs read *Food trucks will need to come through the parking lot. Please don't camp here.*

Many had listened. The area closest to the store sat empty, but tents peppered the far end.

Brooke knew of other roads that connected Liberty to Commercial. The problem was, she would have to back up to get to them and had no way of knowing if they would be as clogged with cars as this intersection.

If I try, will I just end up farther away from where we need to go with an empty tank of gas? She shook her head, wishing she could look on her phone's map for areas of congestion, but she knew the internet would still be down even if she had a charged phone.

So we walk from here, she decided. Gratitude filled her, knowing she and Maddie were lucky they'd gotten as far as they had without a traffic jam or flat tire.

Her hands on the wheel at ten and two, Brooke sat stone-still. She didn't want to open the door. The drive had warmed the engine, and precious heat poured from the car vents. It had been so long since she'd felt heat. The muscles throughout her body felt relaxed, their continuously cramped state from the past week melting away.

She and Maddie were about to leave that warmth, the safety of the car, and walk the streets to a building. Would they have room for her and Maddie? Would the building be seismically safe? Would there be food and water? How many would be ill, exposing Maddie to God only knew what? Would Ian and the others be there?

No choice, she reminded herself. "Come on, kiddo."

Placing her hand on the latch, Brooke pushed the door open and felt the cold flood in.

Chapter Forty-Six

Maddie sat swinging her legs in her stroller. Some of her and Brooke's most essential possessions were loaded in the area underneath. The rest were in Seth's oversized camping backpack, which Brooke threw over her shoulders.

The weight of both slowed her down and, in an irony that infuriated Brooke, large drops of rain pelted down on her. When they'd gotten in the car, she hadn't even seen rain clouds.

Just a few blocks from where they'd left the car, they passed a LifeSource Natural grocery store.

Brooke looked at its dilapidated state, her heart breaking in so many ways for the town, the families, and the small business owners. She pushed forward along the final city block until she saw the building.

Several people stood outside. The relief at seeing them was huge.

Shakily, she pushed the stroller from the sidewalk toward the driveway and the sign that read *Support Services Center: Salem-Keizer Public Schools.*

The single-story building, with its red-tiled roof, swarmed with activity. Brooke scanned the adults and children going in, groups coming out, and others talking in groups near the three tall city trees in front.

The thin parking lot sat empty of cars. Instead, large canvas canopies occupied the space.

"Yo, Brooke! What's up, girl? Come on under the canopy out of the rain. You hungry?"

Brooke turned and smiled. There, waving her over from the middle of the three canopies, stood the boy she'd volunteered with at the shelter.

"Tommy, hey!" She waved. Though she'd only met him once, it felt so good to see a familiar face.

She pushed Maddie over and squeezed in front of a plastic folding table where people were gathered.

"Are you staying here? Please tell me this is an official shelter."

"Double yes on that one."

Brooke felt her heart soar. As scared as she was about going into a building, she and Maddie needed food. They needed water, too, and while she figured she could go home to collect water from the current downpour, Brooke no longer felt good about depending on rainwater as their only source.

Besides, she didn't have much faith the car would get them all the way back home. Even if they could grab a week's worth of food, Brooke knew she didn't have the energy to walk the entire four-and-a-half miles home. They didn't have room for a week's worth of the food in the stroller, at any rate. She and Maddie needed the shelter.

Tommy frowned at her. "Ah, but you're looking for one. Um, I'm afraid this shelter, though, has been full for a couple days now. I can check with our HAM radio guys and see if they know of any others that are open with room if you'd like."

Feeling despair swamp her, Brooke nodded.

"This your daughter?"

Brooke looked down, saw Maddie shyly eyeing the stranger.

Daughter. Brooke had accepted the role, yet hearing someone else say it out loud had the gravity of it slamming into her.

"Maddie, I'd like you to meet my friend Tommy," Brooke said, evading the question.

"Sup, Maddie. You hungry?"

"Oh, I am. I am very hungwy. But no MEEs."

Tommy's eyebrow furrowed in confusion.

"MREs." Brooke clarified.

"Oh, gnarly." Tommy laughed. "Man, me neither. Luckily we are fresh out. Have some water and chocolate protein bars, though."

"Chocolate!" Maddie bounced, her seatbelt the only thing containing the girl's excitement.

"We'd love some."

He walked over, opened a box, and pulled out two bars. Then he grabbed two bottled waters from a thirty-two pack.

Brooke's hand shook as she took one of the water bottles. "Thank you."

"Yeah, you bet."

Brooke started to help Maddie to open her bar.

"No," Maddie said. "I do it my own self!"

Smiling, Brooke handed the bar to Maddie. Maddie put it in her lap and drank a third of her water before picking the bar up and struggling with the wrapper.

To Brooke's delight, Maddie got it open and took an enormous bite.

Brooke felt the back of her eyes sting. She stood, ripped open her bottle, and drank deeply.

"Thank you," she repeated.

Tommy nodded.

"I take it you're volunteering here too. You sure get around."

"I'm a CERT member. That's how I got involved with the warming centers."

"I saw the CERT letters on the canopies. What is it?"

"Community Emergency Response Team. This is what we do," he told her, gesturing with a wide sweep of his hands. "My parents were Red Cross," he explained. "Volunteering is kinda a family requirement."

"A good one."

Making sure Maddie was focused on her snack bar, Brooke lowered her voice. "We need a place to stay. Can you check with the radio guy?"

With a solemn nod, Tommy left her. He meandered around a woman who provided snacks to an older gentleman, his gaunt face telling Brooke she'd been lucky to have eaten as well as she had over the week.

"This is Juan. He's your guy. Hope you find a pad." Tommy gave her a good-natured grin and wandered over to a newly-arriving family.

Brooke turned to Juan. Wiping water from her forehead that streamed from her wet hair, she hoped Juan could provide her a miracle. "Please tell me you know of another shelter with beds available."

He frowned slightly. "I'm sorry. We've been searching all day. City's just not openin' up many yet. It's a big to-do, you know." He scratched his head. "Fact is, I'm shocked they have this one up and running so soon. You're welcome to hang out here for a while. One of us is monitoring the radio. If we hear of anything, we'll let you know."

Chapter Forty-Seven

Maddie looked up, her face peering through the window in the stroller's umbrella. Feeling silly for leaving it up now that they were under the larger canopy, Brooke folded it back and bent to face Maddie.

"How you doing, kiddo?"

"More. I want more chocolate. Pweeese."

Brooke handed her own bar to the girl's waiting hand, then turned to see all the families, the individuals, the couples around the building. Were they all there hoping to hear the same news?

Two large men in their forties stood like bouncers at a club, Brooke thought, controlling who went in and out of the shelter. Regardless of the condition of the shelter, the food and water would need to be rationed. No one would be sneaking in.

She turned back to Juan and nodded. "We'll stay for a bit. Please let me know if you hear of anything."

What other choice do I have?

If they stayed, they might get lucky. Perhaps a new shelter would open, and because these people gathered around would have the inside scoop, so to speak, they'd be the first ones to get beds and meals.

But if a shelter like that didn't open soon, what then?

She'd walk back to the car with Maddie, Brooke decided. If no one had parked behind her after she'd abandoned their car, she'd back out of the lot. She'd drive toward home until they ran out of gas, then walk the rest of the way in the frigid and the wet.

At least the rain she hadn't expected to fall would undoubtedly have filled some of their rainwater collection bins. She and Maddie would return home to relatively warm beds, which certainly beat sleeping outside, but they would still have no food—unless, of course, Ian and the others had returned with magical amounts. But from where?

God, she was tired.

Looking at the building, she thought of her neighbors, wondering if they'd made it to the shelter before it filled up.

Brooke turned from the Student Services building back toward Juan.

"Is it alright if I go in for just a minute? I'm looking for someone."

Brooke's eyebrows furrowed. She was actually looking for many *someones,* so why had she used the singular? Okay, so she had Ian on the brain. Up until that moment, she hadn't realized how focused on seeing him—just him—she'd become.

Juan glanced over his shoulder, stuck his thumb and pointer in his mouth, gave a quick whistle. A woman toward the far end of the canopy automatically broke eye contact with the person she'd been helping and looked at Juan.

Brooke watched him gesture his thumb towards the Student Services building, then tap his watch and hold up five fingers. *Heading inside. Be back in five.*

The woman nodded and went back to her conversation so smoothly that Brooke had to assume the silent conversation had happened many times over the past few days.

"I'll take you in. I'm afraid I can't let you go in without a volunteer."

"Thanks for letting me check. I'll feel better knowing if they're here."

He nodded toward the front entrance. Shoving the stroller to the corner of the canopy, Brooke lifted Maddie out. Brooke had to assume the shelter would be too packed for a smooth stroller ride.

Holding Maddie, Brooke followed Juan to the front door. The smell hit her first, washing over her: soot and urine. Memories of Salem's poorest flooded back to her, but she wasn't entering the building as a volunteer this time.

Maddie's legs wrapped around her right hip. Brooke hugged her—an unspoken apology. They were the homeless today, and worse, this shelter couldn't even take them.

What the hell am I going to do?

Tears threatened. She squeezed her eyes shut for a solid three seconds before trusting her control. Opening them, she walked into the single-story office building with its cheap carpeting so prevalent in office space.

"Do you see who you're looking for?"

Brooke shook her head. Unlike the warming center, this place was filled with people who were wide awake. The noise level boomed, shocking to her system after days with Maddie as her only companion.

"Brooke." The voice came from across the room and she tried to see who had called her.

"Brooke." The voice, closer now, nearly shouted.

"Ian." A huge smile broke out on her face.

He walked toward her, cutting through a group of men talking near the entrance. Then careful not to smush Maddie, he leaned down and placed his lips on hers, lingering for only a moment.

Her heart hammered. When he broke the kiss, she stood speechless.

"What are you doing here? God damn, am I glad to see you."

Juan smiled. "I see you've found who you were looking for," he said to Brooke. "Would you guys mind catching up outside? I really can't leave a non-registered guest in here without a volunteer, and I need to get back out." He tapped his watch.

Still reeling from the kiss, Brooke hardly managed to get the 's' in 'sure' out before Ian interrupted.

"Thanks for bringing them in, Juan. This is Maddie." Ian pinched Maddie's nose, making her burst into giggles. He smiled and then met Brooke's gaze. "And this is my wife."

Chapter Forty-Eight

Brooke hoped Juan wasn't a big fan of Paul Eckman and his training on micro-expression detection because she knew there was no way she'd been able to hide the shock from her face, however fleeting.

Juan smiled. "I didn't realize you were separated from your wife."

Married?

Brooke understood he'd said it purely to get her and Maddie a place to stay, but knowing why he'd lied hadn't stopped her heart from racing. The kiss afterward had sent her soaring.

She took a breath. "Maddie and I were on vacation visiting my dad," she told Juan, trying to spin a believable lie. "We'd come home a day early. I didn't tell Ian because I'd wanted to surprise him."

She looked at Ian. "Our plane landed at PDX about twenty minutes before the earthquake. Then we had to make it from Portland over with . . ."

"No way for us to get in contact," Ian finished for her. "I've missed you."

In that last part, Brooke heard pure truth.

"Well," Juan said, "we have some room to allow immediate family members to stay, I suppose. Not much, but some. Does my heart good to see families reunite. Welcome to our shelter, Brooke." With that, he gave Ian a light pat on the back before heading out the door.

Ian, his eyes on Brooke's, unwavering after the kiss, whispered, "You and I are gonna discuss that first date. Soon."

She remembered Fawn teasing him about wanting to ask. It made her smile. The moment made her smile, too. She and Maddie had a place to stay.

After setting Maddie down to walk beside her, Brooke followed Ian to the back left corner of the building.

The heating system sat quiet, a sharp contrast to the human noises flowing throughout the building. In order to fight off illness and odor, doors were propped open for fresh air flow, dropping the temperature further. However, the crowd added body heat to the space.

The crowd flowed with mixed emotions, Brooke noted. Like her, some had found loved ones and were celebrating. But not all. The look of grief showed out of many bloodshot eyes—a perfect reflection of her own heart.

Brooke scanned more faces as they walked, noting some whose anxiety seemed to pour from their very skin. Plenty to be anxious about, Brooke knew.

Are my loved ones okay? When will I see them again? Where will I live? Does my insurance cover earthquake damage? How do I get ahold of my boss? Do I still have a job? How will I buy food? When will things return to normal?

Brooke could all but hear the thoughts. Then, there were the sick and injured. Doing a slow turn as she walked, she took note of how many lay in makeshift beds in need of medical attention. Though Brooke wasn't a nurse, her teaching career required First Aid and CPR certification.

There were so many who needed help, and like the warming center, by Brooke's gage, the shelter was short on staff. Determined to earn her keep, Brooke decided she'd help out in any way possible.

First thing's first.

"Where are the others," she called up to Ian. "How's your dad? Fawn? The baby?"

"See for yourself."

Winding through the final pod of people, Brooke finally caught the first glimpse of her neighbors. Relief flooded through her as she watched Ian's grandparents, Irene and Henry, playing a card game with George and Carol, the four of them sitting on the floor in a small circle.

Behind them, Fawn sat in an uncomfortable-looking chair holding what looked like nothing more than a rolled-up, fuzzy blanket. From her distance and the angle, Brooke couldn't see the face peeking out just yet. Her feet moved more quickly, eager to see.

Then, her heart stumbled in her chest. Lying on a dark blue cot, Bill smiled. He wasn't old, barely sixty, yet his face appeared much older in his current state of pain and fatigue. Brooke watched as Alex supported Bill's hurt leg while Laura did her best to wrap it.

No one else around to help, Brooke thought again, more determined than ever to get to work.

"Baby!" Maddie let go of Brooke's hand and took off running toward Fawn.

"Hold on there, cowgirl." Ian swept Maddie up and onto his hip as she tried to pass him in the crowded room. "That's what we call a mini. You don't want to scare her."

"Mini. Right." Maddie giggled. "No scare, nope, nope."

"Oh, thank goodness." Laura cut the Comprilan compression material, fastened it with a bobby pin, and then stood to wrap her arms around Brooke. "We have been so worried."

"We're fine." Brooke hugged her back and then looked down at Bill "How are you feeling?"

"Wish everyone would stop fussing so much," Bill grumbled.

"He's been a tough patient," Laura said, rolling her eyes.

Bill waved an arm for Brooke to come over. She knelt and gave him a gentle hug.

"Glad to see you, kid."

Brooke nodded. "You, too."

"Ready to see the baby, Maddie?" Brooke asked.

Maddie squirmed in excitement for Ian to set her down. Hand in hand, she and Brooke made their way over to Fawn.

"She's beautiful," Brooke said and meant it. She marveled at how small, even compared to Maddie, the baby's hands and feet were. Savanna Russick had a head full of blond hair like her dad and beautiful blue eyes.

Brooke spent a solid twenty minutes cooing over Savanna with Maddie before shifting gears. Turning to face the room, Brooke watched the crowds.

She saw a woman about her own age, hair pinned up on her head haphazardly. The woman's expression, different from many around her, was pure disheveled overload.

A blanket hung over her right forearm. She carried two water bottles cradled between that forearm and her side. In her hands, she held a one-foot square piece of plywood that supported two plates of food like a restaurant serving tray.

Brooke turned back towards her neighbors. "Laura, can I talk to you for a minute, please?"

"Always." Laura patted her husband's hand. "Ian, can you watch Maddie?" she asked her son.

"Done," he told her and scooped Maddie into his arms. Her legs around his waist, he tipped her upper body so that she hung nearly upside down, making her giggle.

"What's going on?" Laura asked, moving beside Brooke.

"I know you're already busy helping Bill. I hate to even ask, but I'd like to help out around here. Could you, well...Could you guys all watch Maddie for a couple of hours?"

To Brooke's surprise, Laura beamed at her. "Brooke, I'd be delighted."

Brooke had known Laura would agree. It was just the kind of woman she was, but with Bill's current condition, Brooke had expected to see Laura experience some internal hesitation before deciding.

Good people. They always had been.

Laura laid a gentle hand on Brooke's cheek. "You go help these poor people. They need you. Maddie will be fine with us for a bit."

"Thank you."

Turning, Brooke found the girl with her arms overflowing and offered to carry the tray.

Chapter Forty-Nine

The single sheet of lined paper in Seth's hand felt heavy, as if it supported the weight of his crumbled heart.

He forced in a shaky breath. Willing his vision to clear, he reread the first few lines.

> *Seth, if you are reading this, I'm grateful for the miracle of that. We heard the news out of Seaside. So many days have passed, but we've held onto hope you will somehow make it home. What I'm about to write is impossibly hard. We've lost Jen. She died saving Maddie when the earthquake struck. I'm so sorry. We've buried her in your backyard, beyond the grass.*

His body began to shake.

It had taken him, Isaac, and their fellow coastal refugees nearly seven days to walk the sixty miles from Neskowin to Salem, though some had split off early, heading to Corvallis and McMinnville.

Throughout the journey, nightmares had filled Seth's sleep. Though the logical side of his brain knew he couldn't have gone down to the beach to save Isaac's friend, Seth's heart didn't seem to give a damn what logic said.

Guilt swamped him.

Images of the tsunami's wrath, and the mangled bodies left behind, haunted him alongside that sharp edge of guilt. Together, they'd left him punchy during the days, longing for that double-shot expresso he'd never had the chance to drink.

Frigid temperatures and unstable pathways—slippery with rain-soaked mud—had slowed the pace at every turn. It had been an obstacle course for the mighty. They hadn't felt mighty. But they hadn't given up on each other either.

After the waves, the thought of losing more people had constricted Seth's heart. He'd worked his ever-loving ass off every mile of the trip to the Willamette Valley, ensuring no one else died. From building stubborn-to-light fires to filling water containers from the river and filtering it to drink and cook meals, he'd pushed on.

He'd missed his wife and daughter, and while his worry had laid an invisible hand against his back to push him faster, he'd stood his ground. He'd pushed back.

Now, he wished he hadn't.

"What?" Isaac, the only traveler who'd stayed with Seth all the way to Seth's home, came up beside him. "What's the letter say?"

The letter gripped in his hand, Seth bolted from the kitchen out the back door. It didn't take long for him to spot it. The grave rose in a mound of soft soil and gravel. He ran toward it, feeling lightheaded. The muscles of his legs screamed from the exhaustion that pure stubborn will had overcome on his journey home.

He and Isaac were down to half a protein bar each. Seth had only managed to save that much by living the past week on half the calories he usually consumed. He hadn't had much fat on his body to start with. His ribs waved visibly under his shirt, and the bones of his cheeks jutted out.

He needed sleep. Believing that he'd arrive at his home, reunite with Jen and Maddie, and then sleep for a solid ten in his own bed had kept him going.

He felt his breath catch. Beside the grave was a rock he recognized from his wife's garden.

Jennifer Monroy
Loving wife, mother, and friend
March 3, 1998–February 19, 2029

Seth's stared at the words, his fist covering his mouth. "No!"

He fell onto all fours, sobs retching from his shaking body. "I'm. . . man. I'm so sorry."

Seth's eyes, full of devastation, met Isaac's as the boy knelt beside him.

"Jennifer. That was your wife, right? Jen?"

"Yes."

After several minutes, Isaac asked, "Where's your daughter?"

"I don't know."

The simple truth of it took his breath. In the years since he'd become a father, Maddie had given him and Jen more than a few scares, but he'd always known where she was.

"We'll find her," Isaac promised. Before I head for Portland, I'll help. We'll find her."

Seth nodded. Lifting the paper, he read the last few lines.

*Maddie grieves for Jen and misses you. I have done the best I
can to care for her with incredible help from the neighbors, but the
rains have stopped. Our water collection buckets are empty, and
we are nearly out of food. I'm taking Maddie in search of a
shelter. Come find us. – Brooke.*

Seth swallowed hard, fighting back panic, and looked at the sporadic display of pots, buckets, and pans in the yard, now full to the brim with water.

When had Brooke and Maddie left? he wondered. He'd seen Brooke's home. How had she survived while his wife lay beneath him, lacking the very breath that came too quickly in his own chest? Had Maddie and Brooke found a shelter? How far had they traveled? Were they even still alive? *Oh, God.*

Come find us.

Seth knew he'd never stop looking until he did.

Chapter Fifty

"Thank you so much. I was abso-toodles sure I was going to drop the stupid thing."

Brooke smiled. "Yeah. What else can I do to help? I'm Brooke."

"Melody," she replied, smiling. "And we'll see if you still want to help in a couple of hours. This place is a capital-Z zoo!"

She spoke with a smile and kindness that made the statement more wistful than insulting.

Brooke liked her instantly. "How long have you been at it?"

"Honestly, pretty much since the beginning," Melody said, making her way to where two women sat together on a blanket knitting. She placed the water bottles beside them. "Here you go," she said, then she laid a folded blanket on top of the one they sat on. "Now, you two won't have to share tonight."

"Thank you, dear."

Melody turned and took the plywood tray from Brooke. "Found you some food, too."

"My heavens, I'm famished. Oh, you dears, thank you," the second woman said, beaming at Brooke and Melody.

"We'll check back later if we find more." Melody winked at the women and started heading off, with Brooke following behind.

"Anyways," Melody said, "my son goes to Candelaria."

"You have a son. How old?" Brooke asked.

"He's in Kindergarten." Melody stopped walking, faced Brooke, and lowered her voice to a whisper. "Thankfully, he was at recess when the shaking hit. The school's library on the second story, well, the weight of those books on crazy high shelves in the center of that stupid room. . . When the shaking hit, that part of the building collapsed."

Brooke's hand, fisted, raised to cover her mouth. She shook her head. "No. The kids?"

"I work full time, well, normally," she amended, "so I don't do PTA or anything, and as a Kinder-mom, I just didn't know that many moms until this week. But then, it's a pretty tight-knit community, so I think we'd have heard by now. No way to know for sure with phones out and the internet a bust. Some of the parents aren't here, and it's hard to know why."

Brooke felt a chill run down her spine. She thought again of the state of Liberty Elementary. The image of the wooden cross flashed in her mind.

"Are you saying most of the people here are from Candalaria?"

Melody nodded. "I need to get some more water for a family." She pointed to the water station.

Brooke followed.

"This building was in the school's Earthquake Emergency Plan as a place to take the kids after the shaking stopped. They kept the kids outside the school for several hours, waiting for families to come to pick them up, but didn't want to attempt camping in that field with all of them."

"So they took the kids here?"

"Yeah, that afternoon. I work on the opposite side of town, and the roads were like bananas crazy, so I had to walk. The kids were all gone when I got there."

"Did you panic? I would have."

Brooke and Melody stopped at a table where two burly guys stood as guards. "Hey Steve, I need four more, please. Actually, on second thought, make that eight."

One of the men nodded at Melody. He bent behind the table and started pulling out bottled water for her. Brooke and Melody, each taking four, headed off again.

Melody looked over at Brooke. "Thankfully, I knew where the school had taken the kids, or yes, I would have panicked big time!"

"But how? Does your phone work?"

"No. Candelaria held this awesome Pie and Preparedness night in October."

Brooke smiled. "A what?"

"It was basically a way for the school to tell parents what to expect when the earthquake happened. The principal gave a talk, telling everyone the plans. It was in the evening, one of those rare school events I could actually attend, so I went."

"Where's your son, now?"

"With my parents. I'll have to relieve them before too long. He can be a handful."

"I could watch him."

Brooke suddenly felt better than she had in a long time. There were kids here. And there were parents, like Melody, who could and would help in the shelter if they had someone to watch the kids. Who better than the teachers?

Melody stopped walking, looked at Brooke, considering.

"I teach fourth grade. I love kids. Do you know of other teachers who are here? Maybe I can team up."

"Yeah, sure. Some of the teachers are doing that sort of thing already, but some are injured. Others have kids in other school districts and had to leave or had to bounce to care for relatives."

Brooke scanned the crowd, thinking of how it looked like a very rough child's birthday party: kids out of control, parents exhausted.

They made their way around the room, delivering the eight water bottles, taking notes of requests for supplies from those they passed.

Brooke wiped sweat from her eyebrows. "Everyone seems to know you."

"Like I said, here from day one. It's the only reason this became a shelter so fast, really. Initially, it housed the kids. Volunteers showed up with supplies to help out, and parents showed up, but this is an old neighborhood."

"Meaning?"

"Like, most of the homes were built way before they knew about the risk of earthquakes in this area, you know. They weren't built to survive that kind of shaking, so instead of sending the kids and parents out into the cold, the school invited the parents to stay."

"That's…pretty awesome," Brooke decided. Then realization struck. "Did you lose your home too, then? Initially, I just assumed you were a volunteer."

Melody's eyes welled. She nodded.

"Me, too. I'm so sorry."

She shrugged. "We're all in this together. Come on. I'll introduce you to some of the teachers. I'm sure they'll be thrilled to have you."

Chapter Fifty-One

Brooke found a man in his early forties named Hank, or Mr. H to his fifth-grade students. She got the impression that he usually held an orderly, calm classroom.

But they weren't in a traditional classroom. Hell, she thought, they weren't in a recognizable heart-space.

The kids were homesick and hungry, and many felt helpless in the face of the disaster that had unfolded around them. Naturally, the emotions came out in waves of hyperactivity, short attention spans, and listening skills that, well, sucked, Brooke admitted.

Not that she blamed them. The whole situation sucked, but if she was going to make this her home for the next however long, they needed some structure.

Beside her, Hank looked as though he might cry or just up and quit.

"Do me a favor?" Brooke asked him.

"What?" he half-shouted at her, unable to hear over the commotion.

Brooke squeezed her eyes shut. God, she couldn't collaborate if she couldn't communicate. Something had to give. She held up a finger signaling she'd be right back and headed for the front entry.

She stepped outside to find that the rain hadn't let up. Wind whipped through her hair. "Tommy?" she called.

At the middle canopy, Tommy stood and met her halfway. "Yo, Brooke, you're still here. Figured you'd be long gone."

"No, I, uh." She took a deep breath, hating the fact that she was about to lie to him. Tommy had earned her respect. Brooke wanted to earn—wanted to deserve—his respect in return.

A wind gust pushed against her back; it was strong enough to force her to take a step forward. That's it, she thought. She'd had enough of the nasty weather, enough of not knowing if they'd have enough food or water for the day.

"Turned out my husband was inside, so they are letting us stay."

"Sick. So, what's up?"

"I need the megaphone I saw on the table. Can I borrow it?"

"The blow horn? Sure, but that's not going to go well with some inside. People are sleeping all hours of the day."

"Something's got to give in there."

He shrugged, walked over, and grabbed the city-issued loudspeaker.

Taking it from Tommy, she walked back into the shelter and headed back to where she'd left Hank. She slid two office chairs side by side, stood on one, then signaled for Hank to join her. Eyebrow raised, he joined her.

She clicked the button and heard the electric tones reverberate, so strange in a world that had gone mostly quiet in that area.

"Excuse me," she tried. "Can I have everyone's attention, please?" she said louder and finally had the volume of the room dropping.

"Hi everyone, I know most of you don't know me. My name is Brooke, and I need your help. We have, as I'm sure you've noticed, an extremely full shelter at the moment."

She paused as murmurs filled the space.

"I know, it's chaotic. But for the moment, it's home. Less than two weeks ago, I volunteered at one of the local Warming Centers in town. There was ice on the ground, and the center struggled to find seven volunteers to help out."

She paused for effect. "That can't be us now. We need each other. I'm asking that everyone over the age of ten who's physically able, help. This is an all-hands-on-deck moment. Hank here is going to help divide us into work teams, so please gather around."

Hank's expressive eyebrows shot up in shock this time, but he nodded, took the megaphone.

Together, they spent the next thirty minutes talking with members of their new community. Despite the moans from some, they separated into food and water support, medical, communication, childcare, and janitorial teams.

Brooke took the mic back. "Okay, thank you, everyone. Let's work for the next hour, then rotate if needed. If we take shifts doing this every day, it'll make a huge difference."

The noise level rose again, but this time, it held a pattern—a purpose.

Chapter Fifty-Two

Joy. Of all the emotions coursing through her, it dominated. Scooping up a spoonful of white rice, Brooke nearly moaned.

A generator, given to the shelter by one of the guests, buzzed. The shelter only ran it during dinner time when the sun had gone down. After the dinner was cleared, Brooke was told that everyone went to their sleep areas for lights-out.

Having the artificial light fill the room filled Brooke with gratitude. It had been a good day. Though it had cost her a lie that tightened the food and water rations of the entire shelter, she had a hard time feeling too guilty. She and Maddie were waiting out a nasty storm in the comfort of a sturdy building.

And while orderly wasn't how she would have described the afternoon, she and Hank had done a kick-ass job turning things around in the shelter.

Not only had the place gotten cleaner, but Brooke had also watched purpose replace despair among the community members. Adjusting to the new emotional atmosphere, even the younger children relaxed into calmer play, and now, like an evening meal at a summer camp, they all sat in groups enjoying a much-needed meal.

Ian sat down next to Brooke, opposite Maddie, with a plate of rice and black beans in one hand. He scooted closer to her until she could feel his body heat radiating off him.

"Auntie Brooke?"

"Yes, Maddie?"

"I made friend today. Can I have friend yesterday?"

"Tomorrow? Are you asking if you can play with friends again tomorrow?"

"Yes."

Joy, Brooke thought again. Despite all that had been awful since the earthquake, Maddie had finally had a day that excited her—a day she wanted to repeat.

"Oooh, there a friend," Maddie said, pointing.

Brooke glanced over and saw the young girl Maddie had bonded with during their impromptu shelter-school day.

"You can go say hi."

Maddie jumped up and ran over.

"I wish we had some soy sauce," Alex muttered, scooping up his rice. "I miss soy sauce."

Irene shook her head at her youngest grandson. "Soy sauce? I miss bathroom lights that turn on when I've got to use the lady's room at two a.m. Toilets that actually flush."

Sitting in a circle, the neighbors were reunited for the first time since Bill's injury, content as the wind screamed outside.

"I miss my TV to watch sports," Henry added, putting a loving arm around Irene.

"Water," Laura said. "Not just flowing water that comes out of pipes on demand but temperature-changing water. My lord, I miss hot showers."

"Drugs."

Eyes huge, the group turned to stare at Fawn. She giggled. "Not the illegal kind. But I really could have gone for an epidural during the delivery with a good dose of aspirin afterward."

Alex winked at her. "Next time."

Fawn laughed. "I might need a few years before next time."

"I'm with Fawn on the drug thing." Bill rubbed absently at his leg.

Brooke smiled, loving the honesty of the moment. "I miss my cell phone, the careless ease of cooking a meal on an actual stove, the sound of popcorn in a microwave, and going out to the grocery store."

Carol stood and grabbed a cup of water for herself from a nearby table. "Gardening," she said when she came back over. "Reading a book by my bedside lamp until my eyes close."

"Driving to the river to look for agates and petrified wood. Heck," George added, "I just miss driving."

"I miss the sounds of cement mixers and staple guns," Ian put in. "This new world is too damn quiet."

"My poor baby," Laura teased, ruffling Ian's hair. "I miss sleeping in a soft bed with sheets that smell like fabric softener."

Alex ran a hand over his new beard. "A razor. And beer."

"Yeah." The single statement came out in unison from the other four men.

Ian slung an arm over Brooke's shoulder.

"What are you doing?" she whispered.

"Holding my wife," he replied with a mile-wide grin.

She tried to glare at him, but her lips betrayed her, corking up at the sides.

He laughed.

Alex held up his plastic fork. "So when's the big day?"

Ian tossed his balled-up napkin at his younger brother. Alex deflected. "I'm betting within the year."

"Alex," Laura admonished. "Don't tease."

"Be a helluva better match than his first one," Bill chimed in. "Shelly was great. Don't get me wrong. But the match just never seemed right."

Ian looked at his dad. "I didn't know you felt that way."

"It wasn't my place," Bill said. "But I'm saying it now. This one," he said, nodding his chin at Brooke, "does. Took damn good care of me today, too."

"I'm pretty sure we would need to go on an actual date first," Brooke said before taking another bite of rice.

Bill looked at the arm wrapped around her shoulder. "This doesn't count as a dinner date?"

Looking at Ian, Brooke laughed and shrugged.

The room held close to eighty guests who hadn't showered in nearly two weeks. It housed the broken, the sick, and the sad. Bandages were as much the décor as gym bags and backpacks—the cheap hotel carpet mixed with mud and the occasional dry leaf.

Certainly no Gala, Brooke thought, but she had to admit that sitting next to Ian with his arm around her had her stomach doing butterflies. Again. And the way he looked at her had her heart racing.

Holding her gaze another moment, Ian grinned at her. Then he dropped his arm to hold out his empty water cup that one of the high school kids was offering to fill. "Thanks."

"Yep." The kid held the pitcher out for Brooke. When she thanked him, he gave her a brilliant smile before moving to fill Carol's cup.

"Better get on it," Henry told his grandson when the high schooler left their group. "That boy isn't the only one giving Brooke here considering glances today."

"He wasn't—," Brooke began. "No one . . . I—" she fumbled, then felt a blush rise in her cheeks.

"I'll pummel um—"

Henry shook his head. "Joke all you want, Ian, but I bet this girl's got them youngsters lining up to ask her on a proper date, don't you?" he finished, aiming the last part at Brooke.

Finishing her plate, Brooke set it down in the center on the other dishes to be cleared.

"I plead the fifth," she decided.

She seriously doubted any guy had been checking her out. After all, she was one of those people who hadn't showered in too many days. Her hair was greasy, which made her head itch.

The nail polish she'd applied for the job interview two weeks earlier now resembled a drunken splatter painting, and the idea of makeup was so absurd that Brooke felt a bubble of hysteria threaten.

She swallowed it down. Pressed and polished didn't define anyone in Salem at the moment, she supposed. "I'm going to go check in with Maddie."

"You do that, child," Carol told her. "These boys don't know when to stop teasing."

"Who's teasing?" Brooke heard Henry say.

Chapter Fifty-Three

As the rain pounded like a nail gun against the roof, Ian watched Brooke make her way over to Maddie and Maddie's new friend. He saw the two girls talking as Brooke knelt beside them.

She got to him, Ian admitted, knowing full well his dad was right.

Ian had loved his first wife, Shelly. They'd been young when they'd married. Then they'd grown up. He'd wanted to move a bit closer to his family; he had wanted to start his own family. There was something about having his kids grow up around his parents that had just felt right.

Of course, when they'd started dating in college, he hadn't felt that way. Like most young adults, Ian remembered craving distance from his parents and his hometown; he remembered how much he'd loved the independence of it all.

When Shelly told him a year into their marriage that she wanted to switch majors and had, in fact, applied to a culinary school in France—France for Christ's sake—Ian had been caught off guard. Then Shelly's acceptance had come. She'd been thrilled at the idea of spending her first few years after getting her degree as a chef in France, wanting to learn from the best.

Time had moved at a much faster tempo those next few months, spending the time before her first semester abroad trying to get on the same page. Should they move there and raise kids for the first few years? Family was an integral part of Ian's life. Having his parents halfway around the world during the early years of raising a family hadn't sat well.

They'd considered waiting to have kids. At the time, he'd been okay with waiting a couple of years, but the more they'd talked, the more Ian realized Shelly had the next ten-plus years planned in France if she could make it work.

Ten years away from family, from familiarity, from friends. He loved to travel, would have enjoyed a six-month stint there, but ten years...

He hadn't blamed her. The fact was, his need to separate from his family and to feel that independence had lasted only his first year out of high school. It had been a *need to prove himself, need some space* thing, but not something he'd wanted to drag out into decades.

They'd divorced as friends. Rare, he thought. The courts had called it "irreconcilable differences." And now, here he sat, two years later, knowing his dad was right. The marriage hadn't been right.

Not only because they'd chosen different paths but because doing so hadn't broken them. The separation had been sad but not devastating.

Ian looked at Brooke, doubting a separation from her would ever feel that simple. Taking a slug of water, Ian ran a hand through his hair.

He and Brooke weren't the type to just dive into marriage, but Ian wanted that first date. They cared for each other. They were attracted to each other. He wanted badly to give an actual relationship with her a try.

He stood, ready to walk over and join Brooke and the two girls, when another gust of wind cascaded through the valley. Something slammed down hard outside the shelter. The hum of the generator, along with the lights it provided, died.

Chapter Fifty-Four

Instinctively, Brooke reached out in front of her and grabbed Maddie's hand.

"Someone give me a flashlight," Brooke commanded.

Her heart pounded. She wanted the lights back as much as she wanted to know why they'd gone out. She'd just gotten electricity back in her life. Losing it now was a sharp blade to her heart.

Holding on tight to Maddie's tiny hand, Brooke tried to breathe. Panic flowed through the room. Nearly two weeks of pain, fear, loss, and so much uncertainty coursed through the air, almost palpable. The darkness, unexpected and total in the office building, was like being tossed back into a pit they'd just managed to escape.

Someone grabbed her shoulder. "Brooke?"

"Laura?"

"Yes, oh good, I thought I heard your voice. Are you with her?"

"I've got Maddie," Brooke confirmed, her voice booming over the raging storm outside, the chaos within.

A flashlight came on, its single beam piercing the dark. Though not the brightest, it brought a collective sigh of relief.

Brooke glanced down to smile reassuringly at Maddie, then gaped. The young face looking back up at her *wasn't* Maddie. Brooke stood, holding hands with Maddie's new friend. Forcing a reassuring smile for the girl now, Brooke fought for control. Her breath was coming too fast.

Where is Maddie?

Brooke looked around the room frantically but saw only silhouettes in most areas. The flashlight illuminated only a small section of the room.

Keeping hold of the girl's hand, Brooke turned toward Laura, who was scanning the room. "Help me find her."

Confused, Laura pivoted, glanced down, quickly realizing what had happened. Her eyes grew huge. "I'll get the others."

Watching Laura move toward the group, Brooke felt steadier. The first time Maddie had run off after the initial earthquake, Brooke remembered panic scorching her from within. She'd been alone then.

She wasn't alone this time.

Another flashlight came on. Brooke scanned the area again.

Where are you?

Parents scurried throughout the building, looking for kids, hollering. Chaos, Brooke thought again, thinking of the earlier activity during lunch.

Five flashlights now illuminated the space. Brooke spotted many older kids, but like Maddie, the younger ones appeared to have vanished.

Laura walked up. "They're going to start looking."

"Come on." Brooke grabbed Laura's hand, pulled her and the young girl toward the middle of the room. Bending, she scooped up the megaphone from under the table where she and Hank had played pick-a-team that afternoon.

"Maddie's not the only one missing. We can't find the kids like this."

"All hands on deck," Laura said, nodding.

They climbed onto a white plastic table where food had been served during dinner. *The hell with the mess their shoes would make. Cleaning and hygiene could wait a damn minute.*

"Alright, everyone, freeze."

Ian's mom bit her lower lip, trying not to laugh. "Don't scare 'em, sweetie."

"Right. Can I please have everyone stop for a sec?"

"We're a little busy at the moment," came the voice of an angry woman.

With the group quieter, Brooke set down the loudspeaker but made sure to project her voice so that she would be heard above the remaining chatter. "I know some of the kids are missing. We're going to find them, but we need to stay calm."

"Do you have kids?" she replied angrily.

"I have a three-year-old daughter," Brooke replied, swallowing down a quick flash of sadness for Jen and Seth.

"She needs me. I need to know she's okay. This is scary for all of us, but we need to be clear-headed *for them*. Right off, I've got a little girl here who was near me when the lights went out." Brooke lifted the girl onto her hip so those in the back of the room could see her.

"Audrey." A man came through the crowd, and the little girl in Brooke's arms wiggled down to meet him.

Brooke straightened and faced the crowd who'd reluctantly gathered, their desperation to find loved ones making it hard to stop looking, even for a moment.

"Tell us what you need, Brooke."

Brooke followed the sound of the voice and found Mr. Neilson, the principal who'd interviewed and turned her down for the job at Candelaria, not more than an hour before the megathrust earthquake had hit.

She swallowed hard now. She hadn't known he was staying in the shelter. How hadn't she seen him? she wondered. Had he just arrived? She cleared her throat.

"I'm up for suggestions," she said, "but I'd like us to work like we did this afternoon and break into teams. We need people to check bathrooms, look under bedding, and walk the parameter just in case they ran outside." She thought of the darkness outside, the rain, and hoped the kids hadn't ventured out.

"What if we separate into five groups, four taking separate sides of the building indoors, one going outside?"

Brooke nodded at Tommy, grateful he was there.

Another man chimed in. "Should probably keep voices down, too. Never hear the kids if we're too busy calling for them."

"That's good."

"Mom!" A boy about six years old came running out from behind a closet door, barreled through the crowd, and all but launched himself at a woman.

She hugged him, then looked at Brooke. "Shouldn't more kids be coming out to us?"

Brooke shrugged. "Let's have all the kids under ten come up here. Bring the others as we find them here to this spot. Laura will be here to watch over them."

Laura nodded. "I could use three more adults to assist."

"Everyone else, including any kid over the age of ten, is now officially part of a search and rescue pod. We don't stop looking until every kid is right here." Brooke paused.

"We need the list of those staying at the shelter so we can take roll," she said. "Someone get us that list. The rest of you, pick the wall closest to you. That's the side of the building I want you to look at first. Stay with your group. Be as methodical as possible."

The crowd parted. Fawn, carrying her baby girl, came over with Carol and Irene.

"We'll help watch the kids."

Brooke nodded. "Perfect. Thank you."

A man walked up with a clipboard in hand. "Here's the list of residents."

"Appreciate it," Brooke told him. She took the board, handed it to Laura. "I have to find Maddie."

Laura kissed her cheek. "You will."

Brooke pivoted and frowned. "Why is the front door open?"

"I saw someone open the door just before the power went out. They were taking out the trash from dinner, caring it to the parking lot around back," Laura explained.

Brooke stared at the garbage bag sitting to the side of the door. *Clearly it never made it outside before the outage—and the door was left open.* "No. She wouldn't have."

"Who?" Laura asked.

Brooke closed her eyes, trying to stay calm. "Maddie. When the earthquake hit, I found Maddie outside. She'd taken off running. If she was scared enough when the lights went out and the door was open, she may have run outside again."

"In this weather?"

"Hopefully not, but I've to check."

Chapter Fifty-Five

Brooke stepped out into the raging storm. She lifted an arm, fending off the unrelenting rain coming at a nearly horizontal angle through the gusts of bellowing wind.

"Maddie!"

Her voice barely pierced the thrashing. She yelled even louder. "Maddie!"

"Noooo."

Brooke heard the word, but in the storm, she couldn't tell if it was Maddie. She called for her again.

"No. No, no, no."

Following the direction of the cries, Brooke finally recognized them as Maddie's.

Alive. Maddie was still alive. But where? Why wasn't she coming out? Was she hurt?

"Where are you? I'm coming, Maddie. Help me find you."

Another scream. Was that pain? Fear? Anger? The past two weeks had helped Brooke differentiate the emotions behind Maddie's cries. But this was different.

Shining a flashlight in front of her did nothing to break the limited visibility of the storm. Brooke aimed it instead at her feet, letting the small beam guide her over curbs and fallen limbs until she came around the side of the building.

She stopped abruptly. Whatever she'd expected to see hadn't prepared her for the moment. Two men walked toward Brooke in the darkness. The man on the left wielded a long and wickedly angled knife. It glinted in the beam of Brooke's flashlight when she aimed it at him. The man on the right held Maddie over his shoulder.

"She yours?"

The man's voice, a low growl, reached Brooke in the shortened distance between them.

"Yes." *That's my daughter, you son of a bitch.* "Let her go."

The man with the knife, taller and more gangly than his companion, laughed, reminding her of a hyena. It sent a chill down her spine.

"Screw that, girlie girl. You know how much this little morsel is worth right now?"

"What do you want. I'll give you anything. Just let her go."

Now the bulky man let out a guffaw. "Hear that, Shane? Bitch is staying at a shelter and thinks she has what we need."

Maddie kicked her feet, pounded her fists on the large man's back.

"I can get it." Brooke hoped her voice sounded sturdier than she felt. They were right. She hadn't had cash to grab, had no food and water to her name, and she doubted they'd be interested in the spare pairs of clothes she'd brought with her.

"Shit, Levi," Shane said. "Let's see what the girl can get."

He lifted the knife to his temple, pretended to slice it across his forehead as he grinned at her. Crazy, she thought. Not just desperate. Crazy.

Maddie wailed. "Auntie. I want my Auntie. No. No. No."

Brooke had to bite down hard on the inside of her lip to fight back the tears at the sound of pure terror in Maddie's voice.

Levi shrugged. "How about a helicopter ride out of this apocalyptic hell hole."

His words slurred. Brooke watched as the wind shoved against him. Though she'd held her ground, he'd stumbled, letting Maddie rock precariously before Levi regained his balance.

Drunk? High? Shit.

Brooke pushed her sopping hair from her face, furious at the rain for making the situation harder than it already was. When the wind whipped it right back, she held her hair in a side ponytail. With her hair finally under control, she could keep her eyes on Maddie.

Brooke couldn't see Maddie's face because of how the little girl laid over Levi's shoulders, but she could see the faces of the men who were holding Maddie.

Looking into their eyes, Brooke saw crazy, intoxicated desperation. The situation wasn't something she could handle, not on her own.

"Fresh out. But what would you say to a week's worth of supplies?" She couldn't get it, but she needed an excuse to get inside.

Shane, no longer grinning, stomped toward her. "You screwing with us?" he asked. "A whole week?" He held the blade to her belly. "I'll gut you just like that if you're lying. *Don't* lie to me."

"Us." Levi patted Maddie on the butt. "You lie to us or get help, we'll take this sweet thing and sell her in exchange for a flight outta here. Come to think of it, maybe we should."

Shane grinned again. "That's right. We could, but I'm starving. We can find another kid to sell. Tell you what," he said to Brooke. "We'll give you five solid minutes to get those supplies. Kicked some highfalutin owners out and got ourselves a ripe good home."

"Yeah. Buncha pansies."

"But we ain't had a good meal to eat in too damn long."

"Starvin," Levi agreed. "Want me some damn meat."

"Hells yeah. So you make sure the food is damn good, or the deal's off."

"Tick tock."

Brooke didn't hesitate. She turned into the wind and rain, stumbling over debris as she raced for the front door of the shelter.

Chapter Fifty-Six

Ian opened the door just as Brooke rushed up the walkway.

"Where . . . ?" She slapped a hand over his mouth, then held a finger to her lips.

His eyebrows furrowed. Brooke motioned for him to go back inside. When he didn't hesitate, relief swamped her.

The door closed at their backs. "Spill," Ian told her.

"Two men, they're . . . oh, my God, Ian. Maddie ran outside when the lights went out. I should have guessed. Right away. That's exactly what she did when the earthquake hit, but I didn't think."

Ian placed his hands on her shoulders. "Where is she?"

"Two men are holding her hostage."

Ian turned to open the door.

Brooke grabbed his arm. "No. No, don't. One has a huge knife, and they are both batshit crazy. I have less than five minutes to come up with a plan."

Ian nodded, turned, and made his way quickly through the dark and crowded room full of its own chaos. Most were still searching for the kids hiding inside, but Ian found Alex with two other young guys he'd gotten to know during their brief stay.

"Need you. The three of you, actually."

"Yeah," Alex said. "What's up?"

Brooke knew even if she could find a week's worth of food and water for two grown men, it wouldn't guarantee Maddie's safety, so she had something else in mind.

Ian stood with his thumbs in his front pockets. He looked at her. "Tell us what you need."

Brooke wheedled a wooden piano dolly out the front door. On it sat a large black garbage bag normally used for yard maintenance.

As she came to the parking lot, the wind sent rainwater off the roof to strike her eyes. She used her shoulder to wipe at them. In the raging storm, Brooke pushed the weighty supplies toward Maddie and her captors.

Even on the relatively flat ground, the short distance was a battle in the raging wind. Brooke hoped the wind's howl would be loud enough.

Shane's high-pitched laughter echoed in the darkness. "Heee, girl. You brought us dinner."

Levi no longer held Maddie over his shoulder but instead had something tied around her ankles and wrists. She sat shaking, crying in the driveway. "I want out. No. Out." She screamed at the men, but they ignored her.

Seeing Maddie tied up made a new level of fury boil inside Brooke. She stopped rolling the dolly a few feet from where the two men stood, not daring to look on the roof.

"Here's your food and water. You let her go, and it's yours."

"Screw that." Shane took two steps and reached for the bag with his knife still gripped in one hand. With the other, he began working out the single knot Brooke had tied in the bag to prevent the contents from spilling. Though she'd kept the knot loose, Shane's impaired state didn't mix well with the darkness. The rain-slicked lining whipped in the wind, slowing his pace even more.

From above the men, Brooke caught a glimpse of movement.

Game on.

"Levi, Shane has the supplies. Can I have Maddie now?" She aimed her voice between polite and pleading, not wanting to give him any reason to grab for Maddie. Brooke took a few steps from the supplies, making her way to stand near Shane, hoping he'd let Maddie go. He didn't budge.

Behind her, she heard Levi grumble. Even with the knife in his hand, he couldn't get the knot untied. Sheathing it, he grabbed at the material and pulled until it ripped. From under the empty food boxes that sat on top, Ian jumped out of the bag like a soldier leaping from the Trojan Horse.

He pulled his arm back, then let his fist connect with a satisfying crack against Shane's nose. Blood went spurting from it. Shane wailed.

Taking her cue, Brooke moved in and shoved Levi away from Maddie. He turned, ready to charge her. From the roof, Alex launched a brick. It connected with the back of Levi's head.

Levi went down with a solid thud as Alex's two friends held Shane down. Brooke dropped down beside Maddie. Carefully, she loosened the rubber, oversized twisty ties binding Maddie's feet and hands.

Pulling Maddie in for a full hug, she held out the ties to Ian. "Nice. GearTies."

Brooke looked at him, puzzled.

"We use them all the time at work to hold stuff down. They work great." Ian turned. He tied Shane's wrists behind his back and secured his ankles.

"The other guy dead?" Alex asked.

Ian walked over, felt for a pulse. "No."

Alex let out a breath. "Good. I'm not sure I could handle *that* tonight." He walked over to Brooke, smiled at Maddie. "You were brave today, kiddo. Like, my hero kind-of-brave."

She sniffled, smiled, and curled her face closer to Brooke. Brooke kissed the top of her head. "I'm going to take her in. You guys got this?"

Ian nodded. "Oh yeah. We're taking them a few blocks over to a doggie daycare facility."

Puzzlement flooded Brooke's face.

"They have some heavy-duty, cell-sized crates for the dogs to sleep in at night. These two are going to be guests of that fine establishment until we can find actual cops to handle this. No one's kidnapping kids tonight."

Brooke let out a watery sigh. "Thank you."

He walked up to her, knuckles bruised from the punch, skimmed them gently over Brooke's cheek.

"You were right," he said, his short hair whipping as if he sat in a convertible on I-5. "We were able to lean the ladder on the side of the building and scale it onto the roof without them hearing a thing in this wind. It was a good plan. She's lucky to have you."

I couldn't have done this, any of this, she thought, without you, your family, and our neighbors. "I owe you." She turned and carried Maddie into the shelter.

Chapter Fifty-Seven

The adults were exhausted. In all, they'd found twenty-two out of twenty-two missing kids. Though Maddie had been the only kid to run outside, it had taken time to find them all.

Brooke figured the last two kids should have qualified for some sort of hide-and-seek award.

After all the commotion, getting those twenty-two kids to sleep had only added to the grown-ups' exhaustion.

Despite their hard work and tired bodies, most of the teens and grown-ups couldn't fall asleep, their brains unable to shut off after the evening's events. Leaving the young children sleeping, they gathered. They needed each other and the normalcy of social time and casual laughter.

Brooke heard it gently wafting over the crowd. She could have wept. The people in the room, she thought, had been through Hell. So had *millions* of others in the Pacific Northwest. They needed laughter and support as much as they needed food and water.

"May I join you?"

Brooke pivoted to see Mr. Neilson. "Of course."

He sat, holding a cup of water for himself and handing her one.

"Thank you," she replied, trying to keep her expression calm rather than baffled.

"Has anyone told you why, aside from location, so many Candalaria families are here?" he asked.

She nodded. "It was a pickup spot for the parents that morphed into a shelter."

"Yeah. Hell of a thing." His head dropped. "I've been between here, the school, and homes of the parents all week."

That explained why she hadn't seen him much. "You're checking in with the families. That's wonderful."

He lowered his voice. "We lost two kids."

The cup in Brooke's hands jolted.

"I've been with their families, mostly, doing . . . what I can, I guess."

"I'm, I'm so sorry."

The principal blew out a breath. "It would have been much worse if the ShakeAlert warning hadn't come through. That helped us at least get some kids out. But twenty-six seconds isn't enough time to evacuate more than three hundred kids. It's just not."

"No."

"I know this is impossible to hear. I wish I could tell you that's the worst of the news. Do you know there are sixty-five schools in the Salem-Keizer School district?"

"I. Yes, I read that," Brooke managed.

The ghost of a smile played around his mouth then. "I thought you would have. You came well prepared for the interview." His smile faded completely. "Did you also know that in a 2006 assessment, the state found eight of those schools had a one-hundred percent chance of collapse? DOGAMI, the Department of Geology and Mineral Industries, classified them as *Very High-Risk.*"

Her hand rose to cover her mouth in horror. Brooke shook her head.

"Another nineteen schools fell under the *High-Risk* category for building collapse, which placed the possibility of a collapse somewhere between ten and ninety-nine percent."

A tear slid down Brooke's face to still on her jawline. She hardly felt it over the pounding of her heart.

"Candelaria, along with eight others, fell in the *Moderate* risk group." Mr. Neilson rubbed his hands on the thighs of his jeans. "The district did retrofits about eight years ago."

"It's a lot of schools."

"Yes, and you'll have to excuse my saying so, but it's a political pain to cut red tape sometimes. It took years to get the city to approve the bonds that paid for the retrofitting, but then the Covid pandemic hit. Prices of building materials skyrocketed in the middle of construction. Maybe that's why part of our building collapsed. Maybe corners were cut. I just don't know."

"You're afraid the same is true for other schools too?" Brooke asked.

"Yes. I really hope I'm wrong. Either way, our community is devastated and forever changed."

Brooke had to swallow twice before she was certain she could keep more tears from falling. "I'm so sorry."

"Teaching here would be a choice far different from somewhere outside the impacted area."

Teaching? "I don't—Sir, I don't understand. Are you offering me the job?"

"When you interviewed, your answers were good, except I didn't get the impression you were much of a team player. A good teacher with the kids, maybe, but at my school, I hire for the team, not the individual. You showed me today I was wrong."

"No."

Principal Neilson looked at her with such confusion that despite everything, she relaxed a little.

"You weren't wrong. But a lot has changed since the earthquake. I've changed."

"You've grown emotionally, I'd say. People—depending on them takes courage."

"Yes, it does." She shuddered out a breath. "I don't want to leave Salem. I don't want to teach anywhere else."

"If you don't mind me asking, why is that?"

"My mom was born and raised here."

Brooke stopped, hesitated, knowing oversharing would be unprofessional. She sipped the water he'd given her while she tried to decide how much to say.

Across the room, she watched Ian talking to his brother and holding his new sleeping niece. It made her smile. Growing up, Ian had always been the one to leave Salem before she did. Without a job, she and Maddie would go this time. They'd have no choice.

But now, Mr. Neilson sat next to her, offering her a job that meant so much more to her than a paycheck. She didn't want to screw that up.

The hell with professionalism.

They weren't in some stuffy office. In fact, the moment felt as distant from the day in his office with its plaques and books as she could fathom.

Neither of them had showered in nearly two weeks. They weren't dressed in business attire, and she wasn't about to drive to the store for ice cream.

Everything had changed. In unison with the quivering earth, her hopes of putting down roots, her city, her heart, had all crumbled.

It was time to put some pieces back together.

"My mom died when I was fourteen," she told him, leading with honesty.

"I'm sorry to hear that."

Brooke nodded. "It was hard. It's still hard. After, my dad would bring me here to stay with my grandmother every summer. Every time I came, I felt connected to my mom in a way I couldn't seem to find anywhere else. I felt safe. This place has always felt like home."

"It's a good place," Mr. Neilson acknowledged. "Who was your mom?"

"Barbara Halliwell. Well, Barbara Noel, before she met my dad."

His head tilted as he looked at her, and then to Brooke's surprise, he smiled. "I knew your mom."

"Really?"

"She was one of my students during my first year of teaching. I taught English for ten years before transitioning to administration, and I'll be damned—you look like her."

Brooke smiled, but it faded quickly. She gripped her water cup with both hands and scanned the crowded room as she spoke.

"I understand the struggles ahead and appreciate you being honest about it, but Salem is my home. I've loved this place for a long time. There is no way I can turn my back on it now."

She looked at Maddie, wondering how she'd make it work. Fawn, Alex, and their baby, as well as Laura and Bill, would eventually return to their homes outside of Salem. Maybe Carol or Irene would be willing to babysit Maddie during the day until preschools were fully back up and running, Brooke thought.

"I don't know when we will be opening the doors again, but there will be a ton of work to do to get classes open. Can I count on you then? Will you accept my offer?"

She thought of the kids in the school, kids who had lost friends, lost homes. Kids who were afraid. They would need stability. They would need grownups around to help them through the next several years, and they would need to know it was okay to depend on others. Brooke wanted to be a part of that.

"I'd like that very much. Thank you."

"Good. That's good. I wish it were under different circumstances, but welcome aboard. Let's talk more tomorrow. We can work on some of the details then. I need to rest."

Brooke's heart felt ripped in two; one half was grateful for the stability she'd just earned, while the other was devastated by the news of the fallen schools.

She watched her new boss walk toward the front door, wondering where he was headed. She hadn't asked him about his home and wondered how it had held up.

Despite the situation, she felt the massive weight she'd been carrying lift off her chest.

She had a job. With it, she could find a place for Maddie to call home. She could support her daughter.

Chapter Fifty-Eight

Brooke felt alive. And she was smiling. God, it felt good to smile. She sat on a yoga mat with twelve kids facing her in a semi-circle. She'd spent the past twenty minutes quizzing the second- to fourth-grade kids on geography.

"Alright, Cassady, you're up."

The third-grader, taller than her peers with a very long nose, squirmed.

"Name three countries in Central America?"

The girl thought about it. "Panama, Costa Rica, and Honduras."

"Good! Who can give me three more?"

Cassady smiled and sat quickly enough to tell Brooke she wasn't a fan of being on stage.

Brooke waited as the group whispered, trying to find someone who knew all three. Over the two days since she'd been offered the teaching job, Brooke and three other teachers had started classes within the shelter.

Since most of the kids attended Candalaria, they knew each other and took comfort in being together. The school routine kept the shelter running more smoothly during the day and gave parents time to go to their homes, clean up, or salvage what they could of their personal belongings. It also gave the parents time to check on loved ones and check in with their bosses.

For Brooke, her core identity had been entwined with teaching for so long. Being without it since leaving New Mexico had left her feeling incomplete.

She didn't feel incomplete anymore. Watching one of the kids in the group stand, Brooke marveled at how much the moment filled her.

"Belize, Nicaragua and El Salvador."

"Nice, Jason!"

"I'd say you guys have earned a break. Go get a glass of water from the—" Brooke broke off mid-sentence, staring at the table by the front door.

Her fingertips went up to her mouth. She felt her heart lodge in her throat, her eyes swim.

Maddie's teacher had a funny elephant stuffy. It made her laugh. She liked the teacher, except if she sat too close to him. His breath was stinky.

Sitting by her new friend, she listened as the teacher sang. Maddie liked when the elephant talked, but she liked singing best. except she didn't really like this song.

She sat on the ground, tapping her toes to the tune, wiggling her bottom to try to warm it. The floor was so cold. She wanted to go home where it was warmer. She wanted a blanket. The song stopped. When the teacher started the song again, Maddie pouted.

"New song. I want a new song."

The teacher held up a finger to his lips, finishing the song.

Maddie's pout turned into a scowl. She was bored. Wiggling, she rose enough to put her feet under her. At her new height, she could see over some of the other kids. That was fun.

She liked the kids, but she missed Auntie Brooke. She wanted milk, too, but all they had was boring water. Maddie scowled over at the place where they kept the water and cups.

Then her face lit up. She took off running toward the table.

Ian made his way over to Brooke, squeezing in between two of the kids. "Brooke, what's going on?"

Eyes still swimming, she met his confused gaze. Her hands fell from her mouth, and with tears cresting, spilling, she smiled widely. Placing her hands on his very confused face, she turned him.

Brooke felt Ian's body go still. Then they rose in unison, and watched as Seth Monroy, looking more like a mountain man than the IT geek he was, fell to his knees.

"Daddy! Daddy, Daddy! You're here!" Maddie's words floated above the noises in the room. She flew into his arms.

Brooke's tears became a soundless laugh of joy as she watched them, the emotions coursing through her so powerfully she wasn't sure she could breathe. She held her breath as Seth stood, lifting his giggling daughter into the air. He did a single turn before bringing her tiny body back down for another hug.

Coming out of his own shock, Ian shook his head and shouted to his mom, "Watch the kids a minute, will you?"

She looked up from where she'd been tending to Bill's bandage. Her face creased in a mix of motherly confusion and concern when she met Ian's gaze. Laura finished securing the bandage and walked over.

"Thanks, Mom." Ian kissed her on the cheek. "Seth's back."

Laura's eyes widened. "What?"

Ian pointed. "We'll be right back."

Laura gave Brooke a gentle push. "Go. Oh, thank God. Go."

They left her with the kids and jogged toward a friend they'd both been sure they'd lost.

Chapter Fifty-Nine

Brooke leaned against one of the three slim trees in front of the shelter. The sun shone warm on her face, reminding her that spring was just around the corner.

She lifted her face to the warmth, needing it as much as the fresh air. Both helped her heart to steady, her mind to calm.

She loved just being in the moment. Taking a slow, deep breath, Brooke listened to the CERT members in the tents to her right talking about the plan for the afternoon. She listened to the call of birds and watched a squirrel run up a tree. Closing her eyes, she felt the light breeze flutter the ends of her hair.

"There's a call for you."

Brooke's eyebrows furrowed in confusion as she opened her eyes and looked at what she now recognized as a HAM radio.

"Who?" she asked Ian.

He just smiled and handed it to her.

"Hello?" she began awkwardly.

"Brooke. Oh but damn, is it good to hear your voice, sweetie."

"Dad!"

"Yeah. Took me forever to locate you. I've been worried half-stupid. You're okay? No broken bones? No major cuts? Burns?"

The emotions flowing through Brooke had her head going light. She sat. "I'm. I'm not hurt. It's been a tough couple of weeks, though. I miss you."

"Yeah, lucky for you, your dad's a fire chief. Had to call in a few favors to get on a chopper—as a volunteer, of course."

"Of course," she said, smiling. "You're here?"

"I am. I just landed up on a place called Jory Hill out by your new home. I'm headed your way. Not sure on the time frame based on road conditions, but soon. You thank Ian for getting me the message with your location."

"I." Fumbling, she felt tongue-tied. "He what?"

No response.

"Dad?"

"I think he hung up on you." Ian stood leaning a shoulder on the wall behind him, his grin making her heart trip. "It's good he found a flight."

"You called my dad? How?"

"It was more of a group effort, actually," he said. "George and my grandpa used their connections."

"Uh-huh."

She watched him as he stuck what looked like nervous hands into his pockets.

"My parents knew which city he was living in." He shrugged. "I'd had Henry looking in New Mexico for the first three days," he admitted. "I didn't know your dad had moved."

"But you asked."

Ian looked at her. "Huh?"

"They were looking. They were all trying to contact him. For me. Because you asked them to."

"Oh. Yeah. I knew he had to be worried sick about you and that you've been trying to get texts to him. You've had your hands full with Maddie, so I just…"

She kissed him.

Brooke felt his arms come around her waist as Ian deepened the kiss. She nearly sighed when his lips fell away from hers.

He met her gaze. "So, about that date?"

She tilted her head, considering. "This doesn't count? And here I thought you were my husband."

"Don't tempt me," he teased.

Brooke laughed.

"I'm serious about the date, Brooke. We have somethin' here. Always have. Let's give it a shot."

She looked around. "It might be a while before we get to go out for an actual dinner or something."

Ian nodded. "How about we start by goin' for a walk this evening after you've spent some time with your dad?"

"I . . ." she trailed off, realizing she was about to tell Ian she'd need to bring Maddie.

Brooke moved to the main door that sat propped open in the mid-day heat. Looking into the shelter, she saw Maddie perched on her dad's hip while he talked to one of the other shelter members.

After Maddie had fallen asleep the night before, Seth had come to Ian and Brooke with his questions. And he'd wept.

Brooke knew a part of him would always grieve, but at the moment, Brooke watched him smile at the three-year-old who'd nearly become her daughter.

Brooke wanted, badly, to be there for them both.

Thinking of her recent job offer to work with the Salem-Keizer School District, she relaxed. Salem held her heart. Even in all its current chaos, Salem was her home, her roots, her stability.

She wanted to be there to help the city heal.

With her new job, she could rent a place. Then maybe she would have a new home built on her grandmother's land, on the quiet road south of town. She could build the life she'd always wanted in the city her grandmother had raised her mother.

Roots.

Turning, she met Ian's gaze, felt her heart soften and her belly flutter. Ian, who'd been there for her when her mother had died, who'd been her friend for as long as she'd known Jen. He'd brought her hot chocolate, stood by his family and friends with a fierce loyalty she admired, and had fought the worst Salem had o offer during a nasty storm to save Maddie.

In all that had crumbled, he'd been there to help her pick up the pieces every step of the way. "It's a date."

"Yeah?"

"Absolutely."

Ian crooked his finger, motioning for her to come closer. In the glow of he warm spring afternoon, she leaped into his arms and laid her lips on his.

A Note to My Readers

While *All That Crumbles* is a work of fiction, the Cascadia Subduction Zone poses a very real threat to communities across the Pacific Northwest. I often think of earthquakes as some of the greatest ghost stories ever told. They're nowhere, then suddenly they surround us—unseen but for the destruction they cause.

Be ready.

After a megathrust earthquake, the Willamette Valley in Oregon is expected to go:

50 days without natural gas
100 days without electricity
400 days without water/sewer

Current estimates are that only 5% of the Willamette Valley population is prepared to be self-sufficient for two weeks. Be ready so that you don't become one of many victims in need of saving. Some people can't prepare in advance the way you can, and others depend on you. Be ready so you can help them when the time comes.

Be ready.

Because, you see, for most people in the region, the biggest risk won't be the earthquake itself. The true risk is not being prepared for its aftermath. As a local Community Emergency Response Team member, inspiring people to prepare for a CSZ earthquake is a passion of mine. I hope you found inspiration, however small, within the pages of this book, and I encourage you to take a step today that will move you toward being 2-Weeks-Ready. Every step you take is a step in the right direction. Those steps will make a difference.

There is a ghost on our horizon.

For more information on the topic, please visit
SurvivingCascadia.com

Acknowledgments

To my wonderful kids, Renee, Evan, and Logan, my husband, Forrest, and my amazing family, April, Nathan, Diana, Sam, and Aaron, thank you for supporting my writing dream! Publishing a novel has been a bucket list item of mine for as long as I can remember. I couldn't have written this without you guys, and I'm so grateful!!

To my beta readers and editors, I've enjoyed working with each of you. It truly does take a community, and I'm so grateful you are part of mine. Thank you for helping craft this novel.

April Waters
Nathan Good
Emily Blanton
Annie Greensprings
Luc Charwin
Lynn Nakvasil
Micayla Lally
Kim Evans
Benjamin Baca

Thank you to all who work in emergency management. From CERT and OEM to FEMA and the EIS Council—my family is more prepared for what lies ahead because of you. You inspire me.

Made in United States
Troutdale, OR
08/05/2024

21783999R00170